W9-DGV-275

CHOKE

Also by Stuart Woods

Imperfect Strangers

Stuart Woods

CHOKE

WHEELER
PUBLISHING, INC.
ROCKLAND, MA

★ **AN AMERICAN COMPANY** ★

Published in Large Print by arrangement with
HarperCollins Publishers
in the United States and Canada.

Wheeler Large Print Book Series.

Set in 18 pt. Plantin.

Library of Congress Cataloging-in-Publication Data

Woods, Stuart.
  Choke / Stuart Woods.
    p. cm.—(Wheeler large print book series)
  ISBN 1-56895-265-1 (hc)
  1. Tennis Players—Florida—Key West Fiction. 2. Key West
(Fla.)—Fiction. 3. Large type books. I. Title. II. Series.
[PS3573.O642C58 1995b]
813'.54—dc20   95-44009
                                                    CIP

This book is for William
and Susan Kinsolving

prologue

WIMBLEDON
EARLY SEVENTIES

Chuck won the point, won the game. He sat down at courtside, picked up a towel, mopped, then reached into his bag for a dry shirt.

Bud: Well, Dan, young Chuck Chandler has come a long way in this tournament.

Dan: I'll say he has, Bud. Coming into Wimbledon, this boy was ranked number one hundred in the world. He started strong, then clawed his way up through the seeds, defeating two former champions along the way, and now he stands at the threshold of a whole new career. Would you say that, Cynthia?

Cynthia: I certainly would, Dan. This young man has the talent to beat anybody when he's playing this well, and the charm and looks to become a new matinee idol of tennis for the young female spectators. Off the court he handles himself with the kind of assurance that we have only just begun to see on the court at this Wimbledon.

Bud: And now Chuck Chandler has the
reigning champion tied at two sets all and
down five games to four, and he's just about
to go out there and serve for the greatest
of all tennis championships.

Chuck slipped into the clean shirt. He wanted
to be cool and dry when he accepted the gold
trophy from the duchess, smiling for the cameras,
basking in the glow of his new fame. He thought
ahead to the ball that night. He'd be dancing with
the women's champion, pressing his crotch into
hers, as he had the night before in her hotel room.
They'd make quite a pair for the press, "the dark-
haired eighteen-year-old beauty and the handsome, golden twenty-two-year-old who came
from nowhere to win Wimbledon." That's what
the press would be saying.

"Mr. Chandler?"

Chuck jerked back to the present.

"Mr. Chandler," the umpire said, "would you
please take the court?"

Chuck strode out to the baseline to a swelling
roar of approval from the crowd. They had loved
him from the moment he had defeated the first
former champion in the first round, and now they
showed it to the fullest. Chuck flashed his perfect
teeth at them. They roared anew.

He accepted three balls on his racquet from
the ball boy, tossed away the fuzziest, and tucked
one into a pocket. He positioned himself at the
baseline, looked down the court at the waiting

champion, began his backswing, tossed the ball, and slammed an ace down the centerline.

The crowd went wild.

"Fifteen-love," the umpire said over the loudspeaker.

Chuck walked to the opposite side of the court, positioned himself, and sent another serve straight down the centerline at 125 miles an hour.

The crowd went nuts.

"Thirty-love," the umpire announced.

Chuck accepted balls from the ball boy, took his place, and this time, just for variety, slammed his first serve into his opponent's forehand corner for a third ace.

The crowd went berserk.

"Forty-love," the umpire announced.

Bud: Well, now. Young Chuck Chandler is standing on this court with three match points in his pocket and a very shaken champion staring helplessly back at him. Let's see if he can put this championship away with the next serve.

Chuck thought about the Porsche Cabriolet he had seen in the showroom in New York. His first phone call after this match would be to the salesman, whose card was in the pocket of his tennis shorts. He'd call from the dressing room, before he even got into a shower.

"Mr. Chandler?" the umpire said.

Chuck snapped back. The crowd chuckled.

3

Dan: Dreaming of glory, no doubt.
Bud: Who could blame him?

Chuck served with all his power. The ball slapped against the tape at the top of the net and fell back into his court.

A groan from the crowd.

Chuck served again. The ball struck the net again.

A noise of pure misery from the crowd.

"Forty-fifteen," the umpire announced.

Dan: Well, I suppose he can afford a double
   fault at this point.
Bud: Remember, with double faults it's not
   how often, it's when.

Chuck felt a swell of anger at himself. He'd let his concentration wander, and he had to settle down and think. He walked to the other side of the court and served again, straight into the net.

A sound of shock from the crowd.

Chuck took a deep breath and served again without delay. The ball struck the tape and died.

A worried, almost angry murmur rose from the crowd.

"Forty-thirty," the umpire announced. "Quiet please, ladies and gentlemen."

Bud: That's two wasted match points, and he's
   only got one left. Can Chuck do it?
Dan: We're about to find out.

Suddenly Chuck's fresh shirt was soaked. He wiped the sweat from his eyes and glanced down the court at the champion. Was that a small smile on the bastard's face? His heart seemed to be beating irregularly. *I'll do this one by the numbers,* he thought. Foot pointed at the netpost, feet a shoulder's width apart, racquet held for a flat, hard serve, straight-armed toss, mighty swing. The ball hit the tape and bounced off the court.

The crowd gasped.

Dan: This is difficult to believe, Bud. For a player who has come this far to put five consecutive serves into the net is absolutely astonishing.

Bud: I'm speechless, Dan. Chuck is still at match point, though; let's see if he can pull this one out.

Chuck stood, sweat pouring down his face into his eyes.

"Second service, please, Mr. Chandler," the umpire said, not without sympathy.

There could be no second serve in this position; he had to pull just one more ace out of the hat. He walked to courtside, picked up a towel, wiped his face, and returned to the baseline. By the time he arrived the sweat was in his eyes again.

Please, God. He set himself up, taking his time, tossed the ball, and put his last match point unerringly into the net.

The crowd was absolutely silent.

"Deuce," the umpire said.

Twenty-four minutes later in the dressing room, Chuck knelt before the porcelain throne and puked his guts out. He had lost the next two points; he had lost the next two games; he had lost the Wimbledon championship. He had lost the best opportunity a boy ever had to become a hero.

He had lost more than he knew.

Dan: Bud, what happened out there on the center court?

Bud: There can be only one explanation, Dan, just one. Chuck choked.

CHAPTER

1

KEY WEST
FEBRUARY 1995

Chuck woke in a sweat, his heart pounding as hard as it had twenty-odd years before. The Wimbledon dream was back. The brass clock on the bulkhead said 9:20, and he was starting his new job at 10:00. He dove into the boat's tiny shower and sluiced away the sweat.

At a quarter to ten, freshly shaved and dressed in clean whites, he stepped ashore at Key West Bight, the racquet bag in his hand and the sunglasses perched on top of his blond head. He looked around him. It was a pretty odd collection of vessels compared to the marina at Palm Beach. There were sightseeing catamarans, a large schooner or two for the more traditional-minded tourists, and a weird submarinelike vessel, along with the usual assortment of fishing boats and live-aboard yachts.

His own boat was a thirty-two-foot twin-screw motor yacht that had been custom-built in the fifties at an old-line yard in Maine. He had lived aboard her for nearly three years, since the time when he had had to choose between the condo and the boat. The condo had never had a chance. He worked hard at keeping the boat beautiful, and she rewarded the effort. Her black hull was unmarked, her mahogany trim was bright, and her teak decks were clean and well oiled.

She was named *Choke.* He preferred to make the joke himself, before somebody else brought it up, as somebody always did.

He'd have to rig up the gangplank, he thought, looking at the three-foot gap between the boat's stern and the concrete wharf. The women wouldn't like making that jump.

He walked to the parking lot and stopped in his tracks. The car was a late-fifties Porsche Speedster, bright yellow, restored to a fault, and her radio antenna had been snapped off by some passing sonofabitch. Chuck sighed. He wasn't in Palm Beach anymore.

He got into the car and drove the length of the island to the Olde Island Racquet Club, three courts and a tiny pro shop, owned by the big hotel across the street. He walked in at the stroke of ten.

Merkle Connor looked up from his computer and peered at Chuck. "Oh, hi," he said. "That's right, you're starting today." He seemed to have forgotten.

"That's right, Merk," Chuck said, offering his new boss a smile.

"Sit down a minute, Chuck," Merk said, pushing back from his desk in the tiny office and moving a crate of tennis balls away from the spare chair.

Chuck took a seat. Here it came.

"Let me give you the lay of the land," Merk said.

This is not Palm Beach, Chuck predicted.

"This is not Palm Beach," Merk began. "We're not fancy, but we're busy. If you work hard at developing a clientele here, you can knock down seventy-five grand a year, maybe more."

Stay away from the broads.

"You're going to have to be careful with the female talent," Merk continued. "I had a guy last year who was shacking up with a hotel guest *in her fucking room,* and the manager went freaky on me, made me fire the guy. Basically, I don't give a damn who you screw, as long as it's not in the hotel and it doesn't, you know, *reverberate.* You get my drift?"

"I get your drift, Merk. There won't be any problems."

"Good, because I got problems enough, what with running two programs, this one and the one in Santa Fe. In April I head west, and it's up to you and Victor to run this place."

"I'm Victor," a voice behind Chuck said.

Chuck turned and stuck out a hand. "Hi, I'm Chuck Chandler."

"Victor Brennan," the man said. He was mid-forties, bushy mustache, tousled hair, permanent

9

grin. Something of a belly hung over his shorts; he looked more like an ex-football player than a tennis pro. "Welcome to paradise."

"Thanks. I'm looking forward to it."

"Then you must believe all of Merk's lies."

"Okay, Victor, lay off and listen," Merk said. "Chuck, I'm going to divide the work roughly between you and Victor; you get the better players, the hotshots and the comers. Victor does the daily clinic, which is mostly hotel guests, plus the housewives, the kids, and the duffers. He's temperamentally suited to that kind of teaching."

"I am," Victor confirmed. "I'm the sweetest guy in the world, and I can teach *anybody* to play tennis."

"You're welcome to it," Chuck said. "I've never been any good with the beginners and the duffers."

"I'm going to charge more for you, Chuck, because you have a reputation," Merk said. "We get folks who'll gladly pay just to hit with you; I've already lined up a few. Victor will give you the rundown on them."

"That I will," Victor said. "Come on out to the courts, and I'll show you the lay of the land."

Victor led him out of the pro shop, past the ball machine and the cart of practice balls. He tapped in a code on the gate lock and let them in. "The code is three three three this week," he said, handing Chuck a key. "This is for the other gate down there. I teach on court one, you take three, we'll rent the middle one." He waved at a bench. "Take a pew and I'll enlighten you."

"Do that," Chuck said, sitting down.

"There are some good regulars. There's Larry, the writer, who plays the best players in town three or four times a week. He'll try you out pretty soon, and if you want him to keep coming back, you'd better let him win two out of three."

"Gotcha," Chuck said.

"There's Holly, the freelance personal trainer, who is stronger than you are, believe me, and who will run you right into the ground if you're not careful."

"Okay."

"There's a seventeen-year-old boy named Bill Tubbs who you might be able to do a lot with. He's got a hell of a lot of talent, and he's very strong; has dreams of being a touring pro. I haven't been able to do a lot with him because he's too stubborn, thinks he's always right. And you'll have to deal with his old man, the beer distributor, who thinks the kid is Pete Sampras."

"Okay," Chuck said. "Who else?"

"Over there," Victor said, nodding toward the parking lot.

Chuck turned to see two people getting out of a shiny new Mercedes S-class sedan. The man was sixtyish, tall, slim, and looked to be in good shape. He had thick, snow-white hair, brushed straight back, and a deep tan. Getting out of the other side of the car was the most beautiful woman Chuck had seen since he'd left the pro

11

tour, and that was a long time ago. She was tall—
five-eight or -nine—had high breasts, long legs,
a tiny waist, dark hair in a ponytail, and a tan
nearly as deep as her companion's. She was thirty
years younger than he.

"Wow," Chuck said.

"Wow indeed," Victor replied. "They turned
up a few months ago, and they're both pretty
good. Names are Harry and Clare Carras."

"Married?" Chuck asked.

"That's the bad news."

"What else do you know about them?"

"Not a hell of a lot. He seems to be filthy
rich and retired. They bought a big old Victorian
house in Old Town and apparently spent a
fortune fixing it up. He's got one of those little
portable cellular phones, and he talks on it a lot.
You'll have to get used to that."

The couple opened the main gate to the courts
and walked in.

"Come on, I'll introduce you," Victor said.

Chuck watched the woman walking toward
him, and he was suddenly aware that her husband
was watching him watching her.

"Harry and Clare," Victor said, "this is Chuck
Chandler, our new head pro."

Chuck shook Harry's hand first. It was soft,
but strong. "How are you, Harry?"

"Good," Harry replied.

"Clare?" Chuck said, turning to her. He felt
a stirring in his crotch.

"Hello, Chuck," Clare said. "We heard you were coming."

Her hand lingered in his.

"Glad to be here," Chuck said, trying to tear himself away from her large green eyes. "I hear you folks play good tennis."

"Let's find out," Harry said. "Victor, you want to make a fourth?"

"Sure, Harry," Victor said. "I'll play a couple of sets; I don't have anything scheduled until eleven."

"Good," Harry said. "Me and Clare against you two." He led his wife onto a court.

Chuck followed them, unable to take his eyes off the woman. She was made for tennis clothes, he thought. Or no clothes at all.

Chuck watched them both carefully as they warmed up; they were both smooth players who hit the ball well. He decided to start with his low game, just to see how it went. The low game wasn't enough; soon he and Victor were down love-three.

Harry chipped and sliced a lot and knew where to put the ball—the mark of a good older player. He had abandoned power a while back and had substituted craft.

Clare had more power than her frame had indicated, and she seemed able to return almost anything. Chuck raised his game a notch and left it there. It was enough for a close finish; he and Victor won the set in a tiebreaker.

They all shook hands, then adjourned to the water cooler.

"Chuck, that was a good game," Harry said. "We'll take you next time."

"I'll watch out, Harry."

"Why don't you join us for dinner this evening? We'll officially welcome you to Key West. Victor, you too?"

Both pros accepted.

"Good. Eight o'clock at Louie's Backyard."

"Thanks, Harry," Chuck said. He glanced at Clare. "I'll look forward to it."

There was a tiny curl to Clare's red lip. Chuck took it for a smile.

CHAPTER

2

Chuck found Louie's Backyard on the second try. Key West was only one mile by four, but he needed a map, and still it was tricky. There were only two or three streets that ran the length of the island; the rest were narrow and crowded with frame dwellings called Conch houses. Louie's was on one of these little streets, a good-sized Victorian place that looked more like somebody's home than a restaurant.

"Mr. Carras hasn't arrived yet," the headwaiter said, "but the other member of your party is waiting at the bar outside. Just walk straight through."

Chuck emerged from the rear of the house onto a three-tiered deck filled with tables; the bar was on the lower level and nearly in the water. The sea lapped at the deck, and a rising moon illuminated the diners, mostly tourists, Chuck figured, come south for some sun.

Victor waved at him from the bar, and Chuck slid onto an adjacent barstool. "Where are our hosts?" he asked.

"Harry and Clare are not great at on-time performance," Victor replied. "Buy you a drink?"

"Thanks. I'll have a vodka gimlet, straight up, very cold," he said to the bartender.

The two clinked glasses. "Welcome to paradise," Victor said.

"That's what you said this morning. Is it really?"

"Can be. Depends on your attitude."

"My attitude's pretty good."

"Then you'll like it. There are a lot of very strange people in this town," Victor said. "It's the end of the road, figuratively, for a lot of them. They couldn't make it anywhere else, so they decided to come down here and not make it. Not making it is what folks do here."

"My attitude's not *that* good," Chuck said, laughing. "I gotta make a living."

"Found a place to live yet?"

"I brought it with me."

"Trailer?"

"I haven't sunk that low; it's a little motor yacht. I found a berth at Key West Bight."

"That's where it's all happening, boatwise," Victor said. "Say, is the yellow Speedster yours?"

"Yep. I restored the thing from scratch when I was living in Palm Beach."

"I guess Merk told you, this isn't Palm Beach."

"I'm glad to hear it."

"Listen, Chuck, you and I don't know each other very well, but I've got to ask you . . . "

"Yep, I choked."

"Not about that."

"About what, then?"

"About Palm Beach. We got a whiff of the rumor down here. Did you really get the club president's wife pregnant?"

Chuck shook his head.

"I didn't really believe it," Victor said.

"It was the chairman's wife. And it was a hysterical preg-nancy."

"A *hysterical* pregnancy?"

"Hysterical, isn't it? She actually missed two periods."

"I don't believe it."

"Neither did her husband. Of course, by the time she was running on schedule again, I was out of the club." Chuck looked out over the moonlit water. "It's beautiful, isn't it?"

"It is," Victor agreed.

Chuck watched as a boatload of people left a

good-sized motor yacht anchored offshore and made their way to Louie's aboard a Boston Whaler. The skipper tied up the boat, and a party of six scrambled ashore.

Chuck glanced at his watch. "Our hosts are twenty minutes late," he said. "You may have to buy me dinner."

"They'll show," Victor said. "Harry's the type to keep his promises."

Another half hour passed before the Carrases turned up, and the whole restaurant turned to watch their entrance—or rather, Clare's entrance. She came down the stairs in a white strapless dress that Nature held up, and for a brief moment, not a word was spoken within sight of her.

Chuck stood up and watched her walk toward the bar. "Hello, Harry," he said, shaking the husband's hand first. "And Clare."

Her cool hand squeezed his again. He stopped himself from fantasizing.

"Sorry we're late," Harry said, "but our table's ready, so let's sit down and have a drink there."

Chuck and Victor followed the couple to a well-placed table and ordered another round. Harry ordered scotch; Clare ordered a glass of sauvignon blanc.

Harry raised his glass. "Welcome to Key West," he said.

"Thank you, Harry," Chuck replied. "I think I'm going to like it here." He tried not to look at Clare as he said it.

"So you're down from Palm Beach," Harry said. "Are the rumors true?"

"No, they're not," Victor said. "It was a hysterical preg-nancy."

They all burst out laughing, and Chuck joined them.

"Chuck," Harry said when they had stopped laughing, "do you make a specialty of other men's wives?"

"No, Harry," Chuck replied. "But from time to time, they seem to make a specialty of me."

Everybody laughed again.

Clare put a hand on Chuck's arm. "Who could blame them?" she said, and there was just a touch of sarcasm in her voice.

"You're too kind, Clare," Chuck replied.

The talk turned to tennis as the menus arrived, and they stayed on that subject through two courses, until Harry changed it.

"You do any diving, Chuck?" Harry asked.

"I do. I live on my boat, over at Key West Bight, and I'll be happy to take you out sometime."

"We'll take you," Harry said.

"I'd love to."

At that moment a gust of wind struck, so sharp and so sudden it knocked over a wineglass, and a split second later a roar filled the air. Suddenly everyone in the restaurant was standing, looking in the same direction.

Chuck followed their gaze. A column of yellow fire rose into the sky, and debris was falling into the water in a large circle. The motor yacht Chuck had noticed earlier had now become a flaming hulk.

"Holy shit," Victor murmured.

"Gas," Harry said. "Gotta be gas."

"Gas *and* gasoline," Chuck replied. "Diesel wouldn't blow like that."

"Do you suppose anyone was hurt?" Clare asked.

"I don't think so," Chuck replied. "We saw a large party leave the boat and come ashore here a little while ago."

As if on cue, a woman screamed.

Chuck looked toward the bar. The woman had now covered her mouth with her hand and was pointing toward the fire. Tears streamed down her face.

"What's she bitching about?" Harry asked. "She's alive, isn't she?"

CHAPTER

3

Tommy Sculley was on his feet with the rest of the diners, gawking at the explosion. Then he got hold of himself, reached for his pocket cellphone, and dialed 911.

"I knew it," Rose said. "I knew you'd do something to fuck up this dinner, but I'll admit, I hadn't expected anything quite so elaborate."

"Rosie, shut up and eat your dessert," Tommy said.

"Key West Police Department," a woman's voice said.

"This is Detective Sculley. A boat has exploded a hundred and fifty yards off the east end of the island, and there may be fatalities. I want you to . . . "

"Who did you say this is?" the woman asked.

"Detective Thomas Sculley of the Key West Police Department," he replied.

"I don't know any detective named Sculley," she said.

"Sweetheart," Tommy said, "if you don't listen to me and do what I tell you *right now*, you're going to get a very personal introduction. I'm new, okay? Now you get hold of the Coast Guard and tell them to scramble a cutter and to make sure there's a medic on board."

"You sure this isn't some kind of joke?"

"What's your name?"

"Helen Rafferty."

"Helen, as one Irishman to another, this is the straight scoop. Now, does this department have a boat of some sort?"

"Yeah, but it's hauled out getting some work done at the moment."

"Swell. You call the Coast Guard, and I'll find my own boat."

"Are you sure . . . "

"Do it, Helen, and think about it later." He raised a hand. "Waiter!" he yelled. "Check!"

Five minutes later, Tommy had left his wife to pay the bill for her birthday dinner, collared the young man who had skippered the Boston Whaler to the restaurant, and was on his way to the scene of the explosion, along with a very unhappy accountant from Atlanta.

"I just bought the thing," the accountant said. "This is our first cruise."

"What's your name?" Tommy asked, notebook at the ready.

"Warren Porter," the man replied. "Who are you, and what are you doing in my tender?"

Tommy flashed his new badge. "Key West PD; name's Sculley."

"How did you get here so fast?"

"I was having dinner, just like you." Tommy turned to the man driving the boat. "Are you new on the yacht?"

"No, sir," the young man said. "I worked for the previous owner."

"Were you in charge of maintenance?"

"Yes, sir. She's maintained to the hilt, you can take my word for it."

"Take his word for it," the accountant said. "I'll show you my first yard bill."

"Was there a gas system for cooking?"

"Yes, sir, two twenty-gallon bottles, both stowed on the port quarter. The system is . . .

was first-rate, conformed to all the Coast Guard regulations."

"What kind of fuel did the engines use?"

"Gasoline. Fairly unusual in a boat of this size, but the guy who built her wanted as much speed as possible for the weight of the engine, and diesel didn't cut it for him."

They reached the site of the explosion, and Tommy looked around. "Jesus H. Christ!" he said. "There's nothing left." All he could see were small pieces of flotsam, some of them still on fire. They added an eerie glow to the moonlight.

"There've got to be some bigger pieces," the skipper said, "but they've probably sunk. I mean, nothing short of an atomic bomb could reduce a sixty-foot boat to such splinters. I'll bet we're sitting on top of some major wreckage."

A siren sounded, and from around a point appeared a large vessel wearing a lot of lights.

"Here comes the Coast Guard," Tommy said. "I got to ask both of you some questions before they get here. Anybody aboard the boat?"

"No," the accountant said. "We all came ashore for dinner at Louie's."

"Thank God for small favors," Tommy breathed. "Who cooks?"

"Nell," the skipper said. "She's my girlfriend; we've both been on the boat for over three years."

"Does she know what she's doing with the gas system? How to turn it off and secure it when it's not being used?"

"You bet she does," the skipper said. "She

knows as much about the boat as I do, and she's a careful girl."

"Is it just possible that she might have been in a hurry to get ashore with everybody else and forgot to turn off the gas at the bottles?"

"Well, maybe," the skipper admitted. "Normally we just turn off the gas at the stove and not at the bottles, unless we're leaving the boat for a longer period of time."

"So you could have had a leak?"

"It's possible, but not likely. We'd have smelled it."

"Did you have a gas detector aboard?"

The skipper shook his head. "It went south a week ago. It was on my list of things to replace while we're in Key West."

Tommy nodded. Enough little problems to make an accident were emerging. "Was she insured?" he asked the accountant.

The man nodded sadly. "Yeah, but there's a ten-thousand-dollar-deductible, and insurance won't pay for all the time I put in finding this boat and negotiating the sale."

"Let me say two words to you, Mr. Porter," Tommy said. "Casualty loss."

The accountant looked a little happier.

It was past midnight when Tommy got to the hotel room he and his wife were living in until they found a place. He sneaked in, trying not to wake her.

"Have fun?" Rose asked.

23

"A fucking ball, sweetie," Tommy said, crawling into bed. "The smell of burning yacht does wonders for your digestion when you've just had a great meal."

"Well, I guess you don't have to worry about it being too dull down here," Rose said. "What happened?"

"Looks like an accidental gas explosion that ignited the fuel tanks. Nobody aboard, thank God. I don't think I could have taken the smell of burning flesh after that dinner."

"You like it here already, don't you?"

"I guess we did the right thing," Tommy replied. He had retired from the New York Police Department after twenty years, taken his pension, and headed south. Rose liked Florida, and it had taken him less than a month to find the Key West job. He was forty-two, and he had just started building time on a second pension. When he was sixty-two, they'd be free as birds.

"Let's talk about that when we've found a place to live that we can afford and the furniture has arrived," she said. "Then I'll know if we did the right thing."

"But Rosie, you always loved Florida," Tommy said.

"This isn't Florida, Tommy. This is like some kind of foreign country, some banana republic. It doesn't have anything to do with Florida."

"It's hot as hell and it's humid and it's got a beach. It's Florida."

"If you say so."

He rolled over and dug his arm under her head. "You're going to love it here, Rosie," he said. "Just you wait."

"I'm waiting."

"Rosie?"

"Yeah?"

"You remember the couple who came in right after we sat down to dinner?"

"You mean the couple in the white dress with the tits?"

"That's the one."

"What about them?"

"The guy looked familiar, you know?"

"I don't know."

"You never saw him before?"

"Nope."

"Not even in the papers or anything?"

"Nope."

"You know what he looked like to me? He looked connected."

"Tommy, they don't know from connected down here."

"You never know," he said. "Say, did I wish you a happy birthday?"

"As a matter of fact, you didn't."

Tommy pulled her leg over his, rubbed his thigh against her crotch, and ran a hand up under her nightgown. "Happy birthday," he said, tickling her ass.

Rose sighed and kissed him. "Thank you, Tommy; it's been a memorable evening."

"Memorable starts right now," Tommy said.

CHAPTER

4

Chuck had a light first week at the Olde Island Racquet Club. His only regulars were Harry and Clare Carras; they never missed, and they always came together. Until Saturday.

Clare showed up at 11:00 A.M., alone.

"Morning, Clare," Chuck said. "Where's Harry?"

"In Miami, on business," she replied.

"What do you want to do today?"

She looked at him for a moment. "Let's work on my serve," she said finally. "I'm too erratic."

Chuck nodded. "I've noticed, but you've never seemed interested in any instruction."

"I'm interested," she said.

Chuck grabbed a cart of practice balls and led her onto the court. "Let me see you hit a couple," he said.

Clare picked up a pair of balls and began serving.

Chuck was content to just watch for a couple of minutes. She was wearing a tank top and very short shorts, and every time she reached up for a ball, her buns peeked at him from beneath the white material.

26

She stopped. "Well?"

"A couple of problems," he said, "starting with your grip. You're too far around on the racquet, so all you can hit is a flat serve. Bring your grip around a bit, like this, and you'll get some spin on the ball, make it harder to return."

She tried a couple more serves. "Better," she said. "What else?"

"You're dumping too many serves into the net; you have to watch the ball until the racquet strikes it. Keep your head up, and you'll send more over the net."

He worked with her for a full hour, and by the end she had improved noticeably.

"Thanks," she said. "I enjoyed that."

"So did I," he said.

She put down her racquet and mopped her face with a towel. "Come to dinner tonight," she said without preamble.

Chuck took in a quick breath. "Love to," he replied, trying to sound casual.

She gave him the address. "Seven?"

"Seven's fine; can I bring some wine?"

"A good red would be perfect."

"A very good red."

"See you at seven," she said, then gave him the address. "Don't dress up."

"I won't."

The house was only a block from Key West Bight, a big, three-story Victorian on what seemed to be a double, even triple lot, if the fence was any indication. The door was open, but he rang the bell anyway.

"Come on in!" she called from somewhere.

Chuck opened the screen door and entered the house. There was a short hallway that stopped at a stairway. To his right he could see a large swimming pool.

"Up here!" she called from upstairs.

He climbed the stairs and emerged into a large living room, with the kitchen to his left, separated by a bar.

Clare was rummaging in the refrigerator. She turned toward him, and there was a bottle of Veuve Clicquot in her hands. "Some champagne?"

"Sure." He set his gift of wine on the bar.

She looked at the label. "Very nice," she said. "It will go well with dinner."

"The best the Waterfront Market had," he replied, accepting a flute of champagne. They clinked glasses.

"New friends," she said.

"I'll drink to that."

She came from behind the bar and took a stool next to his. She was wearing a short, sheer dress that buttoned down the front. Two patch pockets covered her breasts, and he could clearly see her panties through the material.

"You look very beautiful tonight," he said.

She laughed, showing even white teeth. "It's my job," she said.

"Your job?"

28

"It's how I earn my keep." She shrugged. "It's how most women earn their keep if they don't have children and don't keep house."

"You make marriage sound very businesslike," Chuck said.

"Harry is a businesslike kind of guy."

"How long have you been married?"

"A little over a year. Harry's first wife died the year before we met."

"Where you from?"

"We're both originally from the coast— Harry's from L.A., I'm from San Diego. You?"

"Small town in Georgia, called Delano."

"How did you get to be a good enough player to turn pro, starting from a small town?"

"I had a high school coach who was very good. He got me a tennis scholarship to the University of Georgia, where I had an-other good coach. I turned pro right out of school. What did you do before you met Harry?"

"Oh, lots of things—secretary, receptionist, manicurist, masseuse."

"I'll bet you were a wonderful masseuse."

She smiled again. "I was, as a matter of fact. That's how I met Harry. I was working at a hotel in Vegas."

"You're far too elegant a woman to hang out in Vegas."

"I thought so, too. When Harry asked me to marry him I made one condition—that I would never have to visit Las Vegas again, ever." She poured them both more champagne.

"You'll get me drunk, feeding me champagne on an empty stomach," he said.

She uncrossed her legs. "Don't I have to get you drunk to fuck you?" she asked.

Chuck set down his glass and tried to control his breathing. "Nope," he said.

She stood up, moved to him, put her arms around his neck, and kissed him lightly, playfully.

Chuck slid up her dress, put his hands down the back of her underwear, and held her cheeks, pulling her crotch to his.

"They come off, you know," she breathed in his ear.

He pushed them down.

She stepped out of the panties, moved back a pace, and started unbuttoning the dress.

Chuck kicked off his moccasins, peeled the polo shirt over his head, and shucked off his shorts. He was fully erect.

She reached out and took hold of his penis. "Come with me," she said, backing across the living room, leading him by his member. They reached a thick wool rug, and she pulled him down on top of her. "Now," she breathed. "No more foreplay." She guided him into her.

Chuck rested on his elbows, watching her face. Her eyes never left his. They moved together slowly, then faster.

Her eyes began to glaze over, and she reached down and held his testicles in her hand, squeezing gently. "Now," she said. "Right now."

Chuck rose to the occasion. He came right

behind her, moving as fast as he could, groaning with pleasure. They stopped gradually, wound down like a clock spring.

"So much for safe sex," Clare said.

"You look pretty safe to me," he replied, rolling off and lying next to her on the rug.

"Don't you believe it," she said, then she got up, went to the bar for some paper towels, and returned. She mopped him gently, then herself. "That was very quick," she said. "Next time you're going to have to last longer to make me happy."

"Making you happy is why I'm here," Chuck said.

"I hope so," she replied. "In a minute, after I've rested a bit, I'm going to cook you the best steak you ever had, and then I'm going to let you make me *very* happy."

"I'm not going anywhere."

"Do you feel guilty? About Harry, I mean?"

"Not really."

"You shouldn't, you know. Harry looks great, but he's not a healthy man. He had bypass surgery a year and a half ago, but he still drinks a lot and eats lots of fatty foods. Then he'll go out there and swim fifty laps in that pool like there's no tomorrow."

"That's dangerous."

"I know. He'll drop dead one day. I'll go out there and find him floating facedown."

"Are you ready for that?"

"Yes, but in the meantime, there's practically no sex. He had prostate surgery last year."

"I'll do what I can to help."

She laughed. "You're sweet; only thinking of me."

"You think Harry knows what we're doing?"

"It wouldn't surprise me."

"How often does he go away on business?"

"Two or three times a month, usually."

"That's not often enough."

"We'll manage." She turned and looked at him seriously. "How old are you, Chuck?"

"Forty-four," he replied.

"Mmmm," she breathed. "It's time you were thinking about your future, your security."

She got up and, still naked, began to prepare dinner.

Chuck watched her move about the kitchen and wondered how he'd gotten so lucky.

After dinner they made love again, then again, before they fell asleep in each other's arms.

CHAPTER

5

Chuck woke late on Sunday morning and had to rush to make it to work on time. As he stepped ashore, a catamaran of about fifty feet was backing into the space on *Choke's* port side.

"Can you take our lines, please?" a young woman called from the yacht's stern. She was young, in her late twenties, probably, not tall, and voluptuously constructed, which was easy to see, because she was wearing only the tiniest of bikinis and barely that. Her hair was shoulder-length and sun-bleached, and Chuck thought she was, for want of a better word, pert.

"Sure," Chuck called back and caught the length of rope just as it was about to strike him in the face. He made the line fast, then took the next one thrown and secured it. On the foredeck a man was paying out anchor rope.

"Thanks," the girl said, stepping ashore and holding out her hand. "I'm Meg Hailey."

"Chuck Chandler, Meg; nice to meet you. I guess I'm your next-door neighbor."

Her male companion walked through the cockpit and stepped ashore. "Hi, I'm Dan Hailey," he said, shaking hands.

"I'm Chuck Chandler, and this is my boat," he said, nodding at *Choke*. "Where're you in from?"

"Fort Myers was our last port," Dan said. "We'll be here for the rest of the winter, I think."

"Let me know if you need any local knowl-edge," Chuck said. "I've only been here for a few days myself, but I'll tell you what-ever I can."

"Thanks," Meg replied. "You can start by pointing me at a grocery store."

"The Waterfront Market is just along the way. I'm headed that way; I'll show you, if you like."

"Be right with you," she replied and jumped back aboard the yacht.

"You here for just the winter, too?" Dan asked.

"Maybe longer," Chuck replied. "I'll see how it goes."

Meg returned wearing a T-shirt over her bikini and carrying a purse. "Be back in half an hour," she said to Dan and kissed him on the cheek. She fell in beside Chuck, and they walked toward the market.

"So, you're new here, too?" she asked.

"Yeah, I came down from Palm Beach just recently."

"You going to play some tennis?" she asked, looking at his clothes.

"I teach tennis," he replied. "Even on Sundays."

"Sounds like a tough life," she said, smiling.

"I bear up." He returned her smile. "Well, here we are," he said, pointing at the market entrance. "Anything they don't have here you'll have to drive to a supermarket for."

"Thanks," she said. "See you later."

He watched her pick her way, barefoot, over the gravel and enter the store. *Thank God she's married,* he thought. Otherwise she'd be real trouble. Not that her being married would slow him down; it was just that if she were single it would be harder to break it off when it was over. Clare was going to be available only when Harry was out of town, and it might be good to have another diversion.

He got into the old Porsche and headed for the other end of the island. As he drove through the intersection of Caroline and Elizabeth streets, Harry Carras's Mercedes crossed just ahead of him. *Good thing I didn't stay the night,* he thought.

He parked the car and approached the tennis club; a teenage boy was hitting with Victor, and he was stopped in his tracks by the boy's grace of movement. He let himself into the court.

"Morning, Chuck," Victor said. "This is Billy Tubbs; he's interested in working with you, I think."

Chuck shook hands with the boy, whose face was nearly blank of expression. He was at least six-two, 190 pounds. He seemed to be looking Chuck over very carefully.

"And this is Billy's dad, Norman Tubbs," Victor said, waving toward a short, thickly built, hairy man who was rising from a courtside bench. He and his son didn't resemble each other.

"How y'doin'?" Norman said.

"Glad to meet you, Norman. Why don't you and I sit down and watch Billy hit with Victor."

"Okay," Tubbs said.

Chuck watched the boy hit ground strokes for a few minutes, making a mental note or two. "Feed him some volleys, Victor," Chuck called out, then watched as Billy returned them for

35

another ten minutes. "Let me see you serve to Victor, Billy," he called.

Billy sliced in a few serves.

"Now let's see you return Victor's serve."

Victor served a dozen hard ones to the boy. He got most of them back, but not particularly well.

Norman Tubbs spoke up, handing Chuck a sheet of paper. "Here's his numbers for last season," he said.

Chuck looked over the sheet. "Okay, that's enough," he called out. "Come on over here and sit down a minute, Billy."

The boy walked over to the bench and stood, leaning against the netpost, breathing hard.

"Norman, do you mind if Billy and I talk for a few minutes? Just the two of us?"

"I'll be the one who makes the decision about who coaches him," Norman said. "You can talk to me."

"The boy has some problems that he and I need to discuss before I decide whether to take him on," Chuck said, not unkindly. "When he and I are finished, then you and I can talk."

Norman looked at him for a moment, then got up and left the court with Victor.

Chuck turned back to the boy. "Have a seat, Billy; let's talk."

"I'm okay," Billy said.

Bad sign. If he wouldn't sit when he was told, there was a lot he might not do.

"Okay, you stand. What kind of a player do you think you are? No need to be modest."

"I'm a damned good player," Billy replied.

"How'd you do in competition your junior year?"

"I was runner-up in the state high school championship."

"Well," Chuck said, "I guess that makes you a *pretty good high school player.*" He waited for that to sink in. "What do you want to do with your tennis in the next few years?"

"I want to join the pro tour as soon as I graduate in June."

Chuck kept himself from laughing. "Well, let me tell you what I saw this morning. I saw a pretty good high school player who's got some nice ground strokes and who's a pretty good volleyer and who has a decent second serve."

"*Second serve?*" Billy said, astounded. "I didn't even hit any second serves!"

"You mean that was your *first* serve?" Chuck asked, looking surprised. He looked at the sheet of paper in his hand. "I guess that explains why you only won fifty-two percent of your first-serve points last year."

The boy glowered at him, but said nothing.

"Let me tell you what I see," Chuck said, "and if you're still standing there when I'm finished, we'll see if we have anything to talk about."

"Okay," the boy said.

"First of all you're using a western grip on your forehand . . ."

"You sound just like my high school coach," Billy said. "My dad says I don't have to listen to that schmuck to be good."

"Your high school coach sounds like he's smarter than you think."

"I'm doing okay with my grip; it feels natural to me."

"Let's go on," Chuck said, "and shut up until I've finished. You're hitting a two-handed backhand, which you've probably been doing since you were six, but you're not six anymore. You've got to learn to move your feet when you volley, and you've got to learn to hit a flat, hard first serve if you expect to get beyond being a *pretty good high school player.* You've got to learn how to place your serve, too, and you've got a long way to go on your return of service. Your returns are weak, just setups for a good player. Am I making any sense?"

"Some, I guess," the boy replied, and his face was red.

"Good. And on top of everything else, you're in lousy shape; you've been drinking too much of your old man's beer. If you sign on with me, there'll be no more of that. I'll run your ass off. However, if you'll shed some of your weight and your arrogance, and if you play the way I tell you to, I can probably get you a tennis scholarship at a good university, and if you keep learning while you're in college, then you might make a pretty good touring pro. Then, if you have a good temperament and strong nerves, you might win

38

some tournaments. In three months, I'll be able to tell you if you can make it."

The boy stared at the ground for a moment. "Okay," he said, finally.

"Okay what?"

"Okay, I'll do it your way for a while."

"You'll do it my way every day for as long as I coach you, kid, or you'll do it for somebody else," Chuck said. "You better understand that up front. I don't need your daddy's money to get along, and I sure as hell don't need any lip from a *pretty good high school player.*" It had been a lie about not needing his daddy's money, but if the boy suspected his coach needed him, he'd be impossible to handle. "Do we have an understanding?"

"Yeah," the boy said.

"Try 'Yes, sir,' " Chuck said.

"Yes, sir."

"Good, now go tell your dad I'd like to talk to him."

Billy walked off the court, and a moment later Norman Tubbs came and sat down next to Chuck. "The boy's good, huh?" he asked.

"Not nearly as good as you think he is," Chuck said. "He's got a lot of problems."

"Listen, that boy beat just about everybody they threw at him last year," Tubbs said.

"Norman, he was playing *high school kids.*"

"So, you want to coach him?"

"If I can do it by myself."

"What do you mean?"

"I mean, I don't want you at practices."

"Why not? I can help you control him."

"I won't have any trouble controlling him if you're not around to take his side."

"I've helped that boy," Tubbs said.

"Norman, the best way you can help that boy is to give him only one instruction: 'Do what your coach says, or I'll kick your ass.' "

Norman looked at the ground. "It's not that I want to interfere."

"Norman, that boy has a very great deal of talent," Chuck said. "But his game is all screwed up, and part of his trouble is that two people—his high school coach and you—have been telling him what to do. He needs just one voice in his ear, and that has to be me, if I'm going to coach him. To tell you the truth, I don't think there's anybody else in town who can teach him what he needs to know."

Tubbs sighed. "All right; I'll stay out of it. What's it going to cost me?"

"Seventy-five bucks an hour, two hours a day, six days a week," Chuck replied, then tried not to hold his breath.

"That's what I figured," Tubbs said.

"Tell him he has to go to college, too, or you won't pay."

"No problem there. I want him to go to college."

"I'll tell you the truth, Norman. If he listens to me and plays the way I tell him to, by the time he's a sophomore, the agents will be all over him.

40

You'll have to resign yourself to that; he's not going to want to come home and go into the beer distribution business."

"That's kind of what I thought," Tubbs said resignedly.

"Okay, then," Chuck said, standing and offering his hand. "Send him over here, and we'll get started."

Chuck played a set with the boy and beat him six-love, ran him all over the court, humiliated him. When they were done he sat him down on a bench. "That's what it's like to play against a pro," he said, "even a forty-four-year-old pro. Are you beginning to get the picture?"

Billy nodded, sucking in wind. "Yes, sir," he said.

Chuck went into the pro shop to see who his next lesson was with. Merk looked up from his calculator.

"How'd you get on with Norman Tubbs and his boy?"

"He's going to do two hours a day, six days a week, at seventy-five an hour."

Merk beamed. "Now *that's* good news."

"The news isn't all good, Merk; I'm going to keep fifty of it."

"*What?*"

"Merk, if you'd dealt with Tubbs, you'd have charged him fifty and kept twenty-five. You're not losing on the deal."

Merk nodded resignedly. "You've got a point."

That was two bluffs Chuck had pulled off in half an hour. He was very pleased with himself.

CHAPTER

6

Tommy Sculley took a seat across the desk from his boss, the chief of police.

"Welcome to Key West, Tommy," the chief said.

"Thank you, sir," Tommy replied, on his best behavior.

"I hear you got off to a roaring start, calling in that exploding yacht."

"Yes, sir; I was having dinner at Louie's, and it came with the dessert."

"I'm going to tell you something you already know, Tommy: Key West ain't New York."

"You're right, I knew that," Tommy replied.

"For instance, I know you spent your last dozen years on the NYPD in homicide, that homicide is your forte, so to speak."

"That's right, sir."

"Well, last year we had a four hundred percent increase in homicides in Key West."

"Four hundred percent?"

"That's right. Of course, the year before, we only had one, so when we had four last year, it looked pretty big."

Tommy laughed. "You had a year with one homicide? The guys in New York would never believe it."

"In a normal year we get two, so you can see it's not worth our while to have a homicide bureau as such."

"I guess not."

"Everybody does a little bit of everything around here. On your tour, you'll take every call for a detective that comes in and some patrolman's calls, too, if we're busy. You'll deal with everything from armed robbery to domestic violence, and in Key West that last category applies to as many homosexuals as heterosexuals."

"Yeah, I heard you had a big gay population."

"Big and valuable. They own shops and galleries, restaurants and bars, they're waiters and doctors and professionals of all sorts, and they make a big economic contribution to the town. So you can see why we treat them with the utmost courtesy and respect, just as we treat everybody else."

"I get the picture."

"I hope you do, because there's no room for a homophobe on this force. If you hold those views, my advice is to keep them to yourself, even with your brother officers, because some of them are gay."

43

"I have no problems with gays, sir."

"You should also know that, generally speaking, a record number of arrests is not something I look at with admiration. I like to think of my force as problem-solvers as well as enforcers. My policy is, if you can deal fairly with a situation, defuse it instead of busting somebody, that's better than an arrest. The exception to that rule is anything involving violence. I won't have it on my streets, and if you come across something as simple as a fistfight, haul in the perpetrator, if you can figure out who he is, and both of them if you can't. We'll sort it out later."

"I understand, sir."

"Something else to keep in mind is that although our population is less than thirty thousand, we have two million tourists a year in this town. They're our lifeblood, and we do everything we can to treat them well. Again, violence is the exception to leniency."

"I'll keep that in mind, sir."

"You'll get the hang of the paperwork in a hurry; it's standard stuff, probably not much different from what you had in New York. Oh, and I have a partner for you." He looked up through the glass door of his office. "And here he comes now."

Tommy turned to see what he took to be a kid of about seventeen—skinny, longish hair, and pimples—walk into the office.

"Tommy, this is Daryl Haynes," the chief said. "Daryl, this is the detective I told you about."

The two shook hands.

"How you doin', Daryl?" Tommy asked, appalled.

"Okay," Daryl replied, then looked at his feet.

"This is Daryl's first day as a detective," the chief said. "He's had two years on the street."

On whose side? Tommy thought. "Oh, yeah, good."

"I reckon you can teach Daryl a lot about investigation," the chief said, "and Daryl can show you a few things about Key West. He grew up here."

Grew up? Tommy thought. *When?*

"Daryl, why don't you start by giving Tommy a tour of the town?"

"Right, Chief," Daryl said. He tossed his head in the direction of the door. "Ready when you are, Detective."

Tommy shook hands with the chief and followed the pimply new detective.

"Tommy?" the chief called.

Tommy stuck his head back through the door. "Yes, Chief?"

"He's smarter than he looks," the chief said.

"Right, Chief." *He'd have to be.*

Daryl was already gunning the engine when Tommy got into the car. The second the door closed, he whipped out of the police parking lot and down the street.

"Pull over here a minute," Tommy said quietly.

"What for?" Daryl asked.

"My underwear is twisted. Just pull over."

Daryl pulled over.

"Okay, Daryl, the first thing is, a detective doesn't drive a car like he just stole it. You notice that there's no markings on the doors?"

"Yeah."

"That's because we're supposed to be inconspicuous. You want people to notice you, you wear a uniform and drive a black-and-white. You get the picture?"

"Right, Detective."

"You can call me Tommy."

"Right, Tommy."

"Now, I want you to start practicing driving like you were, say, fifty years old and had a heart condition."

Daryl sighed and drove on.

"What's this street?" Tommy asked as they turned a corner.

"This is Duval Street, the main drag. It's where most of the bars and a lot of the restaurants are. We get a call a night about a drunk who wouldn't pay his bill or decked the bouncer, you know?"

"I know. What's the worst time of year for us?"

"That's easy, spring break. We get a few thousand college punks down here; they get drunk and drive around with thirteen people in a convertible. The chief has a policy of, when they do something, putting them to cleaning up the streets. Then he makes sure their picture gets in the paper, so the rest of them will know about it. That pretty much keeps them in line."

They continued the tour. They saw the shady streets and neat Conch houses of Old Town, they saw Roosevelt Boulevard, the strip with the car dealerships and the fast food restaurants. They saw the hotels and the schools, then drove up to the next key, Stock Island, and had a look at the new jail. They stopped for some lunch at McDonald's and ate in the car. As they were finishing their burgers Tommy looked up to see the white-haired man he had seen at Louie's on the night of the exploding yacht.

"There," Tommy said. "What do you make of that guy?"

Daryl watched as the man got into a large Mercedes and drove away. "I don't know; rich, I guess."

"You're a wizard, Daryl," Tommy said, scribbling down the car's license number. "Here, run this tag, and let's see who he is."

Daryl called in the tag number.

"Name is Harry Carras," the radio operator conveyed, "of an address on Dey Street, Old Town."

"Harry Carras," Tommy said aloud to himself. "I'll give you two to one, Daryl, that's not his real name."

"Why do you think that?" Daryl asked. "He just looks like a rich guy in a Mercedes. Come to think of it, there's not even a Mercedes dealer in Key West. You'd have to go halfway up the Keys to Marathon to find one."

"That tell you anything, Daryl? A Mercedes 600S, a twelve-cylinder car in a town where the fastest traffic is the rented motor scooters?"

"Tells me he must be *really* rich," Daryl said.

"That's what you call conspicuous consumption," Tommy said, "and I'll bet the folks in this town don't go for conspicuous consumption— of that type, anyway."

"You're right, they don't."

"So that means that Mr. Carras don't give a shit what the neighbors say, right?"

"Right, but so what?"

"Let's test out your local knowledge, Daryl; the chief said you're good at that. Do you know somebody who would run a credit report on our conspicuous consumer?"

Daryl thought for a moment. "Yeah," he said.

The two policemen sat in the tiny office in a corner of a used car lot on Roosevelt. They watched as the fax machine slowly spat out its paper. The salesman ripped it off the machine.

"Weird," he said.

"What's weird?" Daryl asked.

"Three credit bureaus never heard of a Harry Carras on Dey Street."

Daryl looked at Tommy.

Tommy beamed.

CHAPTER

7

Harry's going to Miami on Sunday," she said. "Are you free Sunday night?"

"Sure," Chuck replied.

"*All* Sunday night?"

"I'm teaching until five, but anytime after that, and I'm off Monday."

"Good. I want you to meet me up the Keys a ways."

"What did you have in mind?"

"What I had in mind was, you drive up U.S. 1 just past the twenty-eight-mile marker, then you turn right into a marina parking lot. Allowing forty-five minutes for the drive, I'll meet you at six-fifteen sharp, okay?"

"Okay."

"Bring your toothbrush and something nice to wear at dinner. And I mean six-fifteen sharp," she reiterated. "If you're late, you'll miss the boat."

He laughed. "I'll miss the boat?"

"In more ways than one," she replied, then hung up.

Sunday was busy and there was a shortage of advanced players, so Chuck had to take a pair of Victor's duffers.

"I'm Tommy," the man said, sticking out his hand. "This is Rosie."

They were both on the short side and firmly built. "Good to meet you, Tommy, Rosie," Chuck said, managing a winning smile. "How much tennis have you played?"

"She's played maybe twice, and I've never walked on a court before," Tommy replied.

Swell, Chuck thought. Rank beginners. "Okay," Chuck said, "let's start with the grip. Shake hands with the racquet, Tommy; you too, Rosie."

The lesson went more smoothly than Chuck would have believed. Tommy was a pretty good natural athlete, and Rosie concentrated so much that she made up for her lack of natural talent. By the end of their hour, Chuck had them both hitting a decent forehand and backhand. Maybe it was easier to teach a raw beginner with some talent than to try and correct a more experienced player's years of bad habits. They were just walking off the court when Harry and Clare Carras drove up in the Mercedes.

Chuck felt a pang of disappointment. Harry was supposed to be in Miami. Still, he thought, glancing at his watch, it was early.

"Ain't that something?" Tommy asked.

"What?" Chuck replied.

"That lady," Tommy said. Rosie had gone into the pro shop. "Ain't she something?" He nodded in the direction of Clare.

"Not bad," Chuck said.

"Not bad?" Tommy said. "You must run with a different crowd than me. Where I come from, that's downright fucking spectacular."

"I guess she is, at that," Chuck agreed.

"Who are those people?" Tommy asked.

"Harry Carras and his wife, Clare."

"She don't look like nobody's wife to me," Tommy said.

Chuck laughed. "I guess not."

"Who is Carras? What does he do?"

"Retired businessman, I think," Chuck replied. "I've played with them a couple of times and I've given her a lesson or two, but I don't really know that much about them."

"Uh-huh," Tommy said, and Chuck somehow thought the man didn't believe him. It was time to change the subject. "Where are you from, Tommy?" he asked.

"New York, originally," Tommy said. "Brooklyn. But we moved down here recently."

"Retired?"

"Yes and no," Tommy replied. "I retired from the New York Police Department, and I just joined the Key West PD."

"First cop I ever had for a student," Chuck said.

"You'd told me a month ago I'd be on a tennis court I'd have laughed my ass off," Tommy said. "But Rosie got at me; she said if we're moving to a new place we ought to do some new things."

"Did you enjoy it?"

"Amazingly enough, I did. I want to do it some more."

"Victor and I could make a pretty good club player out of you this winter," Chuck said. "What you want to do is set up a regular lesson, say twice, three times a week."

"I'd just as soon stick with you," Tommy said.

"Our deal here is that Victor works with the beginners, and I handle the seasoned players," Chuck said. "But when Victor's jammed up, as he was today, then I'd be happy to teach you."

"I guess that's okay," Tommy said.

"You'll like Victor. Check with Merk in the shop and set up a schedule for you and Rosie."

Tommy shook his hand and headed for the pro shop.

"Hey, Chuck!"

Chuck turned and looked toward the next court.

"Want to hit some with us?" Harry Carras called out.

"Thanks, Harry, but I've got another lesson scheduled," Chuck replied. "Maybe later, if you're going to be around."

"Nah, I'm leaving town in a couple of hours."

"Good," Chuck said under his breath. "Good."

Chuck was five minutes early at his destination, and there was no sign of Clare. Six-fifteen came and went, and still she didn't show. Had he somehow missed the boat?

At 6:25 the Mercedes pulled into the lot, and she got out. "Come on!" she called, trotting toward a canal cut into the island, toting an overnight case.

Chuck grabbed his bag, put the top up on the Porsche, and ran after her. She was getting aboard a boat, along with half a dozen other people. He caught up, stepped aboard, and took a seat next to her. "Where are we going?" he asked.

"Stick around and find out," she said.

The boat backed down the canal, turned around, and headed out into a stretch of open water, picking up speed. A row of houses on the water to their right fell behind them. To the west a lurid sunset was developing, and to the east, a full moon was rising. The effect was spectacular.

"The sunset's part of the surprise," she said.

Fifteen minutes later they pulled up at a small dock and disembarked. Clare led him into a thatched building, open at the sides, and they were met by a young woman who led them down a path to a palm-thatched cottage. She showed them into an attractive suite, accepted a tip from Chuck, and left them alone.

Chuck snaked an arm around Clare's waist and kissed her. "What a nice surprise," he said.

"Not now, baby," she replied. "We're booked

for the first sitting at dinner. Get changed; we don't want to miss the rest of the sunset."

They missed nothing. They sat at a table at the water's edge and sipped their first drink as the sun sank into the sea.

"Where the hell are we?" Chuck asked.

"Little Palm Island," she replied. "I read about it in a magazine; isn't it something?"

"It is," Chuck said, "and so are you for bringing me. I've never been to a more romantic place."

They ordered from a long menu—seafood with a French accent—and Chuck chose a bottle from a fine wine list.

"By the way," she said, "this is on me. I hope you don't have any qualms about accepting the hospitality of a woman."

"None whatever," Chuck said, tasting the wine and nodding his approval to the waitress. "That would be rude of me."

After dinner they walked slowly back along the path toward their cottage.

"Look!" she whispered, stopping and pointing.

Two tiny deer were emerging from the water; they walked up the beach toward the dining area.

"They're Key deer," he said. "I'd heard about them, but I'd never seen one until now."

"They must have swum over from the next

island," she said, pointing. "And look, they're begging from the diners."

They made love before they paused long enough to talk.

"It's good being here, where nobody knows us, isn't it?" Clare said.

"It certainly is," Chuck agreed. "And I don't have to worry about Harry coming home unexpectedly. When is he coming back?"

"Tomorrow night. We can make a day of it, if you want."

"I want. What does Harry do in Miami? I thought he was retired."

"Oh, Harry will never retire completely. He keeps his hand in, and you ought to be grateful! How could we do this if he didn't go away on business?"

"Do what?" he asked.

"This," she said, and showed him.

CHAPTER

8

Tommy sat in the unmarked patrol car, his head resting against the back of the seat, and half dozed.

Daryl glanced over at him. "You look a little bushed," he said.

"You're not going to believe this, Daryl, but I played tennis on Sunday."

"You don't seem like the type to me," Daryl said. They were driving past Smathers Beach, the island's largest, then past the airport.

"I don't look like the type to me, either," Tommy agreed, "but I'm now the owner of a racquet and a pair of white shorts. Also, I'm sore as hell; it's been a while since I exerted myself like that."

"Good for you," Daryl said. "Do you good."

The radio came alive. "Traffic accident east end of the island, near U.S. 1," the operator said. "Any units nearby?"

Daryl was reaching for the microphone when a black-and-white took the call. "We're headed that way anyway," Daryl said. "Take a look?"

"At a traffic accident?" Tommy asked, incredulous. "That's a waste of my talents."

"Whatever you say," Daryl replied and continued past the airport.

They drove on for a couple of miles, then Daryl pointed ahead. "There it is," he said. "Looks like that . . ."

"That Mercedes," Tommy said. "Pull up over there."

The black-and-white had its lights going, and Daryl steered the car into the lane ahead of it.

Tommy got out. They were at a point where a number of houseboats were moored in the channel that separated Key West from Stock Island. The Mercedes had crashed through a wooden barrier and come to rest balanced neatly on the edge of the highway. Another foot or two and it would have gone into the channel. Harry Carras was leaning against the black-and-white, looking shaken, giving a statement to a uniformed cop.

Tommy hung back until their talk was over, then approached, flashing his badge. "Afternoon, sir," he said to Carras. "You all right?"

"I think so," Carras replied.

"What happened?"

"I don't know, exactly," Carras said. "I was just driving along, and I braked for the curve and nothing happened. The pedal went right to the floor. The barrier stopped me, I guess."

"You were lucky," Tommy said. "A little further and we would have been diving for you."

"I guess I am at that," Carras said. "Is my car drivable, do you think?"

"Not without brakes," Tommy replied. "Officer, will you give the gentleman a ride home, and we'll wait for the tow truck."

"Sure," the cop said. "Mr. Carras, do you want to go to the emergency room and have them take a look at you?"

"No, no, I'm all right," Carras said. "The airbag worked." He got into the patrol car and was driven away.

Tommy looked at the car and smiled.

★ ★ ★

The tow truck unhitched the Mercedes just as Daryl approached with a mechanic in tow. "Tommy, this is Mark, who does all our work. Mark, Tommy."

Tommy shook the man's hand. "Mark, the brakes on this car went, and it nearly ended up in the drink. Could you give it a quick once-over and see if you can figure out what went wrong?"

"Sure," Mark said.

While Mark rummaged around under the hood and under the car, Tommy took the opportunity to go over the rest of the car.

"Don't we need a search warrant or something?" Daryl asked.

"What for? We're just trying to find out what's wrong with a citizen's car," he said, riffling the glove compartment. "Here's the registration. Harry Carras on Dey Street; that much we know." He unfolded another sheet of paper.

"What's that?" Daryl asked.

"Looks like a maintenance bill from something called Island City Air Service. What's that?"

"FBO out at the airport," Daryl replied.

"FB what?"

"Fixed Base Operator. Sounds like Mr. Carras owns an airplane."

"You know anybody at this place?"

"I know a guy who's a mechanic. We went to high school together."

Tommy opened the trunk of their patrol car and extracted a fingerprint kit. He walked around to the driver's-side door and peered at the handle.

"Maybe we'll go talk to your friend just as soon as I lift a print or two."

"Uh-oh," Mark said from under the car.

"What?" Tommy asked.

Mark rolled out from under the car on his creeper, a length of aluminum tubing in his hand. "Here's the problem," he said, standing up and holding it out for Tommy and Daryl to see.

"I don't see anything," Tommy said.

"Right here; not much more than a pinprick; maybe a little bigger than a pin, like the tip of an icepick."

"What kind of tubing is this?" Tommy asked.

"Hydraulic," Daryl said. "Looks like somebody tapped into Mr. Carras's brake line."

"Yeah," Mark said. "Just a little hole. It would leak slowly while the car was parked, but when he was driving, every time he put on the brakes, some fluid would squirt out under pressure. Wouldn't take long to empty the hydraulic fluid reservoir."

"Looks like somebody's trying to make Mr. Carras dead," Daryl said.

"Looks like," Tommy agreed. "Any way this could have happened accidentally?" he asked Mark.

"Not likely," Mark said. "I think it would have to be deliberate."

"Let me lift a print or two, and we'll go back to the station," Tommy said to Daryl.

* * *

The two detectives stood and watched the fax machine spit out the document. Tommy picked it up and read it while Daryl looked over his shoulder.

"No fingerprint record with the FBI," Tommy said.

"That means he's never been arrested, huh?" Daryl asked.

"Or been in the army or done anything else that would get him fingerprinted," Tommy said.

"Another blank, then, like the credit report?"

"Another blank," Tommy said. "Let's go out to the airport."

They were buzzed through the security gate and Daryl drove the car along the ramp, past dozens of parked aircraft, toward the maintenance hangars. They parked, got out of the car, and approached an airplane being worked on by a young man.

"Hey, Buddy," Daryl said, and the two exchanged some sort of teenage handshake.

Tommy stuck out his hand. "So you're Buddy, huh? Daryl says you're the best airplane mechanic around."

"How the hell would he know?" Buddy said, laughing.

"Hey, Buddy, need a favor," Daryl said. "You know a guy named Harry Carras?"

"Yeah, he keeps an airplane here, a Piper Malibu Mirage."

"What's that?" Tommy asked. "I don't know a thing about airplanes."

"It's about the biggest and best piston single on the market," Buddy replied. "Twin turbocharged and intercooled, does about two hundred and twenty-five knots at altitude. We change the oil and do little things to it. He seems to get his major work done on the mainland, probably at Vero Beach; there's a big Piper shop up there, right next door to the factory."

"Where's the airplane?" Tommy asked.

"In a T-hangar," Buddy said. "We only got a few, but Carras has one."

"Locked?" Tommy asked.

"Yep."

Daryl spoke up. "Buddy, I need a favor; can we have a look inside the airplane?"

Buddy looked around. "My boss has gone to town for a few minutes; I guess I can manage that, if you keep it to yourself."

"Right on," Daryl said.

Buddy went to a key safe and rummaged around, then came back with a key ring. "It's the second T-hanger along there," he said, pointing the way. "Maybe I better open the door for you; it's tricky."

The two detectives followed the mechanic and waited while he lifted the hangar door.

"Pretty," Tommy said.

"Yeah," Buddy replied. "It's a slick bird, all right. Wish I had one."

They followed him into the hangar and

61

watched as he unlocked and opened the door. It was in two parts, upper and lower, and the lower half became steps.

Tommy climbed inside the airplane and went forward to the cockpit. Myriad dials stared back at him. The airplane smelled of new leather. He found a couple of little cabinets behind the pilot's seat that contained a cooler and a drawer full of aeronautical charts. Tommy went aft and looked over the rear seats into a luggage compartment. At the rear of the compartment, attached to the aft bulkhead, was a clear plastic envelope containing some documents. He opened the envelope and extracted half a dozen sheets of paper.

"What's that?" Daryl asked.

"Let's see—certificate of registration, airworthiness certificate, radio license. It's registered to Sky Blue, Inc." He put the documents back into the envelope and replaced it, then climbed out of the airplane.

"Buddy, thanks, we appreciate it," he said to the mechanic.

Daryl shook the man's hand, and they got back into the car. "So, what does that do for us?" he asked.

"We'll check out the corporation, see who the officers and the board of directors are," Tommy replied. "Then maybe we'll go see Mr. Harry Carras."

CHAPTER

9

Tommy rang the bell and waited outside the screen door. The front door was open, and he heard a loud splash from the side garden. Sky Blue, Inc., had turned out to be a Florida corporation; the president was Carras and his wife was secretary and treasurer. He turned to Daryl. "While we talk, sort of look around and see if you can see anything that might say something about who he is."

"Like a college diploma?" Daryl asked.

"Like that." Tommy rang the bell again. As he did, he saw Carras's wife enter the house through a side door at the other end of the ground-floor hallway. He got just a glimpse of her wet, naked body before she could wrap the light robe around herself.

"Hello," she said, stopping on the other side of the screen door.

"Mrs. Carras?"

"Yes."

"I'm Detective Sculley of the Key West Police Department; this is Detective Haynes. Could we speak with your husband for a minute?"

"Of course," she replied, opening the door.

"He's out at the pool; you two go on upstairs to the living room, and I'll get him."

"Thank you, ma'am," Tommy replied. He led the way up the stairs, emerging into a large, airy room. "Okay, Daryl, let's see what we can find before Carras gets here."

The two detectives began walking around the room. Tommy thought it was nicely furnished, but not quite complete. There were corners that could use a chair, and there were no curtains in place. He found some snapshots of Carras and his wife on a desk—all of them appeared to have been taken in or around Key West, one of them on a large motor yacht that reminded him of something, he couldn't remember what. "Anybody coming?" he asked Daryl, who was near a window on the pool side of the house.

Daryl looked out the window. "You've got thirty seconds," he said.

Tommy opened the middle desk drawer and found a checkbook from the First State Bank, a local outfit. There was a balance of $81,000, and, he saw as he flipped through the ledger, the checks had been written mostly for household expenses.

"Fifteen seconds," Daryl whispered loudly.

Tommy continued to flip through pages of the check ledger until he heard a footstep on the stairs. He closed the drawer and looked at Daryl, who seemed lost in a leatherbound book from a shelf across the room. Daryl put the book down just as Carras reached the top of the stairs. The man was dressed in a robe and was drying his thick white hair with a towel.

"Oh, hello," Carras said. "You were at the scene of my accident."

"Yes, sir," Tommy replied. "I didn't introduce myself at the time. I'm Detective Sculley and this is my partner, Detective Haynes."

Carras shook both their hands. "You're pretty young for a detective, aren't you?" he said to Daryl.

"Yes, sir, I guess I am," Daryl replied pleasantly.

"Won't you gentlemen have a seat," Carras said. "Can I get you something to drink?"

Both detectives declined.

"How can I help you, then?" Carras asked, sitting on one of the matching sofas while the detectives sat opposite him.

"I just wanted to let you know that we found out what was wrong with your car," Tommy said.

"Good," Carras replied. "It's still on warranty."

"There's no warranty for this, I'm afraid; there was a hole in your brake line," Tommy said. "All the fluid had drained out, and I'm afraid the police mechanic thinks someone deliberately punctured the line." He looked up to see Mrs. Carras at the top of the stairs. Her robe was wet, and he could see the outline of her nipples against the thin fabric. She came and sat next to her husband.

Carras stared at Tommy. "Do you mean that you think someone *sabotaged* my car?"

"It looks that way, sir. I'd like to ask you some questions, if I may."

"But who would have done such a thing?" Carras asked.

"We'll get to that in a minute," Tommy replied. "How long have you been in Key West, Mr. Carras?"

"About seven months, I guess."

"Where did you live before?"

"New York."

"And what sort of work do you do, sir?"

"I'm retired, mostly."

"Retired from what?"

"Oh, I did a bit of this and that. I guess you could call me an entrepreneur."

"I see. And what sort of businesses were you involved in?"

"Varied investments; real estate, commodities, the stock market, that sort of thing."

"You said mostly retired; what business are you currently involved in?"

"I have some real estate deals going around South Florida; the West Coast, mainly. Nothing I have to pay a lot of attention to."

"Are any of your investments in anything to do with gambling? Horse racing, casinos, hotels, that sort of thing?"

"No."

"Are you involved in any sort of business where

66

some of the other investors might have what might be thought of as shady backgrounds?"

"Good lord, no! All my partners are pillars of the community, I assure you."

"Do you have any enemies, Mr. Carras?"

"I don't think so."

"Do you think there might be someone in your past, a business partner, for instance, who might feel that he got the short end of some deal?"

"Certainly not. Everyone who's ever been in business with me has done very well for himself, I assure you."

"Have you had any sort of disagreement or altercation with anyone locally in Key West?"

"No, I haven't."

"Have you ever sued anyone, or been sued?"

"Locally?"

"Yes, sir."

"No."

"How about elsewhere?"

"The only lawsuit I've ever been involved in was more than twenty years ago, and I lost. It was quite expensive, and no one on the other side would have any reason to hold a grudge."

"Mrs. Carras, where are you from, originally?" Tommy asked.

"I'm from California."

"Where in California?"

"San Diego."

"Where did you meet your husband?"

"We met in Las Vegas, where I was working for a hotel."

"And what took you to Las Vegas, Mr. Carras?"

"I was on a golfing vacation; that, and a little light gambling."

"How much did you lose?"

"I won a couple of thousand dollars, as a matter of fact."

"Do you gamble a lot?"

"Rarely."

"Do you have any debts?"

"Nothing more than thirty days old," Carras replied. "I don't like to owe money."

"Mrs. Carras, do you know anyone who might wish your husband ill?"

"No, I don't. Harry is very well liked by everyone who knows him."

"Well," Tommy said, rising. "Looks like we're at a dead end."

"I'm sorry I couldn't be of more help," Carras said, getting up.

Tommy handed him a card. "If you think of anything else that might be of help to us, I'd appreciate a call," he said. "I have to tell you that we take a serious view of this incident, and we think you should, too. Whoever sabotaged your car would be looking at a charge of attempted murder, and he might try again."

"I wish I could take it as seriously as you, Detective," Carras said, walking them down the stairs, "but I just can't imagine that anyone would want to harm me. Clare, will you see the detectives out?"

"Of course, darling," she replied. "This way, gentlemen."

Carras left the house by the door to the pool, and his wife led the two men down the hallway to the front door.

Tommy let Daryl go ahead of him, then paused on the front porch. "Mrs. Carras," he said quietly, "are you having an affair with anyone?"

She was obviously taken aback and didn't speak for a moment. "No," she said, finally. "I'm not."

"I'm sorry if I offended you," he said, "but if there's someone Mr. Carras doesn't know about that you think might want to harm him, please tell me."

"There's no one, Detective," she said firmly, "no one I know who would want to harm Harry."

"Thank you for your help," Tommy said.

Tommy waited until they were around the corner before he spoke. "She's screwing somebody," he said. "She lied when I asked her about it, I could tell."

"That doesn't mean that whoever she's screwing would want to kill her husband."

"Didn't you see the woman, Daryl? Didn't you see those nipples staring at you through her robe? If you were screwing her, wouldn't you want to kill her husband?"

"You've got a point," Daryl admitted. "Oh, by the way, I picked up on something."

"What?"

"That book I was looking at; it was autographed to somebody named Rock."

"You mean like in Rock Hudson? That's not a real name."

"That's what was in the book, though. It said, 'To Rock, with my warm good wishes.' I couldn't read the signature, but it looked like a different name from the author's."

"It looked like an old book; maybe he bought it in a used book store."

"It was leatherbound, but it wasn't old; it looked pretty new to me."

"What was the name of the book?"

"*Investing Wisely*, by John Harrison. It was published in 1989."

"Rock, huh?"

"Rock."

CHAPTER

10

Chuck stood across the net from Billy Tubbs, a cart of balls at his side. "Okay, Billy, I'm going to hit you some forehands and backhands. I want to see a proper grip, and I don't want you to hit the ball hard—just smoothly. Got that?"

"Yes, sir," Billy called back.

Chuck had not let him hit anything but ground

strokes, and only against the ball machine. "And if I see you lapse into your old grip, or start slamming the ball across, I'll return you to the tender mercies of the ball machine, understand?"

"Yes, sir."

"This is only a drill; there's nothing to win."

"Yes, sir."

Chuck fed the boy a forehand and watched carefully as he returned the ball. He fed a backhand and watched again, then he started returning the shots. For fifteen minutes he sent smooth, medium-speed shots across the net and watched Billy return them, just as he had been told. Billy, he reflected, had turned out to be able to follow instructions, when he had to, anyway, and he was pleased with the boy. He stopped the rally and walked to the net, beckoning Billy. "That's very good," he said. "Believe me when I tell you you'll never have to hit a ball any harder than that to win a high school match, as long as you place the ball well. What I want you to do now is to hit your ground strokes just as you have been doing, except I want you to aim this way— right corner, center, left corner, then work your way back. Keep your swing smooth, don't hit anything hard, and concentrate on accuracy."

"Yes, sir," Billy replied.

Chuck walked off the court, grabbed a towel from the stack, and flopped down on a bench next to Victor, mopping the sweat from his face.

"The boy's coming along, isn't he?" Victor said.

"He really is. To tell you the truth, I'm surprised."

"So am I. I thought he would have told you to go fuck yourself by now."

Chuck laughed. "So did I. He really has a gift for concentration, and he's a fine natural athlete. I think if he can develop a good temperament he could make a winning pro."

"You think temperament is something you can develop?" Victor asked. "I always thought you were born with it."

Chuck shook his head. "Some people are, maybe, but for most of us it's a training thing, just like hitting a good ground stroke. I was as hotheaded as Billy when I was sixteen; a good coach drilled it out of me."

"Then why did you choke at Wimbledon?"

"That had nothing to do with temperament; it was all about confidence, and at the worst possible moment, I lost my confidence. I didn't believe I could do it, so I couldn't."

"Well, I guess you've had some time to think about it."

"Plenty of time."

"There's something else you maybe ought to think about," Victor said.

"What's that?"

"Staying out of Clare Carras's pants."

Chuck looked at Victor. "You think I'm messing with Clare?"

"I think you're screwing her socks off every chance you get, is what I think."

"*Why* do you think that?"

"Because I can look at you and look at her and tell, that's why. And if I can figure it out, so can Harry Carras. And I'll tell you something else, I don't think he's the kind of guy to take it well."

"What makes you say that?" Chuck asked. "You know something I don't?"

Victor shrugged. "Let's just say I'm a good judge of character."

"There's more to it than that, Victor; you know something you're not telling me."

"I know a lot about a lot of things I'm not telling you, kid, but your personal life is really none of my business, so I'll keep most of it to myself. Just this one piece of advice: Unless you want to start walking around with your dick in your hip pocket, you'd better watch whose wife you stick it in."

"I guess that's pretty good advice, generally," Chuck said.

"It's good advice, specifically, too," Victor replied. He looked up. "Well, here come the Sculleys, Tommy and Rosie, my most enthusiastic new students."

"How are they doing?" Chuck asked.

"Remarkably well. I wish all my students caught on so fast."

"It must have been their first lesson with me that did it."

Victor laughed, got up, and strolled toward his

73

teaching court. He looked back over his shoulder. "Remember my advice, kid," he called.

"I'll remember, Victor," Chuck called back. *For about five seconds,* he thought. Just thinking about Clare Carras made him hot. Oh, it would end, he knew that, but not for a while. They were a long way from being through with each other.

He mopped his face again and headed for his next session. It was Larry, the writer, and he'd have to remember to lose, but not by much.

CHAPTER

11

Tommy sat at the Raw Bar at Key West Bight and looked out over the little harbor as he munched a conch fritter. Occasionally he tossed the gulls a crumb, and they made a fuss as they went for it. Pelicans sat sleepily on pilings, undisturbed by the gulls, or anything else, for that matter.

Daryl poured himself some more iced tea. "So who you figure is trying to knock off Carras?" he asked.

"Before we know who Carras's enemies are, we have to know who Carras is. You follow?"

Daryl nodded, chewing his calamari. "I guess that makes sense. You don't think it's anybody around here, then?"

"I only know of one candidate here," Tommy replied, washing down the fritter with some tea.

"Who's that?"

"The guy who's screwing Mrs. Carras."

"And who would that be?"

"Listen, Daryl, I'm kinda thinking out loud here, you know? This isn't necessarily serious."

"Okay, it's not serious. Who you thinking about?"

"Tennis pro down at the Olde Island Racquet Club, name of Chuck Chandler."

"Don't know him," Daryl said. "How do you know he's screwing Mrs. Carras?"

"I just know, Daryl. Trouble is, he's not the type."

"To screw Mrs. Carras?"

"To commit murder, dummy."

"Lots of people who aren't the type commit murder," Daryl said.

"Not really," Tommy replied. "Murderers who aren't the type are in the minority. How the hell did you get to be a detective so quick, anyway?"

"The chief is my uncle," Daryl replied, without embarrassment. "My mother's brother."

"That explains a lot," Tommy said.

"Listen, Tommy, maybe we're off on a wild goose chase, you know? Maybe nobody tampered with Carras's car; maybe it was just a defect in the tubing."

"Nah," Tommy said. "I mean, if that was all

we had to go on, you might be right. But we've got more than that."

"What else have we got?"

"Over there." Tommy pointed toward the hotel marina across the way.

"Where?"

"The boat on the end of the dock; the big one."

"Fugitive?"

"That's the one. I've seen another one just like it."

"It's a Hatteras; lots of them up and down the coast."

"The one I saw is on the bottom, the other side of the island."

"The one that blew up?"

"That's the one. It was just like that one, the *Fugitive,* that belongs to Harry Carras."

"How do you know that?"

"There was a picture in Carras's living room of him and his wife aboard it. I could read the name. I wonder if the name means something."

"You think Carras is a fugitive?"

"Of a kind," Tommy replied. "I suppose he could be a fugitive from the law, but maybe he's running from something or somebody else."

"Like what?"

"I don't know, but a guy doesn't change his name at his age unless he's running from *something.*"

"Ex-wife, maybe? Or even a current wife?"

"That's a possibility, but wives, even mean

ones, can be handled with lawyers. You don't have to run from them. Also, Carras obviously ran with some money in his pockets—a lot of money, probably. Look at the way he lives—big house, Mercedes, airplane, yacht. That takes big bucks."

"You're right about that."

"Say you're Carras, in a previous existence. Your work makes it possible to put your hands on a lot of somebody else's money."

"Why somebody else's? Why couldn't it be his?"

"Because you don't have to become somebody else to spend your own money, Daryl."

"I suppose. Unless there's a wife breathing down your neck."

"Forget the wife for just a minute. So you're Carras," Tommy continued, "and you want to take all this money and run, okay? Well, you can't just write a check and get on a plane. That kind of stealing takes lots of planning. You've got to find a way to move the money, hide the money, but still have it accessible. I mean, you don't just fill up the trunk of your car and drive off into the sunset, paying your way with hundred-dollar bills."

"He must deal in cash only," Daryl said. "According to his credit report, he doesn't have any credit cards or charge accounts."

"True, but he has a checking account at First State. He's got to feed that from somewhere. I bet he's got a brokerage account or two, probably in Miami or another city. If he knows about money, it would annoy him to have a lot of cash sitting around earning nothing. He'd want it invested, but where he could get his hands on it."

"He probably doesn't pay any taxes, either," Daryl said.

"Good point. Brokerage houses report your earnings to the IRS. Pretty soon, they'd be knocking on his door. He's been in Key West for seven months, is what he said. That's probably not long enough for the tax people to catch up with him."

"Maybe he plans to move on before they catch up; maybe he plans to change his name again. *But,*" Daryl said, raising a finger, "if he's on the run, why does he have all this *stuff*? House, car, boat, airplane? That's a pretty big tail to drag around with you, isn't it?"

"You're right about that," Tommy agreed. "So maybe he's not planning to decamp again. But let's get back to the boat. Right after I move down here I'm having dinner at Louie's Backyard on my wife's birthday, and the big yacht goes up in flames."

"But it wasn't Carras's yacht," Daryl pointed out.

"But one just like it."

"Ooooh, now I'm getting it," Daryl said. "Whoever is trying to punch Carras's ticket mistakes the other yacht for his and blows it up."

"Now you're following me." The waitress

brought the check. Tommy left some money on the table and beckoned Daryl to follow him. They walked out of the restaurant and down to the water's edge.

Daryl spoke up. "Doesn't make any sense," he said.

"Why not?"

"If you're Carras and you're running from somebody and then a yacht just like yours goes up in smoke, and somebody sabotages your Mercedes, wouldn't you notice? I mean, we couldn't have been bringing him much in the way of news when we told him about the fuel line. Wouldn't all this mean that whoever is looking for Carras has found him and is trying to do him in? So wouldn't Carras be running? 'Course, I'm just thinking out loud here, Tommy."

Tommy looked at him sharply. "Don't be a smartass, kid."

"Okay, straighten me out, Tommy. Make it all make sense."

"I think I'm back to the wife's lover," Tommy said. "That, Carras wouldn't know about, so he wouldn't have any reason to run."

"Okay, I'll buy that, but all we've got for a lover is the tennis pro, and you say he isn't the type."

"Yeah, and there's another problem," Tommy said. "When the yacht blew up, Carras and his wife were having dinner with the tennis pro. I saw them together. So it wouldn't make much sense for the pro to blow up the yacht while he was having dinner with his victim. He'd expect the victim to be aboard, and maybe Mrs. Carras, too. Also, I don't think the tennis pro had been in town long enough to get that involved with Carras's wife at that time. I'll have to check on that."

They stopped beside a pretty little motor yacht tied up alongside. "That's nice, huh?" Tommy said, indicating the boat. "*Choke,* she's called. I wonder why?"

"That's pretty nice, too," Daryl said under his breath, nodding toward a girl in a bikini sunning herself on the next boat.

"We're talking business here, Daryl," Tommy said. "Concentrate!"

"I'm concentrating," Daryl said. "We're back to square one. We've got nothing to tell us who Carras is; we've got nothing on him; we've got nothing on the tennis pro, except your intuition. In short, we've got nothing."

"Great oaks from small acorns grow," Tommy said grumpily.

"Takes a long time, though," Daryl replied.

"Everything is still too confused to make any sense of all this," Tommy said, sighing. "There's a thread here somewhere, but I'm missing it. It'll come together, though, you wait and see."

"Have I got a choice?" Daryl asked.

CHAPTER

12

Tommy looked at his wife in the car seat next to him. "Tell me again how this invitation happened," he said.

"I already told you, Tommy," she replied, sounding exasperated.

"No, I mean *exactly* how it came up. It's important, Sweets."

"Okay," she said. "I was in the pro shop looking at some new tennis shoes, and this Clare Carras struck up a conversation. She was nice, I guess, and I kind of liked her. Later, as she and her husband were leaving the court, she came over and asked if you and I would like to do some snorkeling on Monday and have lunch on their boat."

"How did she know that Monday was my day off?" Tommy asked.

"I don't know that she did; she just asked. Why is all this so important?"

"Come on, babe, you remember that we saw them at Louie's the night of the yacht explosion, right? And I mentioned that I thought there was something funny about him? That he might be connected?"

"Yeah, I remember that."

"Well, I don't think the guy is who he says he is. I've done some checking on him, and things just don't add up."

"Then I would have thought you would welcome the chance to get to know him better," Rosie said, "instead of giving me a hard time about accepting the invitation."

"I didn't mean to give you a hard time, babe, really I didn't, and you're right—I do want to get to know him better. Matter of fact, I'd be real happy if you'd try to get to know *her* better, find out something about her background. By the way, is anybody else coming?"

"She didn't say; I assumed just the four of us."

"Weird," Tommy said. "If Carras is somebody else, you'd think he'd want to stay as far away as possible from a cop."

"So, maybe he's who he says he is."

"If he is, then he's paid cash for everything he ever bought since high school," Tommy said, "and you can't get any weirder than that."

The Carrases were waiting for them aboard *Fugitive*, and so were the two tennis pros, Chuck and Victor. Rosie started to introduce Tommy to Carras, but Carras threw up a hand. "We've already met," he said. "It's Tommy, isn't it?"

"That's right," Tommy replied.

"And I'm Harry," he said. "Well, shall we get under way?" He ran up the steps to the bridge, cranked the engines, and expertly backed the sixty-footer out of her berth, then headed for the entrance to Key West Bight.

Clare produced Bloody Marys for everybody, and they took seats on the broad afterdeck and sipped their drinks, chatting idly and enjoying the winter sun.

They had traveled perhaps ten miles when Tommy noticed smoke coming out of a ventilator. He stood up and shouted, "Hey, Harry! You got a problem down here."

Harry stopped the engines and looked over the railing at Tommy. "What is it?" he asked.

"Looks like smoke coming from down below," Tommy called back.

Harry came down to the deck, looking worried. "I'm afraid I don't know much about the mechanics of this vessel," he said.

Chuck spoke up. "Looks like exhaust to me, Harry. Have you got a tool kit aboard? I'll be glad to take a look at it."

"Sure, Chuck, right under the seat, there, in the locker."

"Let her drift for a few minutes, and turn on your blower. We'll give it a chance to clear out down there."

Harry followed Chuck's instructions, and after a few minutes, Chuck went belowdecks.

"Gosh, I hope it isn't serious," Clare said. "I've been looking forward to getting out on the water."

"Chuck sounds like he knows what he's doing," Tommy said.

Shortly Chuck came back on deck. "Harry, nothing to worry about, just your exhaust tubing for the starboard engine came loose from the overboard vent. I put it back on and put a second hose clip on real tight. You shouldn't have any further problems."

Harry placed a hand on his heart. "Thanks so much, Chuck; I thought I'd burned up an engine or something." He turned back to the controls, started the engines, and they were immediately under way again.

They layed anchor off Sand Key, on the reef, and finished their second round of Bloody Marys.

"Anybody for a dive?" Harry asked.

"Sure," Chuck said. "I brought my gear, and I see you have a compressor down below. I was working right next to it."

"I sure do; I hate lugging tanks back and forth from the dive shop. It's much more convenient to be able to fill them myself aboard. Tommy, do you and Rosie dive?"

"Nope," Tommy said. "We'll stick to snorkeling."

Equipment was produced. The Carrases, Chuck, and Victor got into their diving gear and set off along the reef. Tommy and Rosie donned masks and snorkeled lazily along in their wake.

Rosie was in the galley with Clare, putting together lunch. "So, Clare," she said, "How long you been in Key West?"

"Just a few months," Clare replied.

"Where do you come from?"

"New York. Harry was in business there, and when he decided to retire, we came south."

"We're from New York, too," Rosie said. "What part of town did you live in?"

"The Upper East Side," Clare replied. "Park Avenue."

"We were in Brooklyn Heights," Rosie said. "We've put our house on the market, and I think we've got somebody interested."

"It's nice in Brooklyn Heights," Clare said. "We used to go to the River Cafe. You and Tommy have any kids?"

"A boy, Tommy Junior. He graduated from NYU last spring. How about you?"

"No, Harry and I have only been married for a little over a year, and at his age, he's not too interested in kids. To tell the truth, neither am I, much. We have an awfully good life the way we are."

"I see your point. How'd you and Harry meet?"

Driving home, Tommy grilled Rosie about her conversation with Clare. "Is that it?" he asked. "I already knew all that part of their story."

"That's it, Tommy; I guess I'm not too good at the third degree."

"Don't you believe it, babe; you've grilled me often enough."

"Well, I asked her all the girl questions, and

that's all she told me. It didn't seem to me like she was hiding anything."

Tommy shook his head. "Those two have one hell of a lot to hide. And believe me, before I'm done, I'm going to know it all."

"Tommy, when you own a boat that big, aren't you supposed to have some help on it? I mean, *I* made the tunafish. That girl doesn't have a clue about food."

"Maybe they like to do for themselves."

"Or have their guests do for them," Rosie said grumpily.

CHAPTER

13

Clare Carras looked across at her companion. They were sitting, naked, in the back seat of the Mercedes in a grove of trees on Stock Island, near the huge lump of garbage the locals called Mount Trashmore, and they had just made love. "We're going to have to cool it for a while," she said.

"What's the problem?" he asked.

"This cop, Tommy Sculley, has been too much in evidence the past week or so—on our diving trip, for instance. It was Harry's idea to invite him and his wife."

"Maybe he just liked them."

"It's not like Harry to like cops, let alone socialize with them."

"What's Harry got against cops?"

"Maybe his mother was frightened by one when she was pregnant. How the hell should I know?"

"You're married to him."

"Maybe, but I don't know him much better than anybody else. Oh, I know what he likes for dinner and what he likes in bed, but beyond that, I'm on the outside."

"Nobody can keep his wife on the outside; wives know too much. Mine did, anyway. She always knew fucking everything."

"Maybe I'm not the ideal wife then, okay? Harry's by nature an enigma; he doesn't tell anybody anything he doesn't have to, not even me."

"But you sign on the bank account; you're the sole beneficiary of his will, aren't you?"

"Yes, but the will doesn't say what there is or where it is. I know he deals with some foreign banks. Once in a while I catch part of a telephone conversation from his end, but I don't know which banks or how much is in them. He's promised me that if anything happens to him, his executor will handle everything. I can hardly press him on this."

"Who's his executor?"

"A lawyer in Naples."

"You have his name?"

"Yes."

"That's good to know."

"Oh, don't worry, I'll get the money; there isn't anybody else to leave it to. Harry's life is as devoid of friends and relatives as if he had just arrived from another planet."

"Strange."

"It's just the way he is. He trusts me and nobody else."

"He trusts you, but you know nothing about his financial affairs."

She turned toward him. "Don't get sarcastic, baby." She took his testicles in her hand. "I'll pull them off."

"I love it when you talk dirty," he said.

She changed her grip to his penis and began kneading. "You love it when I do this, don't you?"

He sighed, then caught his breath.

"You want to fuck me again, baby?" she asked.

"You know it."

She pulled him toward her and lay back. "Then come to me, lover. Do it to me again."

It took him longer this time, but she brought him skillfully along until she was ready herself, then she tightened on him. He came in a rush of fast breathing and loud noise.

"There, dear," she said, "is that better?"

"Boy, is that better," he breathed.

"So, we're going to hold off for a while, okay?"

"Why do we always have to fuck in the car or

on a beach somewhere?" he complained. "There are beds available to us."

"You love it in the car and on the beach," she said. "Anyway, beds are risky. You never know when someone will walk in."

"Are you fucking Chandler, too?" he asked.

"Baby!" she spat. "What a shitty thing to say to me!"

"You are, aren't you?"

"If I am, it's for us, sweetheart," she cooed. "Always remember that."

"I'll try to remember," he said.

She pushed him off her and retrieved a towel from the front seat, wiping them both. "So we're going to cool it?"

"I guess."

"Promise me, baby. I can't afford another attempt—failed or successful—while this cop is hanging around."

"Why do you think he suspects something?"

"Oh, he told Harry and me flat out, when he came to the house last week. He said somebody had tampered with the car and wanted to do Harry harm."

"And what did Harry say?"

"He pooh-poohed the whole thing, just like I knew he would. But we don't want to start him thinking about it; that would not be good for our plans. When it happens, it happens suddenly, without warning, and it has to be final; no screwups next time."

"Yeah, the screwing will have to be between you and me."

"You want to screw me again, lover?" She stroked his penis.

"I can't, baby, you've worn me out."

"Bet you aren't worn out yet," she said, bending over and kissing the organ. It twitched in her hand. "See?" she cooed, and took it into her mouth.

"Jesus, how do you do it?" he moaned. "You've got me going again."

"I have, haven't I?" she said, stopping for a moment.

"Don't stop!"

"We're cooling it, then?"

"We're cooling it!"

"Until I say we're ready?"

"Anything you say."

"Good boy; now here's your reward for being good."

"Oh, baby, baby, baby!" he yelled as he came again.

"There," she said. "I knew you could do it."

CHAPTER

14

Chuck first saw the man as Harry and Clare drove up in the Mercedes. He was riding a red rental motor scooter, and he entered the parking lot half a minute after the Carrases, parked in the shade of a tree, switched off the scooter, and watched while Chuck and Victor played three sets with Harry and Clare.

Chuck looked up from time to time to see if the man was still there, and he always was. He was swarthy, very Mediterranean—Greek or Turkish, Chuck thought; tallish, solidly built, with thick, stylishly cut hair and what might be called bruised good looks. He wore jeans, a yellow polo shirt, white running shoes, and Porsche sunglasses, the ones with the big lenses. When the match was over and Harry and Clare moved toward their car, the man started the scooter and drove away. Chuck thought it odd, but he put it out of his mind. There were thousands of tourists in town, hundreds of them riding rented scooters. Then it occurred to him that the man had probably seen Clare somewhere in town and had followed the couple to get a better look at her. Nothing strange about that; all men looked at Clare.

Chuck thought no more about it until after work, when he was leaving Wooley's, a grocery store on Roosevelt Boulevard. He pulled out of his parking space and, as he stopped for traffic at the exit to Roosevelt, he glanced in his rearview mirror and saw the man on the scooter two cars back. He stared at the man, the Turk, as he was beginning to think of him, until the driver behind blew his horn impatiently. Chuck looked both ways, then pulled onto Roosevelt, but instead of turning left toward Key West Bight, he turned right. The scooter turned with him.

What now? He was headed away from home, toward the upper Keys. Should he try to lose the man? If so, where? Key West was one mile by four, and its streets were ill suited for car-scooter chases; he could turn north on Highway 1, but there was only one road all the way to Miami. Anyway, there was ice cream melting in the bag beside him.

He turned into the Overseas Market shopping center, drove aimlessly around for a minute or two, then got back onto Roosevelt and headed toward home. The scooter kept pace, darting among cars a hundred yards back.

Chuck turned right on Palm Avenue and drove across the arching Garrison Bight bridge, past the naval base. Palm became Eaton Street as he headed into Old Town. He turned left on Elizabeth Street, picked up his laundry and dry cleaning, made a U-turn, and drove back to Key West Bight. He parked in his usual spot, put the tonneau cover on the car, and struggled toward Choke, burdened with groceries and laundry. He danced across the little gangplank and dumped his cargo on a deck chair while he unlocked the cabin. As he did so, he looked toward the parking lot and saw the Turk carefully not looking at him. A moment later, the man turned the scooter around and drove away.

As Chuck was putting away his groceries, the phone rang.

"Hello?"

"Hi." Clare.

"Ah . . ." Chuck struggled for the right words.

"Is this a bad time?"

"Call me back in five minutes, but not from home."

She was silent for a moment. "Right," she said finally, then hung up.

Chuck mixed himself a drink and took the cordless phone onto the afterdeck. He sat and sipped, idly watching the sunset, until the instrument rang in his hand.

"Hi," he said.

"Is there a problem?" she asked.

"I'm not sure."

"Are you with somebody?"

"No, I'm alone. Where are you?"

"I'm in the car."

"Good."

"Baby, what's the matter? Aren't we on for tonight?"

"I don't think that's a good idea."

"He's left for Marathon. There's some property up there he's been looking at."

"He may have left a representative behind."

"A representative? What are you talking about?"

"When you and Harry came to tennis today, a man on a motor scooter seemed to follow you."

"What did he look like?"

Chuck described the Turk.

"Doesn't ring a bell. Anyway, it's not the first time I was followed by a man. Maybe he's a breast man."

"Maybe," Chuck said, "but when I left work tonight, he followed me, too, and I don't think it was because he liked my tits."

She laughed. "Are you sure you're not imagining things?"

"I spotted him as I was leaving the grocery store; I took the long way home, and he was with me all the way. He just left, at least I think he did."

"So what do you think?"

"I think there's a better-than-even chance that Harry has put somebody on us."

"Mmmm," she said. "I wonder if he'd do that."

"You know him better than I. Would he?"

"It's unlikely, but you're right, tonight might not be a good idea, considering."

"Considering," Chuck echoed. "Why don't you keep an eye behind you for a couple of days, see if the guy turns up again? I'll do the same."

"I don't want to wait a couple of days to see you," she said, her voice low.

"Believe me, I feel exactly the same way," Chuck replied. "But we don't know if today is this guy's first day on us, or if he's been around for a while."

"My guess is this is his first day," Clare said.

"Why?"

"Because, as hard as Harry is to read, I think I'd know if somebody had reported to him that you and I are screwing each other blind twice a week. That would trouble him."

"Maybe we got lucky. We'll give it a rest for a few days, then?"

"I'm not feeling very restful."

"I'm feeling downright horny just talking to you," he said.

"We'll talk tomorrow."

"But only call me from the car," Chuck said. "If he's Harry's man, he might have done something to your phone."

"Only from the car," she said. "'Bye, lover; I'm going to miss you."

Chuck started to respond, but she had already hung up. He put down the phone, sucked on his drink, and began feeling sorry for himself. He was very randy indeed, and alone.

Then he looked to his right and there was Meg Hailey, dressed in her inadequate bikini, watering the potted plants in the catamaran's cockpit next door.

"Hi," she said, catching sight of him.

"Hi yourself," he replied. "Buy you a drink?"

CHAPTER

15

Chuck mixed them a drink, then set up the little stainless steel grill, which hung outboard in a special bracket, and got a charcoal fire going.

"Haven't seen much of you," Meg said, sipping her drink. She had changed from her bikini to bleached cutoffs and a chambray shirt, unbuttoned and tied in a knot under her breasts. This passed for dressing for dinner in Key West.

"Work, work, work," Chuck said.

"Teaching tennis is work?" she snorted.

"That's what everybody thinks," Chuck replied. "If your work is somebody else's sport, then it's not work. Actually, I put in five or six hours of instruction a day, in the hot sun, on my feet, every week of my life."

"Poor baby," she said. "What's your idea of recreation?"

Chuck looked her up and down. "You haven't had enough to drink for me to tell you."

She laughed heartily and handed him her glass.

"I guess I'd better get to work if I want to find out."

"I was at a cocktail party in Palm Beach once," he said, "and I was talking to a famous writer, a novelist; his name escapes me at the moment. A woman came up to him and told him how much she enjoyed his books, then she asked him what he did for a living! It was like, his books were so much fun to read that writing them couldn't possibly be work."

"Okay, okay, I concede your point," she laughed. "You work hard for a living, even if it is on a tennis court."

"That's better," he said, taking her empty glass. "Now you deserve another drink." He glanced toward the parking lot in time to see the Turk making a slow U-turn on his scooter. Good; now the man had seen him with another woman. "So," he said to Meg, "you been living aboard for a while?"

"Nearly a year. Tell you the truth, when Dan suggested the trip, I didn't think I'd last two weeks. But it grows on you—*if* you can get used to living in a fiberglass coffin and taking showers sitting down."

"Seems to me I've seen you take a shower or two standing up," he said.

She looked blank for a moment. "Oh, you mean in the cockpit. Sure, I'd rather do it that way, even if . . . "

"Even if you draw a crowd?" he asked. "You

do, you know. Half of Key West Bight seems to amble by when you're hosing yourself down."

"Well, what the hell," she laughed. "I'm not going to let a lot of gawkers crowd me."

"You're accustomed to gawkers, I imagine."

She blushed. "My share, I guess. If you spend most of your life in a bikini . . . "

"Half in a bikini."

"Are you objecting?"

"Not in the least. I consider you part of the view from my boat." He put the steaks on the grill. "How do you like your meat?"

"Are you being vulgar?" she asked archly.

"Sorry, your steak?"

"Medium."

"Me too; that makes dinner simpler. Hang on, I'd better go below and put the rice on to cook." He did that, and when he came back on deck, she was turning over the steaks. "They smell wonderful," she said.

He leaned over and sniffed behind her ear. "So do you," he said. As he straightened up, he saw the Turk sitting at waterside in the Raw Bar, eating conch fritters. He kissed Meg on the neck for the Turk's benefit. Well, not *entirely* for the Turk's benefit.

"You keep doing that, and we'll never get to the steaks," she said.

He stepped away to make himself another drink. "I'll back off until after dessert."

"What's for dessert?"

He was tempted to tell her *she* was for dessert,

98

but he thought better of it. "Ice cream," he replied.

"On a boat?"

"*This* boat has a freezer," he said.

"What kind of ice cream?"

"It's a surprise."

"I love surprises," she said.

"Stick around," he replied.

He rolled over and reached for the ice cream, then fed her a spoonful.

"Mmmm," she said, "macadamia brittle, my favorite."

"I knew it would be," he said.

"How could you know that?"

He shrugged. "You just look like a macadamia brittle kind of woman to me." He liked this girl. *Thank God she's married*, he thought. *I could get into serious trouble here.*

She plumped up the pillows and sat up in the double berth, bumping her head. "Ouch," she said.

"Forget you're on a boat?"

"I'm unaccustomed to this much space on a boat."

"Well, there's just the saloon, the head, and this cabin."

"No room for guests?"

"Not unless they sleep with me."

"Somehow I have the feeling I'm not the first guest to share this berth with you."

"I confess," he said. "Before you, there were other women."

"We didn't exactly practice safe sex," she said.

He lifted his head from the pillow. "Aren't you safe?" he asked, half alarmed.

"Of course," she said. "It was *you* I was wondering about."

He raised a hand. "Absolutely safe," he said. "I swear."

"You've had a blood test?"

"About three months ago," he said.

"And how many women since then?"

"Only safe ones," he replied. "Let's not talk numbers."

"Would the numbers be embarrassing?"

"Embarrassingly small," he said.

She snuggled up next to him and ran a hand down his belly. "Me too," she said.

"I should hope so," he replied. "Married woman like yourself."

"Me, married?" she asked. "Not likely."

Alarm bells rang. "But what about Dan?"

"What about him?"

"You have the same last name."

"Our mother wanted it that way."

"He's your *brother?*"

"Since birth."

"Oh, shit," he whispered to himself.

"What did you say?"

"I said, and shipmates, too."

"Oh. Does it somehow bother you that I'm not married?"

"Oh, bother isn't exactly the word," he said. Terrify *is the word,* he thought.

"I don't believe in marriage," she said.

"Well, that's something."

"I guess you don't believe in marriage, either."

"Only for the married."

"The way I look at it," she said, "is if you suddenly come over all hot to get married, what you do is the two of you disappear for a few days, and when you come back you say to your friends, 'We got married.' And everybody says, 'Congratulations.' Then, when the relationship doesn't work anymore, you disappear again for a few days, and when you come back to say to everybody, 'We got divorced,' everybody says, 'Congratulations'."

"I think that makes a great deal of sense," Chuck said. "You're a very levelheaded woman."

"I like to think so."

"But what you're doing down there is not keeping *me* levelheaded."

"I'm so glad to hear it," she said, kissing him on the belly. "And when I'm through with you, you're going to be downright *impractical.*"

And he was.

CHAPTER

16

Chuck sent Meg back to her own boat after breakfast, and he was happy that Dan wasn't around
at the time. He had no particular desire to face
her brother this morning.

Driving to work, a new thought struck him.
For the first time, he considered breaking it off
with Clare Carras. God knew he loved being in
bed with her, but he thought he liked being in
bed with Meg better, and he liked Meg better.
Meg was smarter, funnier, and more lovable than
Clare, and she had the additional advantage of
not having a husband who hired private detectives.

And, speaking of private detectives, the Turk
had vanished. He was nowhere to be seen around
Key West Bight or around the Olde Island
Racquet Club, and when, in the late afternoon,
Harry and Clare showed up to play tennis, he
did not follow them.

There was something different about Harry,
though. He was still affable enough, but edgier.
Then he surprised Chuck.

"You think you're all finished choking in your
life?" he asked Chuck.

"Beg pardon?"

"You choked at Wimbledon. Have you put that behind you? Is your head on straight these days?"

"I think so."

"I think not."

Chuck glanced at Clare. She looked vaguely uncomfortable. "Why do you say that, Harry?"

"I think you're a born loser, Chuck. When the pressure's on, you fold."

"What evidence do you have of that?" Chuck asked, surprised at the direction the conversation was taking.

"My own intuition," Harry said. "I think I know a loser when I see one."

Clare looked at the ground. "Harry, knock it off; you're being rude."

Harry ignored her. "Tell you what," he said, "I'll give you a chance to prove me wrong."

"That's kind of you, Harry," Chuck replied.

"I'll play you three games of tennis for a thousand dollars."

Clare spoke up. "A thousand dollars! That's outrageous, Harry!"

"Three games," Harry repeated. "Any more than that and your comparative youth would give you too great an advantage. I serve two, you serve one; that'll even us up a bit."

"Come on, Harry, I don't want your money," Chuck said.

Victor had heard all this, and now he spoke

up. "What's the matter, Chuck? Can't you use a grand?"

He could, Chuck reflected. He had about twelve hundred in the bank, but he wanted some new equipment for the boat, and a thousand would help a lot. "Harry, I'm the pro here, and I've got twenty years on you. I don't think it would be fair."

"Fair doesn't come into it," Harry said. "I'm just out to prove a point."

"Go on, Chuck," Victor said. "Take the man's money."

Chuck shrugged. "Okay," he said. "I'll take your money, Harry."

They warmed up for a few minutes, then Harry served. Chuck planned a bit of a hustle; he'd lose the first game, win his serve, then let the last game run close before he took it away.

Losing the first game was easy, since Harry seemed to be playing above his usual game. It was in the second game that Chuck got his first surprise. He served a hard one to the outside, one that should have been an ace against a man in his sixties, but to his astonishment, Harry ran to the ball and snapped a forehand straight down the line. It was in by six inches; love-fifteen.

Chuck took aim at the inside corner on his next serve, but the ball went closer than he had planned. Harry took it on the rise, and put an inside-out shot into the opposite corner. That was a shot he hadn't shown Chuck before. Love-thirty. Get a grip, Chuck thought, and he did.

He came back to deuce and, with one ace and another hot serve, won the game. They were tied one-all. Harry's serve.

Suddenly Chuck found himself playing someone new. Harry opened the game with a clean ace, then followed with another. On his third serve, he surprised Chuck by following his serve to the net and putting away a volley. Before Chuck knew what had happened, he was down forty-love.

Chuck won one point back, then another, and then they were at deuce. Harry mopped his brow with a towel, then put an ace down the inside. Advantage Harry.

"Now we'll see what you're made of, Chuck," Harry called across the net. "I think you'll choke; want to double the bet?"

Chuck shook his head. He was one point away from decimating his bank account. "Serve, Harry."

Harry looked determined, and Chuck knew he was going to try for another ace. He moved back a step behind the baseline, tensed, and waited. The toss went back over Harry's head, but Harry reached for it. The ball came high across the net, and Chuck thought it would go out. Too late, he realized that topspin would keep it in. He ran forward as the ball bounced. The topspin carried it high, and Chuck wasn't ready for that. The ball struck him in the chest.

"That's match, I believe," Harry called from across the net.

Chuck's ears were burning; he had been had. Harry had hustled him like a pro. He managed a smile as he shook Harry's hand at the net. "I'll get my checkbook," he said.

Harry put an arm around the younger man's shoulders. "Nonsense, I wasn't serious; I was just making a point about performing under pressure. Believe me, I've had a lot more experience at that than you have."

"Harry, I insist on paying you," Chuck said.

"I won't accept it. If you write the check I won't cash it."

"Harry . . ."

"Tell you what. You come diving with us on Monday and you can buy us dinner afterward, and we'll call it even."

"Okay, Harry," Chuck said. "Tell me, where'd you pick up that goofy topspin serve?"

"I invented it," Harry said, getting his gear together. "See you Monday, about eleven?"

"Fine. And thanks for the tennis lesson."

Harry laughed loudly as he and Clare left the court. She glanced over her shoulder and gave Chuck some sort of look. He wasn't sure just what it meant.

"Well, guy, what happened?" Victor asked, a look of mock sadness on his walrus face.

"Oh, shut up, Victor," Chuck said pleasantly.

CHAPTER

17

On Monday morning Chuck woke up not wanting to go diving with the Carrases. He rolled over and snuggled up to Meg. "I have to get up," he said.

"Why?" she asked sleepily.

"I have to go diving with some people."

"Can I go? I like diving; I'm certified and everything."

"Not this trip, I'm afraid. I wish I hadn't accepted, but this is kind of a kissoff of these people for me."

"Who are they?"

"Tennis clients, people I don't really want a social relationship with anymore. You wouldn't like them, believe me."

"If they're so terrible, why have you been socializing with them?"

"Habit, I guess. When I first came to Key West they invited me out, were nice to me."

"And now you don't want to be nice to them?"

"That's not it, Meg; I've just come to feel uncomfortable around them. Can we leave it at that?"

"I'll fix you some dinner this evening, then."

"Oh, that's another thing; I have to buy them dinner."

"Oh?"

"Don't sound like that. I lost a bet—the guy beat me at tennis, so I have to buy. That's all there is to it."

"What's the name of these people?"

"Carras."

She pushed him back and looked at him. "Do they live on Dey Street?"

"That's right."

"*Now* I'm getting the picture."

"What picture?"

"Chuck, I've *seen* the Carras woman. What's going on there?"

"Nothing. Not anymore."

"You were screwing her?"

"At one time. It was just a fling."

"I'll bet it was." She got out of the bunk and began to get dressed.

"Listen, Meg, this was before you. You're the reason I'm breaking it off."

"Sure."

"I told you that before you there were other women, remember?"

"Yeah, I remember."

"Then what the hell gives you the right to be pissed off about another woman who happened before you came along?"

"I may not have the right," she said, "but I'm

pissed off anyway. Good morning." She stalked out of the cabin and off the boat.

Chuck sighed and got himself out of bed.

"Late night?" Clare asked as he climbed aboard *Fugitive*.

"Don't ask," Chuck replied. "Where are the others?"

"It's just a threesome today," she replied.

"Where's Harry?"

"Getting some beer from the marina shop. We've probably got time for a quick one."

He looked at her, amazed.

"Only joking," she said, smiling. "I would if I could, though."

He knew she would. "That's very flattering, Clare."

"I fucking well hope so," she said sweetly. "Here comes Harry."

Chuck took the paper bag from his host and waited while he climbed aboard. "Where we headed today, Harry?"

"A wreck I know," Harry replied, starting the engines. "A few miles west of here, just outside the reef."

"Won't there be a crowd? The tourist dive boats know all the wrecks."

"The dive boats don't know about this one; I found it myself—a coaster of about a hundred feet. Looks like it's been there for at least ten years."

"Sounds good," Chuck said.

Harry backed the boat out of her berth, motored slowly out of the harbor, and headed west, toward what seemed to be open water. Chuck knew, though, that the water in that direction was shallow, and a skipper had to know what he was doing to go that way. Then they were in deeper water.

They had been cruising at thirty knots for half an hour when smoke began to drift up from below, just as it had on their last trip.

"Harry!" Chuck yelled over the engine noise. He drew a finger across his throat.

Harry cut the engines. "Not again," he moaned.

"I'll see to it," Chuck called out. "Turn on your blower." He gave the ventilator five minutes to work, then went down to the engine room. An inspection revealed a repeat of their last problem; an exhaust hose had come off the overboard vent pipe. The two hose clips he had put in place on that occasion were still there, but loose. Chuck reconnected the hose, tightened the clamp, and safety-wired them for insurance. The whole business took less than ten minutes. As he was leaving the engine room he noticed Harry's air compressor again, bolted to the deck beside the engine, the exhaust of which he had just repaired. Funny place for a compressor, he thought. You'd think he'd want it on deck, where it would be a hell of a lot more convenient for refilling dive tanks.

"Everything okay?" Harry called out as Chuck surfaced.

"Yep; the hose clips had worked loose again. I wired them this time; you shouldn't have another problem."

Harry restarted the engines, and they were on their way again. He was steering from the flying bridge, so Chuck and Clare had the afterdeck to themselves. Clare opened them a beer.

"Sorry about that tennis bet the other day," she said. "I don't know what got into Harry."

"Sure you do," Chuck replied. "He knows; that was his guy following us the other day."

"I haven't seen him around again," she said.

"Neither have I, but we have no way of knowing how long he'd been following us."

"Honestly, I don't think Harry knows; really, I don't."

"We're going to have to let it go, Clare."

"What do you mean?"

"We're going to have to stop seeing each other on the sly."

"*Seeing* each other? Is that what you call it? I'd have said we were screwing each other's socks off every chance we got."

"Okay, then we're going to have to stop screwing each other's socks off." He managed a smile.

"So you're dumping me?"

"Clare, come on; this is dangerous, and we can't go on with it."

"So I'm stuck with a husband who's had five

bypasses and a prostate operation, and I can't have a sex life?"

"If you want a sex life, leave him and find somebody else. That would be a snap for you."

"Are you asking me to divorce Harry for you?"

"Of course not," Chuck replied, flustered.

"You don't want me, then?"

"Clare, we had some good times, but that's all they were. Don't come on like a woman scorned, okay?"

Harry leaned out from his perch. "You two all right down there?"

Clare flashed him a big smile. "Just perfect, darling."

Harry went back to steering the boat, and Clare was quiet for a while.

"All right," she said, finally.

"All right what?"

"We'll stop seeing each other. After all, Harry could fall off the perch at any time. Maybe we'll have another chance."

"Maybe," Chuck said. But he was thinking, *Never.*

The engines slowed. "Here we are," Harry called. "Chuck, will you get on the anchor? Clare, will you get out our gear?"

The two ex-lovers parted, one to the bow, one to the stern lockers.

As Chuck let the anchor chain out he tried to feel relief, but he was still uncomfortable about being on this boat with Harry and Clare Carras.

He wanted the day to be over. Later, he would wish it had never begun.

CHAPTER

18

Chuck handed down the three tanks, each a different color, to Harry, who was standing on the teak diving platform, inches above the water. Harry was all ready to go in his swimsuit and a T-shirt. He slung the red tank onto his back and buckled it in place.

"Aren't you wearing a life jacket, Harry?" Chuck asked.

"Never do," Harry replied. "Too much gear; gets in the way."

Chuck thought he had worn a jacket the last time they'd dived, but he wasn't sure. He got his own inflatable jacket out of his bag and slipped into it. Clare emerged from the master cabin wearing a white one-piece swimsuit that might have been sprayed on. Chuck sighed. And he was giving this up.

"You wearing a compass?" Harry called up.

"Yep."

Harry pointed to the north. "You see the reef?"

"Yep."

"The wreck is in about sixty feet of water

outside the reef, bearing about zero-three-zero from here, maybe a hundred yards."

Chuck looked at the compass on his wrist and oriented himself.

"I'm off," Harry called. "You two come on when you're ready."

"Harry, wait up," Chuck called. "Let's all go together."

But Harry had dropped into the water. A trail of bubbles followed him toward the wreck.

Chuck climbed down to the dive platform. "Give you a hand with your tank?" he called up to Clare.

"You go ahead; Harry should have someone with him. He's always doing that."

"Okay. Does it matter which tank?"

"The blue one is the guest tank; the yellow one is mine."

Chuck got his flippers on, then strapped his harness onto the tank, and slung it onto his back. "You're wearing a life jacket, aren't you?"

"Sure. Go ahead after Harry; I'm right behind you."

Chuck pulled on his mask, bit the mouthpiece, and tested his regulator. Clare was coming down the ladder. He gave her a wave and dropped into the water.

The gin clear waters off Key West were not so clear today. There was a breeze and, since they were outside the reef, no shelter, so a light swell had roiled the sandy bottom a bit. Visibility was no more than thirty feet, Chuck reckoned as he swam after Harry, constantly checking his compass. It was peaceful, though; one of the things Chuck most enjoyed about diving was the peace. It was impossible to think about anything else when underwater.

He was descending a little too quickly, so he blew a little air into his vest to neutralize his buoyancy. That done, he continued his descent, checking his compass and depth meter, on opposite wrists, as he went. He felt a little queasy; too much wine with dinner last night, maybe. He reckoned he'd covered a hundred yards, but the wreck was still not in sight. At fifty feet he stopped his descent and blew more air into his vest. The bottom was in sight, and for the first time he had a fixed reference to let him know that a current was running—a knot, maybe two. A nurse shark swam idly underneath him, giving him a start.

He made himself relax. The creatures weren't dangerous unless stepped on while they were sleeping on the bottom. Still, a fish that size nearby was enough to get his attention. He continued on his course of zero-three-zero, compensating for the current, which seemed to be at ninety degrees to his course.

A moment later, something large came hazily into view, and a moment after that it was clearer. The ship lay upright on the sandy bottom, intact, it seemed. Only the encrustations on its superstructure and rigging made it seem at home on the bottom instead of the surface. Harry was right; it was a good one. Harry was nowhere in sight; Chuck swam for the wreck.

Then he stopped. A little wave of nausea swept over him. Jesus, he thought, maybe he shouldn't have come diving with a hangover. Only it wasn't much of a hangover, not enough to make him sick. Chuck belched a couple of times; there was an awful taste in his mouth. He took a couple of extra-deep breaths and continued on. Then he saw Harry.

Harry was on deck, near the little wheelhouse, and he wasn't wearing his tank, which lay on the ship's deck. He still had his mask on, though, and it was all that was keeping him in one place. His body flowed out, parallel to the ship's deck, his arms waving idly in the current.

Chuck accelerated toward him, and as he approached, he saw through Harry's mask that his eyes were open, staring. No bubbles were rising from him. There was blood in his mask.

Chuck reached the unconscious Harry. His own heart was racing, his lungs pumping air out rapidly. He felt very sick. He decided to forget the tank, since Harry wasn't breathing anyway. He yanked the mask off the inert man, grabbed him by the wrist, and started for the surface. He had only gone a few feet when suddenly he vomited. He spat out his mouthpiece and heaved his guts out, expelling the air in his lungs. He tried to put the mouthpiece back in for some air, but he vomited again. Involuntarily, he tried to breathe and sucked saltwater into his lungs.

Panicked now, he let go of Harry and yanked the CO_2 cord on his life jacket. The jacket inflated immediately, and he shot toward the surface, kicking wildly to increase his ascent, terrified every foot of the way. What seemed minutes later, he broke the surface, gasping for air, choking on seawater and vomit, still unable to breathe. Then he retched again, bringing up bile and saltwater, and that cleared his breathing passage. He bobbed on the surface, gulping down great lungfuls of air, trying not to vomit again. He saw *Fugitive* at anchor, maybe a hundred and fifty yards away, upcurrent, then he saw Clare's yellow tank. She was clinging to the diving platform.

He thought about Harry, about going down again for him, but he knew he could not. He was still nauseated. He began swimming weakly toward the yacht, but he made little progress. He unbuckled his harness and sloughed off the tank and his weights; then he was able to make better progress. As he neared the yacht, nearly exhausted, he could see that Clare had vomited, too.

He swam up to her and grabbed hold of the dive platform. "Clare, are you all right?" he gasped.

"Sick," she said weakly. He undid her harness and got the tank off her, letting it fall into the water. He was too weak to deal with both Clare and the heavy tank. He heaved himself onto the diving platform, then got hold of Clare and dragged her up beside him.

The two of them lay there for a couple of minutes, taking deep breaths. Clare rolled over onto her stomach and vomited again. "Oh, God," she moaned, "what's wrong with me?"

"Me, too," Chuck said weakly. He knew he had to get up the ladder and to the radio, but he couldn't manage it just yet. He lay there and tried to gather strength.

"Harry," she said. "Where's Harry?"

"Gone," Chuck replied, then started slowly up the ladder.

CHAPTER

19

Chuck felt remarkably well now, considering how ill he had felt twenty minutes before. "How are you feeling?" he asked Clare.

"Better," she said. She was huddled in a beach towel across the cockpit; she had hardly said a word since he had gotten her out of the water.

"Here they come," he said, looking east. The Coast Guard cutter was steaming toward them at a great rate of knots, and he was glad to see it.

The cutter's skipper, a lieutenant, seemed impossibly young to be in command of such a vessel, something Chuck noticed about a lot of authority figures lately.

"Are you both all right?" the young man asked as he clambered aboard.

"Yes," Chuck said, "we're fine."

"Then why did you send out a mayday?" he asked.

"We've got one still in the water, dead," Chuck said.

"How do you know the man is dead?" the lieutenant asked.

"Because he's been underwater without a mask for at least half an hour," Chuck replied. "But he was dead when I reached him."

The lieutenant nodded. "Where is the wreck?"

"Zero-three-zero, a hundred and twenty yards, is my best guess," Chuck replied, pointing in the direction of the reef. "There's at least a knot of current running east."

The lieutenant leaned over *Fugitive's* railing and began crisply giving orders. "Two men in full diving gear," he said, then told them the bearing and range. He turned back to Chuck. "Now tell me what happened."

"We were going diving. Harry—that's Mrs. Carras's husband—went ahead of us, toward the wreck. I was worried because he'd had some surgery the past couple of years, and he wouldn't wear a life jacket."

The lieutenant turned to Clare. "What sort of surgery, ma'am?"

"He had five bypasses and prostate surgery,"

Clare said listlessly. Tears began to roll down her face.

"He was in very good shape, though," Chuck said. "He beat me at tennis yesterday."

"Go on," the lieutenant said.

"Harry said the wreck would be a hundred yards away, but it was farther," Chuck said. "I finally came upon it, and Harry was lying on deck—well, not exactly lying; his tank was on deck, like he'd gotten out of it, and his mask was holding him in place against the current. His eyes were open, and there was blood in the mask."

"What did you do then?" the lieutenant asked.

"I was feeling nauseated by then, but I pulled the mask off him and tried to get him to the surface. Then I began vomiting, and I guess I panicked. I let go of Harry and popped my jacket. I was lucky to make it, I think. I tried to swim back to the boat, but

I was too weak, so I dropped my tank, and then I made it back. Clare was holding on to the dive platform; she was being sick when I got there."

"What do you think was making you sick?"

"Must have been something in the tanks."

"Where are your tanks?" he asked, looking around.

"I ditched both of them," Chuck replied. "We were too weak to handle them."

"Is that right, ma'am?" the officer asked Clare.

Clare shrugged and said nothing.

The lieutenant leaned over the railing again.

"There are three tanks down there somewhere; bring me all of them, if you can."

The divers went into the water.

The lieutenant came back. "You said there's a compressor aboard? I'd like to take a look at it."

"Below," Chuck said, nodding at the stairs. "In the engine room."

The officer disappeared below. He was gone less than five minutes, and when he came back, he was carrying a foot-long piece of clear plastic tubing by his thumb and forefinger. "Ever seen this before?" he asked.

"No," Chuck replied.

The lieutenant nodded. "Funny," he said, "neither of you look very sick to me."

It was nearly dark when the cutter came alongside the Coast Guard dock near Key West Bight. *Fugitive,* driven by a Coast Guard crewman, docked behind them. Chuck saw Tommy Sculley and a very young man waiting on the dock. He waved at Tommy and Tommy waved back. When the gangplank was down, the policeman came aboard and introduced himself and the young man to the skipper.

"Come to my cabin a minute, will you, Detective?" the lieutenant said.

"Sure," Tommy replied. "Chuck, stick around, will you. Mrs. Carras, we'll take you home in just a few minutes."

Clare nodded. She had changed into shorts

and a tight T- shirt. Chuck thought she didn't look at all like a widow. He went and sat next to her.

"I'm sorry about Harry, Clare," he said. "I had hold of

him, but I think he was already dead; then I got sick, and I had to let him go."

Clare nodded. Her face was still expressionless, and the tears had stopped.

Tommy and the lieutenant appeared on deck again. "Give me another couple of minutes," he said to Chuck and Clare. Then he followed the lieutenant aboard *Fugitive*. Chuck saw the two men go below.

When they returned to the cutter, Tommy approached Chuck. "I need to talk with both of you," he said. "Why don't we do it at Mrs. Carras's house?"

"Sure," Chuck said, gathering up his gear. He took Clare's arm and escorted her down the gangplank to the police car. This police stuff had to be done, he supposed; a man was dead, after all.

Chuck and Tommy sat on a sofa in the Carras living room; Clare was downstairs in her bedroom, changing clothes; Daryl, the younger cop, sat on the opposite sofa, notebook at the ready. Tommy motioned to him.

"Put that away for now," he said to the younger man, then he turned to Chuck. "Listen to me," he said. "I want you to tell me everything that happened, from the time you got on the boat this morning, and don't leave anything out. I haven't read you your rights, so this is off the record, just between you and me and Daryl, okay?"

"Rights?" Chuck said, alarmed. He had watched enough television to know what it meant when the police started advising somebody of his rights.

Tommy put a hand on his shoulder. "Don't worry about that right now; I just want to know what happened out there today."

Chuck started at the beginning and related everything he could remember about that day, from the time he'd set foot aboard Fugitive until they had returned to Key West.

Tommy listened with complete concentration, occasionally asking a brief question. When Chuck had finished, Tommy looked at him with some sympathy. "You've had a rough day," he said. "Why don't you go home and get something to eat. We'll talk more later."

"Thanks," Chuck said. "I'll do that." He was relieved to have this session over with.

"Where do you live?" Tommy asked. "Daryl will give you a ride."

"Aboard my boat in Key West Bight," Chuck replied. "I can walk; it's only a few hundred yards."

"I'll call you tomorrow," Tommy said.

As Chuck left the house he turned back to see Clare leaving her bedroom and starting up the stairs. She was wearing a simple cotton dress, and she looked beautiful. But then, she always did.

Chuck walked slowly back toward the Bight, feeling exhausted. Maybe Meg would fix him some dinner. As he neared his boat, something seemed wrong, but it took him a moment to figure out what it was. The catamaran was gone. The berth next to Choke was empty.

Chuck didn't bother with dinner. He fell on his bunk and was immediately asleep.

Clare waited until the policemen had been gone for an hour, then got into the car and drove north. She parked in an empty supermarket parking lot and dialed a number on the car's phone.

"Hello?"

"It's me."

The voice tensed. "Tell me."

"It's done."

There was a whistle of relief at the other end. "Any problems?"

"No, it went pretty much the way you said it would. I stayed close to the boat, so when I got sick I wasn't in any real trouble."

"How about Chandler?"

"He tried to get Harry to the surface, but he had to let him go. The Coast Guard came and looked for him, but there was a current running, and he had drifted away."

"Damn! I was counting on an autopsy."

"So was I, but they recovered all three tanks, so that may not matter."

"Harry's body might turn up yet," he said. "Sometimes they do; you read about it in the papers."

"I guess."

"Are you okay?"

"I'm just tired. It's been one hell of a day."

"Try and get some sleep tonight," he said. "We can meet tomorrow."

"No!" she blurted out. "We can't go anywhere near each other, maybe for weeks."

"I can't stay away from you that long," he said, and his voice was shaky.

"You have to. Florida has capital punishment, remember? And these days they're in a mood to use it. We have to be very, very careful, and that means staying away from each other until I can get Harry's estate sorted out and make some sort of move."

"I guess you're right," he admitted. "But I'm not going to like it."

"Neither am I," she replied. "I'm going to miss fucking you."

"I know you," he said. "You can't go long without sex. You'll have Chandler in bed again in a week."

"That might do us some good," she said, "but I don't think he's going to want to be anywhere near me."

"Why not?"

"Because before we went diving, he broke it off."

"Why the hell would he do that?"

"I don't know. God knows I was keeping him happy."

"I believe that, but I just don't get it."

"Neither do I. Maybe he was feeling guilty about Harry."

"I doubt it; there was nothing in his history that suggested any guilt about husbands."

"Another woman," she said. "That would account for it."

"I don't believe another woman could stack up to you, husband or no husband."

"You're sweet, baby, but that's my best guess."

"I can sniff around and find out."

"No! Don't you dare follow him, or me either. We have to be very, very cool. Things went well, and I think they're going to go even better. What I told the cops will make sure of that."

"What did you tell them?"

"I have to go now. Remember, no contact at all. I'll call you when I think it's safe."

"Whatever you say, lover. I love you."

"I love you, too. Good-bye for now." She hung up, started the car, and drove back to the house.

CHAPTER

20

Chuck picked up a paper at the Waterfront Market on his way to work. The incident occupied half the front page, and he was prominently featured. The reporter obviously had a source with the Coast Guard, maybe even the skipper of the cutter.

When he arrived at the club, Merk called him into his office, and a moment later Victor walked in.

"What the hell happened, Chuck?" Merk asked.

"I take it you've read the papers," Chuck replied.

"Sure," Victor said, "but what *really* happened?"

"The paper got it right," Chuck said. "They got it from the Coast Guard, I think."

"How about Clare?" Victor asked. "Is she okay?"

"She's fine."

"Glad to hear it," the pro said, smiling. "I'd hate to think of anything happening to that sweet body."

"Oh, shut up, Victor," Chuck said.

"Hey, listen, the husband's out of the way now; you've got a clear shot, haven't you?"

Merk broke in. "That's enough, Victor. Chuck, I take it you'd been seeing her."

"Don't believe everything you hear, Merk," Chuck replied. "My student's here; I've got to go." He walked out of the clubhouse to find Billy waiting for him, and Billy's father as well.

"I hope you don't mind," the father said. "I just want to see how Billy's doing."

"I don't mind," Chuck said. He was too numb to mind.

"Say, listen, what happened out on that boat?"

"The papers got it right," Chuck replied. "That's all I can say about it. Come on, Billy, let's get warmed up."

Billy was sharp that morning, and when Chuck played points with him, the boy won most of them. When they had finished playing the father motioned Chuck to sit down with him.

"What's up?" Chuck asked.

"There's a tournament in Naples this weekend," the elder Tubbs said. "I'd like Billy to play in it."

"That's a pro tournament," Chuck said. "Nothing major, but a pro tournament, nevertheless."

"I'm aware of that," Tubbs said.

"It's too soon," Chuck said. "Anyway, he'd blow the rest of his high school season; they wouldn't let him play again."

"We both know he's too good to be playing high school kids," Tubbs said. "You've done wonders with him; it's time to see how he plays under that kind of pressure, how good he really is."

Chuck shrugged. "I can't stop you," he said.

"Come on, Chuck, we want you there," Tubbs said. "It's important that you see how Billy does against that kind of competition. Assuming you still want to coach him, of course."

"Sure I do."

"Then come with us. I'll talk to Merk, get you off for the weekend, and I'll pay you for your time, of course. We'll fly up in my airplane; it's only half an hour."

Chuck shrugged. "Okay, what the hell." Today he couldn't care less.

Tommy Sculley sat across the desk from the lab technician and tried to see what the woman was typing on the form.

"I'll be just a minute more," she said.

"Take your time," Tommy replied. "I've got all day."

"I haven't." She typed a few more lines, ripped the form out of the typewriter, took it to a copying machine, and punched some buttons. Finally, she handed a copy to Tommy. "Carbon monoxide," she said.

Tommy looked at the form. There were three columns of figures, headed source air, ambient air, and air standard. "What does ambient air mean?" he asked.

"Each tank was tested twice," she replied. "Source is one test, ambient is the other. The results are expressed in parts per million. The right-hand column, air standard, is what you find in ordinary air—what you should find in compressed air from a clean source. All three tanks are high in carbon monoxide, carbon dioxide, and methane. The red and yellow tanks both had more than twenty-five-hundred parts per million. Normal air contains ten parts per million."

"Pretty rich, huh?"

"*Very* rich."

"Enough to kill?"

"Plenty. If your man had put his mouth over a car's exhaust pipe, it couldn't be richer. The blue tank is different, though; while it's abnormally high in carbon monoxide, it contained only about seven hundred parts per million, less than a third of the other two tanks."

"Not enough to kill?"

"Sure, if you breathed it long enough."

"How long?"

"Difficult to say—it would depend on the physical condition of the breather, his respiration rate, other things."

"What would it do to the breather?"

"The symptoms would include weakness and nausea, eventually unconsciousness, finally death."

"How long would it take the red and yellow tanks to kill?"

"Again, a lot would depend on the condition of the breather."

"Say a guy who'd had five bypasses and prostate surgery, but who was otherwise in pretty good shape. Top shape, in fact, for his age. The guy swam, played regular tennis."

"I don't know what effect the prior surgery would have, but even in top shape, the breather wouldn't get far sucking on the red or yellow tanks."

"What do you mean by not far?"

"A few minutes at most—very few."

Tommy thanked the woman and left the lab. He got into the car, picked up the cellular phone, and after a couple of minutes, was patched through to the Coast Guard cutter.

"Lieutenant, this is Detective Sculley."

"What can I do for you?"

"Tell me the locations where your men found the three tanks, by color, if you will."

"The red tank was on the deck of the wrecked ship; the blue tank was maybe twenty feet from the wreck, in the direction of the yacht; the yellow tank was practically under the yacht."

"Thanks, Lieutenant."

"Glad to be of help."

Daryl spoke for the first time. "So Chandler was wearing the blue tank?"

"That's how it looks," Tommy said. "Let's ask him."

CHAPTER

21

Tommy and Daryl pulled into the Waterfront Market parking lot just as Chuck Chandler was parking the yellow Porsche Speedster across the road.

"Hey, Chuck," Tommy called as he got out of the car. He crossed the road to where the tennis pro was waiting, still dressed in whites.

"Hi, Tommy. What's happening?"

"Beautiful car, Chuck; I haven't seen one in years."

"Thanks. I put a lot of work into it."

"You restored it yourself?"

"Everything. I rented a boat shed near Palm Springs when I was living up there, and I restored both the car and the boat over a period of nearly two years."

"Is *Choke* your boat?"

"That's right."

"Daryl and I were admiring her the other day."

"It was a lot of work, but I had a couple of guys helping on the boat. And I got a floating home and a car out of it."

"Could we take a look at *Choke?* I wanted to ask you some more questions, anyway."

132

"Sure, come on down."

The three men walked down to the waterfront and boarded *Choke*.

"Wow," Tommy breathed. "I've never seen such good varnish work."

"Thanks," Chuck said. "That took a lot of work. Can I get you guys a drink?"

"Maybe some coffee or tea for us," Tommy said, catching Daryl's eye. "You go ahead and have something stronger, if you like."

"I think I will," Chuck said. "It's been a hard couple of days. Come on below and have a look around."

Chuck showed them the saloon and the master's cabin, and Tommy poked around while Chuck made tea. The engine room was spotless.

"You do the engine work?" Tommy asked.

"Yeah, with the help of one of the guys. We pulled the engine, overhauled it, painted it, and reinstalled it with new mounts and hoses."

"You're a pretty handy guy," Tommy said.

"Must be genetic; my father could fix anything, and I used to help him in his workshop." He handed each detective a glass of iced tea, then poured himself a gin and tonic in a tall glass. "Let's go sit out on deck; it's cooler."

The three men relaxed in deck chairs and sipped their drinks.

"I know this is a pain in the ass," Tommy said, "but I need to go over yesterday again. I'd like you to tell me what happened from the moment

133

you arrived aboard *Fugitive* until I saw you aboard the Coast Guard cutter. Do you mind?"

"I guess I've got one more retelling left in me," Chuck said. "I arrived aboard *Fugitive* around ten, I guess."

Tommy held up a hand. "Wait a minute, let me go through the drill. You have the right to remain silent, but if you decide to talk to us what you say can be used against you in a court of law; you have a right to an attorney, and if you cannot afford one, one will be appointed to represent you. You understand these rights?"

Chuck looked a little worried. "Tommy, are you arresting me or something?"

"No, no, nothing like that; you'll know it when I arrest you. We always have to go through this form, and I want you to understand that it's important that you tell me the truth at all times."

"Sure; want me to go on?"

"Yeah. You arrived aboard *Fugitive.*"

"Right. Harry was at the marina shop getting some beer, but he came back after a couple of minutes."

"What did you do while you waited?"

"Clare and I chatted."

"About what?"

"Just small talk."

"Anything about your trip that day?"

"No; I didn't even know where we were going until Harry got back."

"Go on."

"Well, we were out, I don't know, half an hour

or forty minutes when the same thing happened as on the day you came out with us—exhaust began coming up from below."

"What happened then?"

"Harry stopped the engines and turned on the fan to clear the engine room, then I went below to fix the problem, which was the same as before. The hose clips had loosened, vibration from the engines, I guess, and the exhaust was being poured into the engine room, instead of overboard."

"What, exactly, did you do to fix the problem?"

"I put the hose back onto the overboard pipe and tightened both clamps. This time I put some safety wire on the clips to make sure they stayed put."

"How long did all this take, exactly?"

Chuck shrugged. "Eight minutes, maybe—ten, tops."

"What did you do then?"

"I came back up, Harry started the engines, and we continued out to our dive spot."

"Who was driving the boat?"

"Harry."

"Where was Clare all this time?"

"She and I sat on the afterdeck and chatted."

"What about?"

"Just small talk—her tennis game, whatever."

"Go on."

"Well, we arrived at the place, and I went forward to deal with the anchor. Then Harry went below and handed up three tanks, one for each of us. There's a compressor in the engine room."

"Harry handed up the tanks?"

"Yeah. Then we started getting into our gear. Harry was ready first, and he went on ahead of us."

"Do you remember which tank Harry was wearing?"

"Yeah, it was the red one, I'm sure. I remember the color when I saw Harry on the bottom."

"Why didn't Harry wear a life jacket?"

"I suggested that he should, but he said he never bothered. Funny, I could swear he was wearing one the last time we dove together. Do you remember, Tommy? You were there."

"I believe he was," Tommy said. "So you gave Harry the red tank, and you chose which one?"

"Harry picked the red tank for himself, and Clare said for me to use the blue one, said it was the guest tank. She took the yellow one."

"You're sure she said that?"

"Positive, just as I'm positive Harry chose the red tank for himself."

"Okay, what happened next?"

"Harry started out before I even had my gear on, and Clare expressed some concern about that, asked me to catch up with him."

"Was she ready by that time?"

"No, I was ready before she was; I helped her on with her tank, then I went after Harry. He had given me a compass course and a distance."

"How many minutes would you say Harry was ahead of you?"

"Hard to say, exactly; maybe two minutes, five at the outside."

"Go on."

"So I followed Harry out to the wreck. It was further than he had estimated, I think, and there was a current, a knot or two, running. I had to correct my course. The visibility wasn't so hot, so I was very close to the wreck before I saw it. I was starting to feel sick."

"Did you see Harry then?"

"Not immediately, not until I got closer. Then he was in plain view on the wreck's deck."

"Describe what you saw."

"He had gotten out of his tank, but he was still attached to it by the connecting hose. The regulator wasn't in his mouth; his eyes were open, and there was blood in his mask. I knew he had stopped breathing, because there were no bubbles coming from his mouth."

"What did you do?"

"I went straight for him, and got hold of his wrist. I pulled off the mask, because I knew it was no good to him. I wanted to get him to the surface as quickly as possible. But then I vomited, spat out my regulator in the process, and I really panicked. I yanked the cord on my life jacket, it inflated instantly, and I popped to the surface, kicking to get there faster. When I reached the surface, I was retching and strangling on saltwater at the same time. I guess I was lucky to survive."

"Did you think about going back for Harry?"

"There was no way I could have done it. It was obvious to me that something was wrong with the air in my tank, so I had nothing to dive with, and Harry was at sixty feet. Also, I was having a lot of trouble breathing properly, coughing up vomit that had gotten into my wind-pipe. I felt exhausted, and when I started back toward the yacht I had to drop my tank so that I could make it."

"How long did it take you to get back to the yacht?"

"I don't know—a lot longer than it had taken me to get out to the wreck, because I was so tired."

"Make a guess."

"Well, it must have taken me five or six minutes to reach the wreck, and probably twice that long to get back."

"Where was Clare all this time?"

"I saw her hanging on to the diving platform, vomiting. I guess she had tried to follow Harry and me, but had gotten sick and turned back."

"Did you ask her what had happened?"

"No, we were both in pretty bad shape. I helped her onto the platform and out of her tank, then I took a few deep breaths and went up to the cockpit and radioed the Coast Guard."

"How long before they arrived?"

"Twenty minutes, half an hour. They must have already been in the area."

"What did you and Clare talk about while you were waiting?"

"I told her about Harry, but she didn't really respond. She seemed to be in shock or something."

"But you weren't in shock?"

"God knows I was shaken up, but I felt better with every breath I took. By the time the Coast Guard arrived I was feeling perfectly normal. I guess Clare was, too, although she didn't say anything. The lieutenant commented on how well we both looked."

"You didn't feel the need of going into a pressure tank, to avoid the bends?"

"No, we were at sixty feet, which is deep enough to make a very slow ascent advisable, but I guess I was down too short a time for that to be a problem; it was sort of what divers call a bounce dive. There was a tank on the cutter, and they offered it to me, but I didn't think I needed it."

"Anything else you care to add?"

"No, I guess that's about it."

Tommy took a deep breath and blew it out. "Well, we've kind of got a problem here, Chuck."

"What problem?"

"Some of your answers don't jibe with some of Clare's answers."

Chuck furrowed his brow. "Such as?"

"Tell me again, how long were you in the engine room?"

"Eight, ten minutes."

"Clare said it was more like forty-five minutes."

Chuck's eyes widened. "That's ridiculous; it was a simple job, and it didn't take anywhere near that long."

"You're positive?"

"Yes, I am."

"Something else: Clare says you handed Harry the red tank and her the yellow tank and chose the blue one for yourself."

"Not true. Clare told me to use the blue tank; she said it was the guest tank!"

Tommy nodded slowly. Then he produced a plastic bag from his pocket and held it up for Chuck to see. Inside was a twelve-inch length of clear plastic pipe. "Chuck," Tommy said, "have you ever seen this before?"

CHAPTER

22

Chuck stared at the plastic pipe as if it were a poisonous reptile. "Yeah, I guess I've seen several thousand feet of that kind of tubing in my time. It's used a lot on boats."

"I don't mean this kind of pipe in general," Tommy said. "I mean this piece of pipe in particular."

He didn't at all like where this was headed. "I don't know how to tell that piece of pipe from other pieces of the same pipe," Chuck said. "What's going on, Tommy?"

"Chuck, I think we've established that you're pretty handy on a boat, or with anything mechanical. Would you say that's a fair judgment?"

"Yeah, I guess so. What's your point?"

"My point is that Harry Carras wasn't handy at all with mechanical things, that he never did his own work on his boat, that he didn't know how machinery worked. But you do."

"I guess I'm a little slow, Tommy. Why don't you just spell it out?" Chuck braced himself.

"Well, it started with the lieutenant on the Coast Guard cutter. After arriving aboard *Fugitive* he went below to the engine room, and he found this piece of plastic pipe on the floor, right next to the air compressor."

"So?"

"He also didn't find any safety wire on the hose clips securing the exhaust pipe."

"That's crazy; I'd put it on there less than an hour before. Safety wire doesn't just come off by itself."

"Never mind that; let me go on with the lieutenant's theory."

"What theory?"

"Listen to me, Chuck," Tommy said. "The lieutenant thinks that this piece of tubing might have been used to join two larger pieces of hose together. Could that be?"

141

"Well, if they were the right diameter, you could put each end of the smaller tubing into a piece of larger tubing and extend the length a few inches."

"Let me ask your opinion on this," Tommy said. "Could this piece of tubing have been used to join together the exhaust hose from an engine with the intake hose of the air compressor?"

Chuck's jaw fell, and he didn't speak.

"Chuck? What's your opinion of that possibility?"

Chuck swallowed hard. "You think I did that, Tommy?" he asked.

"I just want your opinion, Chuck. Could you join those two pieces of equipment together like the lieutenant thinks?"

"Yes, you could. Assuming the different hoses were the right diameters. Is that what happened, Tommy? Did somebody deliberately charge our tanks with exhaust from an engine?"

Tommy leaned back in his chair and sipped his tea. "We had the air in the tanks analyzed. Two of the tanks had enough carbon monoxide in them to kill in a matter of minutes; the third tank was contaminated, too, but not enough to kill in such a short time, just enough to make whoever breathed it sick after a few minutes."

Chuck stared at the detective. "And the third tank was the blue one, my tank?"

"That's right, Chuck. Do you see where I'm headed here?"

Chuck nodded. "I'm afraid I do."

"Help me out, here, Chuck; show me how you couldn't have done this."

"Maybe Harry was running the engine and the compressor at the same time, and the compressor intake sucked in the exhaust from the engines."

"Nice try, but the exhaust pipes are on the stern of the boat, and the intake for the compressor is around on the starboard side, well away from the exhaust."

"I was only below for ten minutes," Chuck replied. "That wasn't enough time to connect the engine to the compressor and fill the three tanks."

"The lady says you were below for forty-five minutes."

"That's not true, but even if it were, the engines weren't running."

Tommy raised a finger. "Good point. I need some more points like that, Chuck. How long would it take to fill three tanks like that?"

"I don't know, without knowing the output of the compressor. Certainly it was smaller than the ones you'd see at a dive shop, where they're filling dozens of tanks a day."

Tommy turned to Daryl. "Make a note of that; I want to know the output of Carras's compressor and how long it would take to fill three tanks." Tommy then turned and pointed to the marina across the bight. "Chuck, how far do you figure it is from here to *Fugitive*'s berth over there?"

"I don't know, maybe a hundred and fifty yards."

"You a good swimmer Chuck? Could you swim over there, at night maybe, and fill those tanks?"

"I'd have to start *Fugitive*'s engines to do that," Chuck replied. "That would get noticed at night. Security's pretty good over there."

"Another good point," Tommy said. "Keep 'em coming."

"All I can do is tell you the truth, Tommy."

"So far you haven't told me the whole truth, have you, Chuck?"

"What do you mean?"

"When the three of you were cruising out to that wreck, what did you and Clare Carras talk about?"

"I've told you."

"Yeah, but Clare has told us something different."

"Told you what?"

"Chuck, how long has the affair been going on?"

Chuck looked back and forth at the two detectives. "What did Clare say we talked about?"

"She said she told you she was breaking it off, that she loved Harry, and that even though he was impotent, she didn't want to leave him for you." Tommy leaned forward. "Is that your recollection, Chuck?"

Chuck sighed. "Just the opposite, Tommy. I told her I was breaking it off."

"How long had it been going on?"

"Almost from the moment I met her," Chuck replied.

"How often were you seeing her?"

"Two or three times a week; whenever Harry was out of town on business."

"Did you take her up to Little Palm Island, so you could spend a whole night with her?"

"*She* invited *me.* I'd never even heard of the place. I met her up there, and we spent the one night together."

"Why did you want to break it off with Clare?"

"Because I'd met a girl I thought I could fall in love with."

"What's her name?"

"Meg Hailey. She lives right over there." He turned and pointed at the empty berth. "At least, she did."

"She lived on a boat?"

"Yes."

"So where's the boat?"

"I don't know. When I came back here yesterday, she had sailed."

"The boat or the girl?"

"Both. She and her brother, Dan, lived aboard."

"I'd sure like to talk to Meg," Tommy said.

"So would I."

"Chuck, that night up at Little Palm Island, did you ask Clare to leave Harry for you?"

"I did *not;* that never crossed my mind. The thing with Clare was just . . . "

"Recreational?"

"I guess you could say that," Chuck replied. "It was for the sex; nothing else."

"That's not the way Clare saw it," Tommy said.

"How did she see it? Tell me."

"Clare says she was in love with you, that you had manipulated her into talking about her leaving Harry."

"Tommy, that's just nuts. Harry was a rich man; I'm a teaching tennis pro, for God's sake. In a great year I might make seventy-five grand. That wouldn't keep Clare in earrings."

Tommy sat back again. "I guess not," he said. "Not without Harry's money, anyway."

All three men were quiet for a moment.

"Tommy," Chuck said finally, "do I need a lawyer?"

"It couldn't hurt," Tommy replied.

CHAPTER

23

Daryl was quiet until they were in the car. "So why didn't you bust him?" he asked Tommy.

"This is a quiz, Daryl," Tommy replied, exasperated. "Why didn't I bust him?"

"Because you don't have enough evidence?"

"You get an A."

"You've got motive and opportunity," Daryl said.

"Motive, maybe; opportunity, maybe. If you buy Clare Carras's end of what happened."

"What do you mean, maybe? He wanted Clare and Harry's money—that's motive; he spent forty-five minutes down in that engine room doing a ten-minute job, that's opportunity. Or maybe he fixed the tanks at night, like you suggested."

"You're buying Clare's story, then?"

"It makes more sense than Chuck's."

"I'll give you that much," Tommy said. "But he might have an alibi, if the girlfriend turned up."

"Even if we found her today, that wouldn't stand up for an alibi."

"Why not, Daryl?"

"He could say to—what's her name?"

"Meg."

"Meg. He could say to her that he's breaking up with Clare, right? That doesn't mean he actually does it; he could just be covering his ass."

"Look at it this way, Daryl," Tommy said patiently. "Let me give you three possible scenarios, just for a start: One, Chuck wants Clare and her husband's money, so he knocks off Harry; two, Clare wants Harry's money, so she sets up Chuck for the murder; three, Chuck and Clare are in it together."

"And which one do you buy?"

"At the moment, I'm leaning a little bit toward they're in it together."

"Why?"

"Because they've both got something to gain."

"But they've forgotten something," Daryl said.

"What's that?"

"In order to make this thing with the tanks work, they've got to give us somebody else who'd look good for the murderer, somebody else who'd want Harry dead."

"Daryl, try to think back as far as the exploding yacht, which was just like Harry's; try to remember the punctured brake line in the Mercedes, which was *actually* Harry's. Does your memory go back that far?"

"Oh, yeah," Daryl said.

"Here's a fourth scenario: Somebody hates Harry. Maybe Harry stole from him; maybe he came out on the short end of a business deal with Harry. Whatever. Anyway, he decides he'd be a much happier person if Harry stopped living. He tries twice and fails, then he gets lucky, and Harry is fish food."

"A possibility, I guess," Daryl admitted. "And a pretty good one."

"Let me give you another possibility, a fifth scenario: Clare is having it off with a third, no, a fourth party, Mister X. She and Mister X want Harry unbreathing, so they knock him off and set up Chuck for the deed."

"I guess that's a pretty good possibility."

"Damn right it is; that's what's driving me crazy."

"Why?"

"We've got five pretty good possibilities; that's too many. Murder is usually simpler than that; you don't usually get multiple choices, not sensible ones, anyway."

"I never thought of murder being simple, I guess."

"Ninety-nine times out of a hundred, it is. Fred loves Sally, kills Sally's husband—or swap the genders; wife hates husband who made her life miserable, puts butcher knife in throat while he's sleeping; jerk owes shark money, won't pay, shark kills him as an example to his other debtors; kid hates dad, wants to inherit his money. Or, most common of all, Joe and Al have a few too many and remember how much they hate each other, so they slug it out in the alley, and one of them forgets to mention he has a knife. Those are your typical murder scenarios, and there are a lot more, but for the most part, they're simple."

"And this one's complicated."

"Very."

"So what do you do when it's complicated?"

"You run down *all* the possibilities, or at least you keep all of 'em in mind while you're working on the most promising."

"And the most promising is that Chuck and Clare are in it together?"

"Technically, yes. But my gut is having trouble with that one."

"Why?"

"Maybe I'm letting my feelings get in the way."

"What feelings?"

"I like Chuck; I think he's a nice guy."

"And nice guys never murder anybody?"

"It's not just that. When I listen to Chuck talk I think I hear the truth."

"Because you like him?"

"Maybe. Or maybe because he's telling the truth. I don't know, I may be letting what I think of him get in the way of what I think of his story."

"Something bothers me about the two of them being in it together," Daryl said.

"Tell me."

"If they're in it together, why is Clare's story different from Chuck's? I mean, if it's their plan together, then Clare must have had second thoughts and is trying to nail Chuck. Problem with that is, she's bound to know that if she tries to nail him, he sucks her into it, right?"

"Daryl, I have hopes for you," Tommy said.

Daryl beamed. "I mean, we're talking human nature here, right?"

"Right, Daryl. If Chuck is after Clare and Harry's money, he wouldn't try to suck in Clare, unless she started it."

"I think I like the Clare option, that Clare has engineered it and is setting up Chuck."

"Tell you the truth, I wouldn't mind seeing it come out that way. Of course, the world would be poorer for the loss of the Clare Carras body."

150

"Yeah, I would have liked to have a crack at that body," Daryl said.

Tommy burst out laughing. "Daryl, I like your ambition, but the odds are, you are never going to have a crack at something like Clare Carras, not in your whole life."

"And why the hell not?" Daryl demanded, sounding hurt.

"Because it is a universal truth that women who look like Clare Carras always end up with men like Harry—older, rich, and very, very generous. A cop could never in his whole life put together enough money to get a sideways glance from something like Clare Carras. So save your fantasies of Clare Carras for nights alone between the sheets and a bottle of hand lotion at your side."

"I guess you're right," Daryl sighed.

"That much, I'm right about. And before this is over, I'm going to be right about who killed Harry Carras."

"I believe you, Tommy."

"You're a smart kid, Daryl. You keep thinking that way, and someday you'll make a great detective."

"Tommy," Daryl said, "you're more full of shit than anybody I ever met in my whole life."

CHAPTER

24

Tommy and Daryl stood on the steps of the Monroe County courthouse, where the county coroner had heard all the evidence at an inquest and declared Harry Carras dead of unknown causes. They watched Clare Carras walk toward her car.

"Tommy, are you absolutely sure I have no chance at all with a woman like that?" Daryl asked.

"Not unless you overpower her," Tommy replied.

"It might be worth the effort."

"Never work; she's probably stronger than you."

"So Carras is officially dead; what does that mean for Mrs. Carras?"

"It means she can get the will probated, and she's a free woman, able to spend her husband's wealth as she sees fit."

"Excuse me, Detective Sculley?"

The two detectives turned to find a man standing behind them. He was solidly built and deeply tanned, with thick black hair. Tommy made him for Italian.

"Yeah?" Tommy said.

"My name is Barry Carman. I'm a private investigator; I wonder if I could have a word with you in private?"

"I'm pretty busy," Tommy replied. "What's this about?"

"About the Carras case," Carman said.

Tommy pointed at his police car. "Step into my office," he said. He opened the rear door and let Carman in, then he and Daryl got into the front seat.

"Okay, what?" Tommy said.

Carman opened a briefcase, extracted an eight-by-ten glossy black-and-white photograph, and handed it to Tommy. "Tell me if you've ever seen this man before."

Tommy looked at the photograph. It was a head-and-shoulders shot of a smiling man who appeared to be in his early forties. He was over-weight and had dark, very curly hair and thick sideburns. "No, who is he?"

"I think there's just a chance he could be Harry Carras."

Tommy looked at the photograph more closely. "How old is this picture?"

"It was taken in 1976; it's extracted from a shot of a group of people at a dinner."

"We're talking plastic surgery here, right?"

"We would have to be talking plastic surgery, in addition to major weight loss, capped teeth and, of course, almost twenty years of aging."

Tommy looked at the photograph again. "Who

knows? It's possible, I guess. What's this guy's name?"

"Rocco Marinello."

Tommy and Daryl exchanged a glance. "And what's the connection with Carras?"

"Marinello was a lawyer in L.A. Well, more than a lawyer, really, he was a kind of financial genius. He represented some clients of mine. Four years ago he decamped and left a note saying he'd gambled away his clients' money and couldn't face the music."

"Was he married?"

"And had a son in college. He had put enough in the wife's name to keep them both comfortable."

"So why are you still looking for Marinello after so much time?"

"Let's just say that my clients aren't the sort of people to forget about him."

"And who are your clients?"

"Business associates of Mr. Marinello's; of course, I can't reveal their identity."

"Of course," Tommy said. "Do your clients also have Italian names?"

"I can't comment on that."

"Pretty juicy assignment, huh?" Tommy said. "I mean, if you never find the guy you still get paid, right?"

"There's a considerable bonus if I find him," Carman replied.

"So what made you look in Key West, Mr. Carman?"

"I got a tip."

Tommy's eyebrows went up. "Oh? From who?"

"Anonymous. A woman's voice, though. She said, 'If you're still looking for Rocco Marinello, try Harry Carras, in Key West.'"

"Not that Marinello *was* Carras?"

"That's right, but I took her to mean they were one and the same."

"What else did she say?"

"Nothing; she hung up."

"What was the voice like?"

"Youngish, muffled; could have been anybody."

Tommy nodded. "So what do you want from me, Mr. Carman?"

"I wondered if you knew anything about Carras that might make you think he was someone else?"

"I hardly knew the man," Tommy replied.

Carman seemed to accept that. "What do you think the chances are of the body turning up?"

"Not great," Tommy said. "The incident took place outside the reef, which means that Carras could be floating in Havana Harbor right now, or he could have caught the Gulf Stream and be on his way to Scotland, or something could have found him delicious."

"Oh." Carman looked crestfallen.

"Apart from this tip, do you have any evidence at all that Carras was Marinello?"

"None."

155

"Did you ever see Carras?"

"Once."

"Did you ever see Marinello?"

"No."

"So you can't make an ID?"

Carman shook his head. "All I have is the photograph, which is apparently the only one in existence. Marinello went through his house and destroyed everything that might have helped find him."

"A thorough fellow, Mr. Marinello."

"You better believe it. The guy seemed to just vanish off the face of the earth. He'd apparently been planning his move for some time."

"Sounds like it. Are you any good at what you do, Mr. Carman?"

"I like to think so. Believe me, my clients wouldn't have hired me if my reputation wasn't solid gold. I'm ex-LAPD, twenty years on the job."

"Are you the only PI they hired?"

"It wouldn't surprise me to learn that they'd hired others, but I don't know. My clients also have full-time employees who are good at finding people."

"Be interesting to see if anybody else turns up in Key West," Tommy said.

"Could happen," Carman replied. "Tell me, do you know how long Carras and his wife were married?"

"Little more than a year, she says. If he was

Marinello, he probably wouldn't have told her, since he was such a careful man."

"I agree," Carman said. "I talked to her yesterday and drew a complete blank. I don't think she had a clue what I was talking about."

"Are you going to report all this to your clients?" Tommy asked.

"I haven't decided."

"You understand what might happen to Mrs. Carras if you do?"

"It's crossed my mind."

"Let me be straight with you, Mr. Carman," Tommy said. "I don't want somebody's goons coming down here to my town and beating up on a citizen, you get my drift?"

"I do. I don't think she knows anything about Marinello anyway."

"That wouldn't much matter to your clients, would it? I mean, they're not likely to take her denials at face value, are they?"

Carman shook his head. "I wouldn't want that on my conscience."

"Let's leave it at this, Mr. Carman: if I find out something that might connect Carras to Marinello, I'll call you; you do the same for me, okay?"

"Okay," Carman replied. "I don't see much point in hanging around this tropical paradise any longer. I'm going back to L.A. Thanks for your help, Detective." He stuck out his hand.

Tommy shook it, then let Carman out of the

back of the car. The PI got onto a scooter and drove away.

Tommy got back in. "What do you think?" he asked Daryl.

"Well, we already knew Carras wasn't Carras. He could be Marinello. Is Rock short for Rocco?"

"Could be; like in Rocky Graziano."

"Then the book I saw at Carras's house could be the connection Carman was looking for."

"Could be, but as far as you and I are concerned, it's moot. Carras is dead, and I'm not going to sic the mob on his widow, are you?"

"Not me. If Carras was Marinello, I'd bet she didn't know it."

"Way I look at it," Tommy said, "if somebody can clip the mob for a bundle and get away with it, it's okay with me."

CHAPTER

25

Clare Carras swam slowly up and down the length of the pool. The underwater light was off, and the house was dark. It was just after midnight. A faint, mixed din of rock music wafted over the fence from the direction of Duval Street; the tourists were stocking the bars.

He came in over the back fence, as he had been told to do, looking around him in the darkness.

"Over here," Clare said quietly. He walked to the edge of the pool, slipped out of his clothes, then slid silently into the water.

After they had made love and he was still begging for another time, she climbed out of the pool and lay on the grass. He came and lay beside her.

"Something's come up," she said. "We have to talk."

"If we have to."

"A man named Carman showed up in town yesterday; he came to see me in the afternoon."

"Somebody Harry knew?"

"No. Somebody who was looking for Harry."

"Well, he's a little late, isn't he?"

"He's not too late to make trouble for us, baby."

"What kind of trouble?"

"He found out who Harry really was."

"Wasn't Harry Harry?"

"Not until a few years ago. He spent the earlier part of his life as somebody else, somebody who disappeared with a lot of somebody else's money."

"Uh-oh," he said.

"I'm glad you're getting the point, baby. We do not want these particular people coming around asking for their money back."

"Who are these people?"

"Believe me, it's better if you don't know any more about that."

"I'll take your word for it."

"Trouble is, they might take Carman seriously about the connection to Harry, and we can't have that."

"We certainly can't," he said.

"Do you think you could handle the problem?"

"For you? Of course."

"For both of us, baby."

"Do you know where he's staying?"

"He's at the Pier House. I followed him home after the inquest. He'd been talking to that cop, Tommy Sculley."

"Not good."

"No, but not necessarily bad, either. I don't think he's likely to tell Sculley who he's working for."

"No?"

"Believe me, no. But we're going to have to take care of Mr. Carman, and we can't do it in Key West. I don't want the people he works for to even know he was here."

"Did he fly in?"

"No, he flew into Miami, rented a car, and drove down. He told me he'd never been to the Keys, and he wanted to know what it was like. In fact, Mr. Carman told me a lot more than he should have. He told me, for instance, during our conversation, that he liked to travel under an assumed name, and that he always paid his travel expenses in cash whenever possible. Mr. Carman is a private detective, and I think he's seen too many movies about his profession."

"So?"

"So what we have to do is to get him back to Miami and deal with him there."

"I'll bet you already have it worked out how to do that."

She smiled. "I have. Mr. Carman was in a bar on Duval Street a couple of hours ago. He could be back in his room by now. Shall we see?"

"Let's."

She picked up the poolside phone and dialed the hotel room directly, bypassing the switchboard.

"Hello?" His voice was sleepy and slurred.

"Mr. Carman?"

"Yes."

"This is the person you talked to yesterday afternoon; do you remember?"

"Yes, of course." He was awake now.

"I'm in Miami, and I have some information about the man whose photograph you showed me yesterday."

"That's very good. When can I have it?"

"You'll have to move fast, I'm afraid; I've left Key West, and I'm not coming back."

"I can move as fast as you like," Carman replied. "Where can we meet?"

"First, you have to promise me that you won't ever tell your clients you spoke with me."

"All right; I won't tell them."

"Do you have a Florida road map?"

"Got one right here; let me turn on the light. Okay, got it."

"Do you see where Highway 1 leaves Key Largo and goes north?"

"Yes."

"That goes to Homestead. From there take Route 997 north until it joins 27, then turn north."

"Got it."

"Highway 27 crosses I-75, and there's a tollbooth. There's a rest stop just before the tollbooth; stop there. I'll leave all the information in an envelope behind the toilet in the men's room."

"What sort of information is it?"

"Everything you need to make the connection. But leave me out of it, remember?"

"Don't worry, you won't even exist."

"That's the way I prefer it. Now, you must leave at once to get there before dawn; after that the rest stop will get busy, and somebody might find the envelope before you do."

"I can be out of the hotel in ten minutes; I've already paid my bill."

"Good. We won't be talking again. You'll make good time on the road this time of night, but don't get any speeding tickets."

"I won't. Thank you and good-bye."

"Good-bye." She hung up. "He's all yours," she said, "but you'd better hurry."

He stood up and started to get dressed.

"Search him and his car for any sign of Key

West—hotel bill, matchbooks—anything. And there's a photograph; bring it to me."

"Gotcha."

She stood up and kissed him. "Thank you, baby," she said. "Next time we meet I'll do something special for you."

"I'll look forward to it," he said.

When he had left, Clare got back into the pool and resumed her laps—slowly and easily. Harry had taught her how.

Carman pulled into the rest stop and switched off his lights. There was a glow in the sky to the east, but the place wasn't crowded; only one other car there.

He got out of his car and walked toward the little building housing the restrooms, wondering if they'd be unlocked this time of day. When he reached the door, he saw that the hasp had been jimmied off the door and hung, useless, with the padlock still on it. He opened the door and felt for the light switch. He found it, but the lights didn't come on. "Shit," he said, feeling his way toward the toilet. It was the last word he ever spoke.

He went through the man's pockets and found no evidence of a stay in Key West. He took a thick wad of small bills and the man's wallet and wristwatch, then stepped out of the building. The sky was brightening now, and he could see the parking lot clearly. He went to Carman's car and, using a handkerchief to avoid leaving fingerprints, rifled the briefcase on the front seat and took the Key West hotel bill . . . and the photograph. He looked at the beefy man with the curly hair; sure didn't look like Harry. Then he took the credit cards from the wallet and threw it toward the pond next to the rest stop.

A few miles down the road, he tossed the credit cards and the wristwatch into a drainage ditch, then headed for Key West, his mission complete. He'd managed very nicely, he thought, and made some money in the process. That would buy a few good dinners.

CHAPTER

26

Clare Carras opened the *Key West Citizen* and looked through the realty ads. There was a display advertisement with photographs of a number of agents. She was stopped by the picture of a very beautiful Asian woman from whom Harry had bought the house. She didn't want to be in the same room with any woman as lovely as that; she chose the man in the next photograph, phoned him, and made an appointment.

Then she picked up a copy of a yachting magazine she had bought, turned to the rear pages, and found a full-page ad for a broker in Fort Lauderdale. She picked up the phone and dialed.

"This is Mike Domenico," a young man's voice said.

"My name is Clare Carras," she said.

"What can I do for you, Miss Carras?"

"It's Mrs. Carras. My husband recently passed away, and I want to sell our boat."

"What sort of boat is it, Mrs. Carras?" He sounded bored.

"It's a Hatteras Sixty. It's less than a year old."

"Well, now," Domenico said. He didn't sound bored anymore. "Where is the boat lying?"

"In Key West, at the Galleon marina."

"Does she have a paid crew?"

"No, my husband operated her himself."

"I see. There's certainly a market for that boat right now, but I think we could do much better with it in Fort Lauderdale."

The doorbell rang downstairs. "Could you hold on a minute, please?" She went to the intercom. "Who is it?"

"It's Tommy Sculley, Mrs. Carras. Could I speak to you for a moment?"

"Yes, come on upstairs; the door is unlocked." She went back to the phone. "I'm sorry, you were saying?"

"I was saying that I think we could do a lot better with the boat in Fort Lauderdale."

"I suppose so," she replied. "What is your usual commission?"

"Five percent," Domenico replied.

She looked around, saw Sculley and his young partner enter the room, and motioned them to a sofa. "That's too much," she said to Domenico. "I'm willing to pay three percent, no more."

"Well, I'd have to talk to my manager about that, but I think we could work something out."

"And you'll have to bear the expense of moving the boat to Fort Lauderdale," she said.

"I'll speak to my manager, Mrs. Carras; I'm sure we can agree on terms. Tell you what, I'll put a contract in the mail to you today, and I'll talk with a ferry skipper about moving the boat. What's she called?"

"*Fugitive,* and I'd like the name removed from the hull as soon as possible."

"Fine. May I have your address and phone number?"

She gave it to him, then hung up. Tommy Sculley regarded her from the sofa.

"Selling *Fugitive,* Mrs. Carras?" he asked.

"I don't have much use for the boat," she replied. "I wouldn't even know how to start the engines, let alone handle the thing."

"Of course," he said. "I'll see if I can have the boat removed from evidence."

"Evidence? What do you mean?"

"It was the scene of an apparent homicide," he said. "I'll have to talk to the chief and see if he thinks it's of any further importance to our case."

"Please do so as soon as you possibly can,"

she said. "Now, I have a rather busy day ahead of me. What can I do for you?"

"I just wanted to see if you had remembered anything about the events of that day that you haven't told me already."

"I'm sorry, I don't know what you're talking about. I answered all your questions the other day."

"I know you did, Mrs. Carras, but often people who are involved . . . are witnesses in a death remember things a few days later that they might have forgotten at the time of the occurrence."

"I don't think I remember anything new."

"I was concerned, you see, about some discrepancies between Chuck Chandler's story and what you told us on that day."

That didn't surprise her in the least. "Do you mean that what Mr. Chandler told you doesn't jibe with what I told you?" She tried to sound surprised.

"That's exactly what I mean. For instance, how long did you say that Mr. Chandler was below repairing the exhaust pipe?"

"Perhaps forty-five minutes."

"Well, that kind of struck me as odd, Mrs. Carras. You see, when my wife and I were aboard and the same problem occurred, it didn't take Chuck more than five minutes to fix it."

"Well, this time it took forty-five minutes."

"I would have thought that would have worried Mr. Carras—I mean, Chuck down in the engine room for three-quarters of an hour, working on something that took only five minutes to fix the last time it happened. Did Mr. Carras question how long Chuck was below?"

"Not that I recall."

"What did Mr. Carras do while Chuck was in the engine room?"

"To the best of my recollection, he sat in his skipper's chair on the flying bridge and looked out over the water."

"Did he say anything to you?"

"No."

"Did you say anything to him?"

"No."

"Had you and Mr. Carras had some sort of spat that day?"

"No, we hadn't; we never had 'spats,' as you put it."

"Your relationship was a cordial one on that day?"

"Yes, perfectly cordial."

"And yet you and your husband sat for forty-five minutes on a drifting boat and didn't so much as speak to each other?"

"Detective, you're married; surely you know that married people can sometimes go for hours without speaking to each other. Harry and I were very comfortable together; we didn't have to constantly converse."

"I see your point, Mrs. Carras; sometimes my wife and I have gone for days without speaking to each other."

The doorbell rang again, and Clare went to the intercom. "Yes?"

"Mrs. Carras, it's Clay McDaniel, from Knight-Prudential Realty."

"Oh, yes, Mr. McDaniel, please come upstairs; the door is unlocked." She turned back to the detectives. "I'm afraid I have an appointment," she said. "Was there anything else?"

"I don't know, Mrs. Carras," Tommy replied. "Can you think of anything else?"

"No, I can't."

"We'll be on our way, then." The two detectives rose, made their good-byes, and left. On the way down the stairs they passed the real estate agent. "Hi, Clay," Tommy said.

"Hello, Tommy; you in the new house yet?"

"Not yet; Rosie wants to get the curtains and other things done before we move in. Also, we have another two weeks on our short-term lease, and she's not one to waste money." The two said good-bye, and the detectives left.

Clare received Clay McDaniel in her living room. After an exchange of pleasantries, McDaniel spoke up.

"There's something we should clear up before we talk, Mrs. Carras," he said. "I believe you dealt with Lynne Kaufelt when you bought this house. Are you sure you wouldn't prefer to deal with her now?"

"I'd prefer to deal with you, Clay," she said, sitting beside him on the sofa and giving him a

169

large smile. "I've heard so many good things about you."

"Well, that's very kind. Now, how can I help you?"

"I'm sure you've heard that my husband died."

"Yes, and may I express my condolences?"

"Thank you," she replied. "How much can you get me for this house?"

CHAPTER

27

Tommy slammed the car door. "She's gonna be gone soon," he said. "She's selling the boat and the house, and there's nothing else to keep her here."

"You ready for lunch?" Daryl asked.

"Yeah, okay. How about the Raw Bar?"

"That's good for me." Daryl put the car in gear; it was a one-minute drive. "It would keep her in Key West if we busted her," he said.

"Don't be crazy; we don't have enough to bust her."

"How about if we bust Chandler, and she's a material witness. Wouldn't that keep her here?"

"For about three minutes. We'd be ass-deep in lawyers before we knew what hit us. We could never make a case that she wouldn't show for the trial of her husband's murderer."

"I see your point." Daryl pulled into the parking lot of the Raw Bar, and the two detectives went in and asked for a table by the water.

"We're pretty jammed, Daryl," the young head waitress said. "You mind sitting at the bar?"

"Not at all, Suzie," Daryl replied. "Come on, Tommy, the tourists have got all the tables; let's eat with the other locals. The noon news is on the TV."

They found barstools and ordered lunch. Tommy ate quietly, and Daryl followed his lead.

Then Tommy's head snapped up at the TV set. "What did she say that name was?"

"What name?" Daryl asked, looking at the TV.

"Somebody got offed north of Miami." He watched as the camera roamed around a rest stop and looked inside a car.

"So? We haven't got enough to worry about?"

"Shut up and listen, Daryl."

The TV cut back to the anchorwoman on the noon news. "This is the latest in a series of murders of tourists up and down Florida," she was saying. "Mr. Carman had rented the car at Miami International four days ago and had apparently been touring the area. The Florida legislature has acted to have the state's license plate system altered so that rental cars will not be recognizable by their license numbers, but unfortunately, the car Mr. Carman had rented had not had its plate changed yet. There are no suspects yet in the murder."

"Holy shit," Tommy said softly.

"That's our Carman from yesterday?" Daryl asked.

"I'm gonna find out," Tommy said. "Finish my lunch for me." He headed for the pay phones.

When he came back, he was nodding. "It was our Carman, the PI from California. Come on, let's do some police work."

Back in the car they drove to Dey Street and parked half a block from the Carras house.

"We'll each take a side of the street," Tommy said. "Talk to somebody at every house, especially little old ladies. They never miss anything."

Half an hour later they met back at the car.

"What have you got?" Tommy asked.

"Little old lady across the street says Mrs. Carras's car hasn't left the driveway since midnight. She got up at 4:00 A.M. to pee, and the car was there at that time. Tommy, you weren't seriously thinking that Clare Carras could drive a hundred and seventy-five miles north in the middle of the night, murder Carman—how?"

"With a large knife."

"Yeah, a knife—and get back here in time to talk to us this morning without batting an eyelash?"

"No, I don't think that, not really, but think about it: Carras runs off with some bad people's money four years ago, and they've been looking

172

for him ever since. Suddenly a private eye gets a tip, then he shows up in Key West, questions Clare. He tells us about it after the inquest, then next morning, bright and early, he's dead. Now, do you think there might be a connection between his murder and Clare Carras?"

"Maybe."

"Maybe? *Maybe?* I can't see it any other way. Look, if she knocked off her husband, then she had to have some help, right?"

"Probably."

"Then who?"

"Chandler?"

"No, not Chandler. She's trying to hand him to us for the murder; he wouldn't help her. She's got another boyfriend."

"And the boyfriend offed Carman?"

"Gotta be; who else?"

"Tommy, remember what the lady on TV said? Tourists have been getting offed all up and down the state—some of them at rest stops. Don't you ever watch TV?"

"And you buy Carman's death as one of those?" Tommy demanded, not without scorn.

"Seems like the obvious answer. Anyway, it's a better answer than somebody from Key West following him to a rest stop a couple hundred miles north and offing him just because he found Clare Carras. Tommy, if he was killed around six this morning, he would have had to drive all night to get there. No, he had to be staying in the Miami area, and Clare couldn't have known where. It's just too much of a stretch, too much of a coincidence."

"Yeah? Let's go back to the station and do some phone work."

"What kind of phone work?"

"I want to know where Carman stayed and when he checked out and what phone calls he got while he was there."

"Tommy, you can be such a pain in the ass sometimes," Daryl moaned.

Two hours later, Daryl put down the phone and motioned to Tommy, who was at the next desk.

Tommy hung up. "What?"

"He stayed at the Pier House; he was out until about eleven- thirty. He paid his bill before he went to bed—said he was leaving early the next morning, had to catch a plane in Miami. They don't know if he got any calls, but someone could have called in on a direct line if they had his room number. He made two calls while he was there, both to the same L.A. number." He shoved his pad toward Tommy.

Tommy glanced at the number. "Okay, good, let's backtrack. If Carman got dead around six, what's the latest he would have had to leave?"

"Well, it's a good four hours to Miami, and he was a bit farther north, say four and a half hours?"

"But he was driving in the middle of the night, so there's no traffic."

"Okay, four hours from the Pier House to the rest stop."

"So he left the Pier House sometime between eleven-thirty and two A.M."

"More or less."

"And Clare Carras's car was parked in her driveway all night, or at least until four A.M."

"Right."

"So somebody had to follow him from Key West. Four hours is a long time without a piss, and the first time he stopped, somebody followed him into the men's room and cut his throat."

"Unless they knew where he was going and were waiting for him."

"Nah, they couldn't predict where he'd stop." Tommy was quiet for a moment. "Or could they?"

"Look, Tommy, I can buy that somebody followed him from Key West and offed him— it's a stretch, but I can buy it. What I can't buy is that Clare Carras knew when Carman would need to piss and have somebody waiting for him. Is it okay that I can't buy that?"

"It's okay, Daryl. But I still connect Clare Carras to this."

"I believe you, Tommy; Clare Carras is a master criminal who can pull the strings on any murder from the reef to the Everglades. I'm with you all the way."

"Don't be a smartass, Daryl."

A secretary approached. "Tommy, Daryl, the chief wants to see both of you."

CHAPTER

28

The chief looked serious as the two detectives sat down. "I read your report," he said. "Why haven't you arrested Chandler?"

Tommy blinked. "I don't think we've got enough, Chief, not yet."

"Is your report accurate?"

"Yes, sir."

"Then Chandler looks good for it, doesn't he?"

"Maybe."

"Maybe? You got anybody else in mind?"

"It's complicated, Chief. I've got four or five scenarios; I just need more time to run them down."

"You've questioned Chandler twice, right?"

"Right."

"Did you read him his rights?"

"The second time, not the first; I wanted the first to be informal."

"Did he respond to being read his rights?"

"It made him nervous, if that's what you mean."

"Good. Arrest him, bring him in here, and sweat him. Let's see how he holds up under pressure."

"He'll just call a lawyer."

"Come on, Tommy, you're more experienced than that. You can talk to him, scare him, make him stumble. Hell, you might even get a confession."

"Chief, my gut tells me he didn't do it."

"Your report tells me he did. Even if he didn't, he's bound to know more about this than he's telling. Get him in here, sweat him, get everything you can. We've got enough for an indictment, the D.A. agrees with me on that."

"You've already been to the D.A.?"

"He's read your report."

"Chief . . . "

"Don't make me tell you again, Tommy."

They parked near the Overseas Market. A lurid sunset lit Key West Bight; music blared from an open waterfront bar along the way. It was a perfect Key West evening.

"I don't want to do this," Tommy said.

"I know you don't, but believe me, when the old man says 'Don't make me tell you again,' you better do what he says. He's a nice guy, but he's got a hell of a temper."

They got out of the car and walked toward where *Choke* was moored.

"His car's not in its usual spot," Daryl said.

"I've begun to get the awful feeling that Chandler isn't in his usual spot, either." He looked at his watch. "It's too late for tennis."

They arrived at the boat and went aboard. It was locked up tight.

"They've got lights over at the tennis club," Daryl said. "Maybe he's got a night lesson."

"Let's find out," Tommy replied.

They drove past the Olde Island Racquet Club, and the lights were out on the courts. They pulled into the parking lot.

"The yellow Porsche isn't here," Daryl said.

"I'm afraid I might know where it is," Tommy said.

They cruised slowly through the airport parking lot; nothing there.

"There's another lot down at the end of the terminal, next to Island City Air Service."

"Let's try it."

The yellow Porsche was parked in the smaller lot, its top up, all buttoned down.

"I was afraid of this," Tommy said.

"What now? An APB?"

"An APB where?" Tommy replied. "You fly from here to Miami or Orlando, and you're connected to anywhere in the world. He could be halfway across the Atlantic by now."

"I didn't think he'd run," Daryl said.

"Neither did I," Tommy replied.

"Maybe the chief was right?"

"Even chiefs are right sometimes."

"Somehow I don't want to be the one to tell him that Chandler skipped."

Tommy said nothing. He stared disconsolately out the window at the Porsche.

"There's something I'd like to know," Daryl said.

"What's that?"

"I'd like to know where Clare Carras is right now."

"You know something? So would I."

They turned the corner into Dey Street. The Mercedes was parked in front, but the lights in the house were off. They found a parking spot a few doors down and walked back toward the house. When they reached the high fence around the Carras property, Tommy held out a hand and stopped Daryl, then put a finger to his lips and cupped a hand behind his ear. There was noise coming from behind the fence.

Tommy strained to hear. Then there was a splash and a girlish giggle, then a man's voice, he was sure of it. "She's got a guy in there," he whispered to Daryl.

Daryl moved down the fence until he found a tiny crack. He motioned Tommy over.

Tommy put an eye to the crack. It was dark inside; the pool lights were off, but he was sure he could see more than one head bobbing in the pool, and the two heads were very close together.

"I want to know who that is," he said to Daryl. "Come on."

On the front steps Tommy paused. "You go around back, in case he skips."

Daryl disappeared, and Tommy rang the bell. He could hear splashing from the pool, and after a moment he rang the bell again. Shortly a light came on in the downstairs hallway, and Clare Carras appeared at the door, dressed in a terry cloth robe. There was a trail of wet footprints on the polished floor behind her.

"Yes, Detective, what is it?"

"Ah, Mrs. Carras, I wonder if you've seen Chuck Chandler today."

"No, I haven't; I haven't seen him since my husband was killed."

"We're unable to locate him."

"You mean he's left Key West? Why am I not surprised?"

"Mrs. Carras, would you mind telling me who was in the pool with you just now?"

"I was alone," she said.

"Mrs. Carras, I was walking along the street next to your fence, and I heard two voices, one of them a man's."

"You're mistaken, Detective," she said evenly. "You may have heard the skimmer intake murmuring. It does that."

"I see," Tommy said. "Would you mind if I had a look at the pool area?"

"What is this about, Detective?"

"Would you mind, Mrs. Carras? I'll only take a moment."

"All right," she said. "Come this way."

She turned and walked down the hallway to the door leading to the pool, then outside. Tommy stayed right behind her. There was no one visible in the darkened pool area.

"Would you mind turning on some lights?" Tommy asked.

"All right," she said, then disappeared into the house. A moment later, lights came on, including the pool lights.

Tommy walked to the other side of the pool. There was a large wet area where at least one person had climbed out of the pool, but there were no discernible footprints. He walked from the pool across the grass to the fence, but the grass was closely cut, and he couldn't tell if anyone had walked across it.

Clare Carras was standing next to the pool when he turned around. "Are you quite happy now, Detective?"

"Thank you, ma'am; I'm sorry for the inconvenience." He began walking toward the house.

"Tell me, what did you hope to find out here?"

"I'm not sure, ma'am."

"Suppose I had had a man here swimming with me; what would that have told you?"

Tommy looked at her, always easy to do, he thought. "I suppose I would have found it odd that a woman whose husband died last week was entertaining a man in her pool in the dark, dressed in . . . "

Her eyes never left his. She undid the belt of the robe and opened it wide.

". . . a bikini," he said.

She closed the robe. "I'm sorry to disappoint

you, Detective, but I've been quite alone all evening."

Tommy apologized again and left.

"See anything?" he asked Daryl when they were back in the car.

"I got a glimpse of something that might have been a man. I ran down to the end of the alley, but it was a dead end. If he was there, then he had to vault a six-foot fence or two to get away."

"Did you hear a man's voice from the pool? Did you see a man through the crack?"

Daryl shook his head. "I'm not sure, Tommy, I'm really not."

CHAPTER

29

Bright and early the next morning, Tommy walked to the chief's office and tapped on the door.

"Come."

Tommy walked in. "Good morning, Chief. Got a minute?"

"Morning, Tommy; have a seat."

Tommy sat down. "Thank you, sir."

"So what did Chandler have to say for himself after he was arrested? Did he demand a lawyer?"

"We didn't arrest him, sir; he seems to be out of town."

The chief stared at him for a moment, then leaned forward on his elbows and spoke in a very quiet voice. "You mean Chandler has skipped?"

"No, sir, I don't think he has. His car's at the airport, and I don't think he would have driven there if he was skipping. I think he would have left the car in his usual parking space at Key West Bight."

"Have you checked at the tennis club where he works?" His voice was still low; the chief seemed to be trying hard to control himself.

"They don't open until ten," Tommy lied. "I wanted to report to you at the earliest moment—without waking you up, of course."

"Listen to me very carefully, Tommy, because I don't want to repeat myself. I want one of two things: I want Chandler in my lockup by noon, or I want your badge on my desk. Do you understand me?"

"I understand you very well, sir," Tommy said, trying very hard to hold on to his temper, "and now I want you to understand me."

The chief's eyebrows shot up, his face reddened, and he sat back in his chair. "Go on."

"I'm not going to arrest Chuck Chandler for the murder of Harry Carras—at least not until I get a lot more evidence—because every instinct that I've acquired in twenty years of police work tells me he didn't commit the murder, and I'm not going to subject a man I believe to be innocent to the ordeal of arrest and all the publicity that follows. I'm going to clear this homicide, one way or another, and if I have to, I'll do it without my badge, so if that's what you want, you can have it right now." Tommy reached into a pocket, retrieved his badge and ID, and set them on the blotter before the chief. "No point in waiting until noon."

The chief looked at him for a moment longer, then opened his desk drawer, raked Tommy's badge into it, and slammed it shut. "Big mistake to try and bluff me, Tommy," he said. "Now take a hike."

Tommy got up. "I'm sorry you thought I was bluffing, Chief." He walked out.

Daryl was sitting at his desk watching when Tommy walked out of the chief's office and out of the squad room. Then the chief appeared in the doorway of his office and bellowed, "Daryl! Get in here!"

Daryl scurried into the chief's office and started to take a chair.

"Don't bother to sit down," the chief said. "I'll be brief. I want you to go down to the tennis club where Chandler works and if he's there, arrest him for homicide and haul his ass back down here. If he's not there, then I hereby authorize a statewide APB. Got that?"

"No, sir," Daryl said.

"Which part didn't you get?" the chief demanded, his face red.

"Oh, I got it; I'm just not going to do it. I agree with Tommy; Chandler didn't do it."

"All right, then," the chief said, his voice rising, "get your ass into a uniform and report for foot patrol on the graveyard shift!"

"Uncle Art," Daryl began.

"Don't you call me that in this station!" the chief bellowed. "You have your orders, so get out of here."

Daryl dug into a pocket, then tossed his badge onto the desk between them. "Stick this up your ass, *Uncle Arthur*!" he yelled, then turned and stalked out.

Tommy was hoofing it down Simonton Street when Daryl pulled up next to him in a sixties-era Mustang. Tommy stopped and looked at him. "That's not a police car, is it?"

"I'm not a policeman anymore," Daryl replied. "Get in."

Tommy got into the car and closed the door. "You weren't supposed to do that, Daryl," he said. "I've got a pension to lean on; you're just starting your career."

"Don't worry about it," Daryl said, flooring the Mustang. "When my mother hears about it she'll be all over Uncle Art like a hive of bees, and so will his wife. I'll be back at work tomorrow morning."

"No shit?" Tommy said.

185

"No shit. Now, where you want to go?"

"The Olde Island Racquet Club."

"In thirty seconds," Daryl said.

When they pulled into the parking lot the first thing they saw was the yellow Porsche, and the second was Chuck Chandler, on the court, giving a tennis lesson to a young couple. They sat at a table next to the court and waited for him to finish.

"Morning, guys," Chuck said, flopping down next to them and wiping his face with a towel. "How you doing?"

"Where you been, Chuck?" Tommy asked.

"Up in Naples at a tournament; Billy played."

"How long?"

"All weekend."

"How'd Billy do?"

"He won the damn thing; there's going to be no living with him."

Tommy looked around and saw a black-and-white pull into the parking lot. He turned back to the tennis pro. "Chuck," he said, "it's time to get a lawyer, the best one you can find."

"Jack Spottswood is awful good," Daryl said. "You want me to call him for you? He's a friend of my folks."

Before Chuck could speak, two uniformed policeman were standing next to the table.

"Morning, fellas," Tommy said. "How's it going?"

"Tommy," one of the cops said, "the chief wants to see you and Daryl."

"Yeah?" Tommy asked. "Tell him I said to go fuck himself."

Chuck's mouth fell open.

"He said to bring you both back in cuffs, if necessary," the cop said. "Tell you the truth, I'd enjoy that." He grinned.

"Oh, all right," Tommy said. "We're right behind you." He stood up and turned to Chuck. "Maybe you could wait a while longer to take my advice," he said.

"Okay, thanks," Chuck replied.

"I'll let you know if it gets necessary. Come on, Daryl."

The two former detectives sat before the chief's desk and waited.

"Okay, we all got a little hot under the collar," the chief said. "Tommy, I respect your judgment; if you don't think Chandler's our man, go on investigating."

"All right, Chief," Tommy replied pleasantly.

The chief tossed both men their badges. "What's your next move?" he asked.

"I want to go to Los Angeles," Tommy said.

"*Los Angeles!*" the chief bellowed. "What the hell for?"

"There was a guy named Carman wasted up north of Miami yesterday. He'd been down here talking to Clare Carras. I think there's a connection, and I want to check it out. It could be very important."

The chief looked at them both for a moment, then pointed at Daryl. "Not you," he said. "Tommy, bring me a travel chit, and I'll sign it."

"Yes, sir," Tommy said, and both detectives rose.

"Travel cheap," the chief said. "I don't want to get any big bills."

"Yes, sir," Tommy replied.

"And you," the chief said, pointing at Daryl. "You ever talk to me that way again, I'll whip your ass, I don't care what my sister says."

"Yes, sir," Daryl replied.

Both detectives got out of there.

CHAPTER

30

It wasn't Tommy's first trip to L.A. Work had taken him there three or four times, so he knew the town a little. He rented a car and drove up to Beverly Hills, then West Hollywood, where he'd booked at a suite hotel on a quiet street. He'd stayed there once before.

Numb from the three-hour time difference, he took a nap that turned into a deep sleep. The California sun was streaming through the windows when he woke up; it was half past nine, and he was hungry. He called down to room service and ordered breakfast.

He hadn't intended to sleep through the night; he'd wanted to visit Carman's office when there was no one around. He had a good breakfast, showered, shaved, and left the hotel. Carman's office was in a three-story, semi-seedy commercial building on Melrose, in a neighborhood that would soon be too expensive for a PI. Tommy found a parking meter up the street and walked back to the building.

He looked up Carman's name on the building's directory, then took the elevator up to the third floor. CARMAN INVESTIGATIONS, the sign on the door read. In smaller letters there was an instruction to leave a message on the telephone answering machine if the office was closed. He tried the door; locked. He bent over to inspect the lock, but the door across the hall opened, and a woman strolled down the hall to the ladies' room. A moment later, someone got off the elevator and went into another office. The place was too busy for messing with locks. He'd have to come back later.

He took the stairs to the ground floor and tried the lock on the stairwell door at each level. He could get into the stairwell, but not out, except to the street, and he couldn't get in from the street. He walked to the side of the building and looked down a narrow alley. The fire escape seemed to mate with the window at the end of the hallway on each floor.

He was hungry; the time change was playing havoc with his appetite, so he found a sidewalk cafe and had lunch in the shade of a large sycamore tree. California could be a very pleasant place, he thought. After lunch he strolled up Melrose, window-shopping, until he came to what he would describe as a very fancy hardware store. He went in.

"May I help you, sir?" a young woman asked.

"Yes, thank you, I'd like to buy an umbrella—a large one, like for golf—one with a curved handle, not a straight one."

She looked vaguely puzzled.

"Something wrong?" he asked.

"Oh, no, sir, it's just that in my three years here, no one has ever asked for an umbrella, and I'm afraid we don't stock them. The California weather, I guess."

"I see. Can you tell me where I might find such a strange object?"

She furrowed her brow. "I'm afraid not; I don't know where you'd begin to look for one."

Tommy nodded. "Thanks; I guess I'll just have a look around."

"Of course; let me know if I can help you with anything."

Tommy wandered up and down the aisles, finding everyday objects for sale at amazing prices—twenty-five dollars for a flashlight; seventy dollars for a small luggage cart; thirty dollars for a set of cheap screwdrivers. Then he saw something interesting. He reached up and took it down from a shelf. "How much for this?"

"Oh, that's the most convenient thing to have," she said. "I gave my mother one for Christmas last year; she has arthritis and can't reach up very easily anymore."

"How much did you say?" Tommy asked.

"That's sixty-five dollars."

"I'll take it," he said, wondering how he would justify the thing on his expense account.

He tossed his package into the car and relocked it, then spent the afternoon walking up one side of Melrose and down the other. He bought Rosie a small piece of silver jewelry and picked up some books and magazines. Back at his hotel he ordered dinner from room service and set his alarm clock for 2:00 A.M.

He was momentarily disoriented when the alarm went off, reaching for Rosie to ask what was wrong. Then he remembered. He showered to get himself fully awake, then slipped into his shoulder holster with the nine-millimeter automatic in its sling and his badge and an extra clip fixed to the strap. He got into a dark blue windbreaker and checked himself in the mirror. He looked respectable enough not to get rumbled by some passing cop, but he'd be hard to see in the dark, too. He wasn't sure why he was packing the gun, except that he had worn one for so many years that he felt oddly lopsided when he wasn't wearing it.

He drove up and down Melrose twice, checking out the area, looking for parked police cars, especially unmarked ones. He passed one black-and-white on the move but saw nothing else. He parked around the corner from the office building, retrieved his recent purchase from the back seat, then locked the car and looked around. He had the street to himself.

He walked down Melrose for half a block, then turned and walked back, on alert for anyone who might give him a hard time, then darted into the alley alongside Carman's building. He put on a pair of driving gloves, then ripped the wrapper from the device and tossed the paper into a nearby garbage can.

It worked as advertised: He took hold of both handles and squeezed them together. The grappler extended a good eight feet. He reached up and grabbed the ladder on the fire escape, then contracted the gadget. A moment later, he had the ladder in his hand. He tossed the grappler across the alley into the garbage can, looked around for a moment, then started up the ladder.

At the top he took out his key ring and switched on the tiny flashlight attached; it worked remarkably well. The window was a double-hung sash with true divided lights. Good; that made for less noise. He looked down the alley to the street, made sure there were no lighted windows nearby, then peered through the window and down the hallway, which was lit by a single bulb.

He turned sideways, drew back, and struck the top pane of the bottom sash sharply with his elbow. The glass shattered and fell into the hallway. He looked around again to be sure that he had not attracted any attention. All was quiet.

Quickly, he reached through the broken pane, unlocked the window, raised it, stepped inside, then brushed together the broken glass with his gloved hands, tossed it into the alley, and lowered the window. He pulled the remaining fragments from the window and pushed them through the now empty pane. He stopped and listened for a full minute. If there was a security guard and he had heard the glass break, he didn't want to be surprised.

When he heard no other sound, Tommy went to Carman's office door and switched on his tiny flashlight again, holding it between his teeth. From his wallet he produced a set of small lock picks and selected two. The lock was a garden-variety dead bolt, and he had it open inside a minute. He put away the lock picks, opened the door, and stepped into the offices of Carman Investigations.

There was a small room with a receptionist's desk, a love seat, and some old magazines, and an inner door led to Carman's private office. Tommy lowered the shade on the only window and pulled the cheap curtains shut, then switched on the desk lamp and looked around.

It was very neat. That encouraged him, because it meant Carman's files would likely also be neat. There was an answering machine on the desk, and Tommy pushed the playback button. A mechanical voice read out four messages, two of them from Carman himself, one saying he would be out of town for a few days, another saying to call the shop where his car was being repaired and find out when it would be ready, so he would know whether to rent a car on his return to L.A. The third and fourth messages were from the same man and the message was the same: "Your new client would like to hear from you as soon as possible." The voice was pure, accentless Californian, and the mechanical announcer placed both of the messages after Carman had died. Tommy wondered who the new client was. Time to go through the desk and the filing cabinets.

Suddenly the overhead light went on, and Tommy spun around to find a small woman pointing a large revolver in his direction. Her hand was trembling, but the pistol was pointing more or less at his middle.

"This is a .357 Magnum," the little woman said, "and if you mess with me it will make some very big holes in your chest."

"I believe you, lady," Tommy said.

CHAPTER

31

Tommy waited for the woman to say something else, but she didn't. During the uncomfortable silence he checked to see if the hammer was back on the pistol. It was. He had been hoping that if she fired, it would be double-action, making accuracy problematic for an inexperienced shooter. No such luck.

"I'm a police officer," Tommy said. "Can I show you my badge?"

"You're a goddamned burglar," she said.

"I promise you, I'm a cop." He held up his left hand and touched the thumb and forefinger together. "Just these two fingers," he said. "I'll pull back my jacket very slowly so you can see my badge, okay?"

"*Very* slowly," she replied.

Tommy pulled back his jacket and waited for a response.

"That's not an LAPD shield," she said.

"It's from Key West."

"Horseshit. What would a Key West cop be doing burglarizing an office in L.A.? Anyway, you've got a New York accent."

"I put in twenty years on the NYPD," Tommy

said, "then I moved south and signed on in Key West."

"Pull back your jacket again," she said.

Tommy did as she asked, revealing his badge.

"No, more; all the way open."

Tommy let her see the automatic in the shoulder holster.

"Take it out with your left thumb and fore-finger," she said.

Tommy lifted the pistol from his holster and held it up as if he had a dead rat by the tail.

"Drop it in the wastebasket by the desk," she commanded.

Tommy turned slightly and let go of the pistol, wincing at the clang.

"Put your palms flat on the desk and assume the position."

Tommy did so and thought the frisking was very profes-sional.

"Now, stand up, move to your right, and sit in the straight chair."

Tommy did as he was told.

"Put your feet on the desktop and clasp your hands behind your head."

Tommy complied.

"Comfy?" she asked.

"Just fine," Tommy said.

She pulled another chair around until it faced him and sat down, finally letting the pistol rest in her lap. "Before you get any ideas about jumping me, you should know that I fired expert with this weapon on the LAPD range. Got that?"

Tommy nodded. "You on the job?"

"I'll ask the questions. Now explain yourself."

"My name's Tommy Sculley; I'm a detective on the Key West force, and I'm investigating the murder of Barry Carman."

"Barry was killed near Miami; the Dade County Sheriff's Office is the investigating authority. Lie to me again and I'll put one in your knee."

"I'm not lying. Barry was in Key West the day before he died; he came to see me."

"About what?"

"Rocco Marinello."

"What did he tell you about Marinello?"

"That he disappeared from L.A. a few years back and that somebody had hired him—Barry—to find Marinello."

"What did Barry want from you?"

"He'd had a tip that a guy in Key West might be Marinello, and he wanted to know what I knew about the guy."

"Who was the guy?"

"Before we get to that, it's your turn to answer some questions."

"I'm the one with the gun," she said. "I ask, you answer."

"Come on, lady, you're not going to shoot me in cold blood. Now I'm cooperating with you, and I want some cooperation back."

"What do you want to know?"

"Are you a cop?"

"I used to be."

"What's your name?"

"Rita Cortez."

"What are you doing here at three o'clock in the morning?"

"Your turn; what are *you* doing here?"

"Trying to find out who hired Barry to find Marinello."

"Why?"

"Your turn. What are you doing here at three A.M.?"

She sighed. "I came to look for some papers. It's the only time of day I can come here without mixing it up with Barry's wife. Excuse me, widow."

"How'd you get in?"

"I have a key; I worked for Barry. In fact, we were supposed to be partners. It was the partnership papers I was looking for."

"You had an agreement with Barry, and you don't have a copy of the contract?"

"I trusted Barry; he said he'd written everything down, in case anything happened to him."

"Why don't you want to see his widow?"

"He told her about our agreement; she'll probably look for the papers so she can destroy them before anyone else sees them."

"Why would she do that? So she can inherit all this?" He waved an arm at the contents of the room.

"There's some money in the bank, and there's the business. She knows I could keep it going."

"Did you and Barry have a little thing going, Rita?"

She nodded. "He had already left her; the divorce was in the works. Your turn again: Why do you want to know who hired Barry to find Marinello?"

"I think there may be a Key West connection to Barry's murder. I want to find out what he reported back to his client, what he found out in Key West." This was less than the whole truth, but he had to hang on to some of his cards.

"You think maybe Marinello's in Key West and that he murdered Barry?"

Tommy shook his head. "The guy Barry thought might be Marinello is dead. He was killed right before Barry arrived in town."

"Shit!" she said.

"Huh?"

"Finding Marinello would have been a big plum for Barry; the money would have gotten us through the divorce settlement."

Tommy nodded. "Tough break. Listen, is there a bar open this late? Can I buy you a drink?"

Rita stood up and laid the pistol on her chair. "I'll buy you one," she said. She went to Carman's desk, opened a bottom drawer, and extracted a bottle of Wild Turkey and two glasses. "Barry didn't drink much. He kept this in the hope that one day, some gorgeous blonde would walk in here in tears and he could whip out a bottle, like Sam Spade, and offer her a drink."

She poured two healthy shots and handed him one.

"Better days," Tommy said, raising his glass.

She raised hers and took a sip, then returned to her chair. "Tell me something, Tommy," she said.

"Anything."

"If Marinello was this guy in Key West, and he died, the money didn't die with him, did it?"

"I guess not."

"Where would it go, do you think?"

"The guy had a wife."

"Then the wife's got the money?"

"Depends on what kind of planner Marinello was."

"Oh, Marinello was a big-time planner, believe me. He couldn't have walked with all that money without being a very good planner."

"Then the wife might have the money. If she's the wife."

"What do you mean, 'If she's the wife'?"

"I've no way of knowing for sure that my murder victim in Key West was Marinello."

"He was murdered?"

"That's right."

She got up and poured them both another drink. "Tommy, you and I have a lot of talking to do," she said.

CHAPTER

32

Tommy watched Rita Cortez as she talked, and he liked what he saw. She was short, like himself. And like Rosie. He didn't have anything in mind, he just appreciated her neat body, her short, dark hair, and the way she seemed to trust him so soon after their bad introduction.

"I only spent a couple of years as a street cop," she said. "The rest of the time I was in Records, and I was good at it. Barry was always coming in wanting somebody's sheet or something, and I always delivered for him in a hurry. Then, when he was having some problems with the captain of the precinct, he decided to put his papers in and go private. He took me to lunch and laid it all out, and it sounded pretty good. I was bored, so when he asked me to come to work with him I took the chance. Worked out well, too. Barry had a lot of friends on the force and down at the courthouse, so he got a lot of referrals. He was a good investigator and he produced for his clients, so we did okay." She got up, went to a file cabinet, and starting flipping through it. "This Marinello thing was our first shot at some really

201

good money, though. Barry was offered a hundred grand to turn him up."

"That's good money, all right," Tommy said. "Who hired him?"

Rita stopped flipping through the files and looked at him. "Later, maybe," she said, then went back to the files.

Maybe she didn't trust him so much after all. "Any luck in the files?" he asked.

"Not yet."

"Did Barry have a safe?"

She nodded. "Right-hand side of the desk, what looks like two drawers is a door. He never gave me the combination."

Tommy opened the door and looked at the safe. "Too good for me." He began opening desk drawers, feeling the edges and bottoms.

"What are you doing?"

"I'll bet he wrote down the combination somewhere. Most people don't trust themselves to remember." He continued searching the desk.

"If it was in the desk, then Myrna has already been into the safe."

"The wife?"

She nodded. "I'm sure she's been through the place thoroughly." She looked up from the file drawer. "The computer," she said.

Tommy turned and looked at the system, which rested on a built-in cabinet along the wall. "Did he use it a lot?"

"Yes, he did, every day; kept all sorts of notes

on it." She went to the machine, switched it on, then sat down and waited for it to boot up.

"What sort of file might it be in?" Tommy asked, looking over her shoulder.

"Probably a file of its own, if I knew Barry. He was very neat and organized, for a cop." She typed "TREE" and watched as the computer displayed a list of directories.

"Try 'Miscellaneous,'" Tommy said.

She switched to the directory and moved the cursor down the list. She stopped on a file called "Security" and opened it.

"Aha," Tommy said as a list of numbers appeared on the screen. "That was easy."

"It might not have been if you hadn't been here," Rita said. "I don't know how long it would have taken me to think about going through the computer."

"There's something else," Tommy said, pointing at a file called "Partner."

Rita opened the file and began reading. "This is it," she said. "He wrote the whole partnership plan down."

"Trouble is, you can't sign a document on a computer," Tommy said. "There must be a hard copy somewhere."

"Time to open the safe," Rita said. She printed out a copy of the combination file, then knelt before the safe and began twirling the knob. In a moment she had it open and was shuffling through papers. "Here it is!" she cried. "Signed and notarized, and only two weeks ago!"

"Good for you," Tommy said, clapping her on the back.

"There's a copy of the will, too." She flipped through the pages until she found what she wanted. "It refers to the partnership document and says I get the business!"

"That's great, Rita," Tommy said, genuinely glad for her. "Maybe you'd better make copies of these and put them back in the safe for Myrna to find. That way she can't stiff you."

Rita went to a copying machine against the wall, made the copies, and returned the originals to the safe. "There's this, too," she said, handing Tommy a photograph.

"Barry showed me this; it's Marinello. I doubt if he still looks like this, though."

"Yeah, this is at least fifteen, twenty years old, according to the client."

"You said you were in Records at LAPD. When Marinello stole the money, did the client beef to the cops? If he did, there might be some good information there."

Rita shook her head. "These are the kind of people who do their own missing persons work, if you get my drift."

"I do. You ready to tell me who the client is?"

Rita flopped down in her chair. "I have the feeling you haven't told me everything about this guy in Key West yet."

"What do you mean?"

"You said he was murdered; who did it?"

"Tell you the truth, I don't have a handle on

204

that yet. There's a suspect, but I don't buy it. My boss does, though."

"Is the wife involved?"

"A possibility."

"If she knew about her husband's past and if she had a handle on the money, is she the type to knock him off?"

Tommy had hardly thought about anything else lately, but he thought about this again. "She's a pretty cool customer, but I don't think she could have brought this off by herself. She strikes me as the type of woman who has always depended on her looks to get guys to do what she wanted, and I think that's maybe what happened this time."

"How old is the lady?"

"Early thirties, I'd say."

"Marinello would be, let's see, early sixties," Rita said. "You think the missus traded him in on a newer model?"

Tommy grinned. "Great minds think alike. You should have been a detective."

She smiled. "Maybe so. What was the murder victim's name?"

Tommy shook his head. "Not yet. There's more involved here."

"What?"

"After you tell me who the client is, I want to go see him, and I don't want him to know about the dead guy yet, if Barry didn't already tell him. There's a better than even chance that my guy wasn't Marinello, and if he wasn't, then I don't want a bunch of goons coming onto my turf and calling on the widow. Okay, maybe she's a regular black widow, but she may not be Mrs. Marinello, and she shouldn't have to pay the guy's dues."

"I see your point."

"So, who's the client?"

"Wait a minute; you want me to tell all, but you're going to hold back. That's not fair."

"Life is not fair, sweetheart, but sometimes it's just. I want to do what I can to keep it that way. To you, too."

She looked at him carefully. "Are you married?"

Tommy laughed. "Very."

"Too bad; all the good ones are married."

"Tell you what, Rita: you put me with the client, and when I'm sure that all my bases are covered, I'll tell you the whole story."

Rita looked at her watch. "He's not open for business yet. Come on, I'll buy you some breakfast." She got up and headed for the door.

Tommy trailed along behind her.

CHAPTER

33

Tommy stood in front of his hotel, freshly shaved and dressed in a suit, and wondered if he had been stiffed. It was 3:20, and Rita had been supposed to pick him up at three. Had he misjudged the woman?

A red Volkswagen convertible screeched to a halt, top down, Rita at the wheel. "Sorry I'm late."

Tommy got into the car. "You had me worried."

"I was primping. This is the first time I've met the guy face-to-face, and I wanted to make a good impression."

Tommy looked her over. "Don't worry about it."

She shot him a smile. "Thank you, kind sir."

"What time's our appointment?"

"Three forty-five. Don't worry, we'll make it. Century City isn't all that far."

"So who is the guy?"

"First I want to know what you're going to say to him."

"What I'm going to try to do is get information."

"What's in it for him?"

"Maybe I can help find Marinello."

"What happens if you do?"

"Rita, baby, I don't want the money, I promise you. I'll see that you get all the credit."

"It's just that the money could help me a lot in making the transition to running the business. A lot of Barry's buddies are going to stop making referrals now that he's gone."

"I understand, believe me; I'm on your side. Now tell me about the client."

"His name is Barton Winfield."

"Yeah? I was expecting a name that rhymed with macaroni."

"Your expectations are not misplaced. The guy's name used to be something else, the rumor is, but I guess he thought he'd get more business and attract less attention if he came on like a major WASP. That's what Marinello did, too. By the time he was in college he'd changed his name to Ralph Marin, like the county, but his friends called him Rock."

"What's Winfield's line?"

"He's a lawyer. In fact, Barry said he was Marinello's law partner in the old days, before our boy decamped with the cookie jar."

"A mob lawyer, huh?"

"Oh, no; he's an arm's-length operator. The gossip in the legal community, if you can call it that, is that Winfield doesn't represent any mob guys directly; he's more of a consultant. He suggests who they hire if they're busted, that sort of thing, and he's supposed to be a key business advisor to the head of one of the families out here, but nobody could ever prove it. It's also rumored that he oversees their money-laundering operation, from a distance. Barry figured that Marinello was doing all this before he lit out, and that's how he got hold of so much cash all at once. Winfield, whom he'd known since Stanford Law School, replaced him."

"So he knew Marinello well, huh? Perfect."

"Perfect is always good," Rita said.

The offices of Winfield & Carrington were like a movie set for a white-shoe law firm. There was lots of shiny paneling, and the furniture looked as if it were out of the Rockefellers' attic. The receptionist was middle-aged and plump; nothing flashy for Winfield & Carrington. After a ten-minute wait they were shown into a corner office.

Winfield rose to meet them. He was sixtyish, widening at the middle, gray at the temples, and beautifully tailored. He was also very gracious.

"Please sit down, Ms. Cortez, Mr. Sculley." He directed them to a grouping of sofas and chairs, rather than facing them across his desk. "Ms. Cortez, I was so very sorry to hear of Mr. Carman's death. He always struck me as an extremely competent man."

"Thank you, Mr. Winfield," Rita replied. "I wanted you to know that since Barry and I were partners, I will now be running the firm."

"Oh, good," he said. "I hope we can send some work your way." He turned to Tommy. "Tell me, Mr. Sculley, are you a private investigator as well?"

"No, sir," Tommy said. "I'm a police officer in South Florida."

Winfield blinked but recovered quickly. "Are you the investigating officer in Mr. Carman's case?"

"No, sir, I'm involved in a more tangential way," Tommy replied. "In fact, my visit here is entirely unofficial and off the record."

"I see," Winfield said, obviously not seeing at all. "And what can I do for you?"

"I'm aware of Barry Carman's work for you, and . . ."

Winfield turned to Rita, and his voice was icy. "You brought the police into this?"

"Oh, no, sir," Tommy said quickly, stepping in to save Rita, "nothing like that at all. I assure you, there is no official interest in your relationship to Barry Carman or his firm."

"Oh, good," Winfield said, relaxing a bit. "So what *is* your interest in this matter?"

"During Mr. Carman's investigation of . . . the missing person in question, he came to me unofficially to check out some things. I wasn't able to give him any pertinent information, but when I heard of the manner of his death, I looked into it, and it occurred to me that there might be a direct connection between Mr. Carman's death and the matter he was pursuing."

"It was my impression that Mr. Carman met his death as the result of one of those ugly tourist killings that seem to be plaguing Florida these days."

"I'm inclined to think that's not the case, sir, although I believe some effort was made to make it appear to be such a murder."

"That's very interesting," Winfield said, his eyes narrowing slightly.

"Also, it appears there might possibly be a connection between the missing person in question . . . "

"His name is Marin," Winfield said; "you may use it."

"Between Mr. Marin and another case I'm investigating."

"And what case would that be, Mr. Sculley?"

"I'm not at liberty to discuss it at this stage, sir, but I believe that if I were able to locate Mr. Marin, it might materially help my investigation."

"Is Marin a suspect in your case? I mean, should you find him would you wish to arrest and try him?"

"No, sir, it's not that kind of connection. I just believe Marin could be of help in resolving a difficult case. Actually, it's a long shot, but you and I may have some mutual interests."

"Should you find Marin, what would be your course of action?"

"I would detain him on a minor charge and notify Ms. Cortez immediately."

"And how long would he be likely to be in custody?"

"I could hold on to him for twenty-four hours, maybe more."

"I see," Winfield said. "And what do you want of me?"

"As I understand it, you knew Mr. Marin well. It would be of great assistance to me if you could tell me as much as possible about him."

"May I have your word that you have no other official interest in Marin than to question him in your other case?"

"You have it, sir."

"Very well. What would you like to know?"

"When did you first meet Mr. Marin?"

"Our families knew each other when we were very young, and we were both at Stanford; he was a couple of years ahead of me in law school. When I graduated I went to see him, and he helped me gain a position in the firm he was working for at the time. Later we left together and opened this firm. We did very well. After many successful years together we occasioned to have a very large amount of money in the firm's trust account, as the result of a real estate transaction we had just closed. Before the funds could be transferred to the client, Marin raided the trust account and decamped with the funds."

"May I ask how much he took?"

"That's not really important; let's say many millions of dollars."

"You went to the police, of course."

"I did not. If I had done so the resulting publicity would have destroyed the firm. I made arrangements to replace the funds—with great difficulty, I might add—and our clients were simply told that Marin had taken his own life, a notion which he took some pains to further."

"If you'll forgive me saying so, sir, that's extraordinary."

"I'm aware of that; nevertheless, it's what I

212

did. To this day, I do not wish for any client of mine to know that a member of this firm behaved in such a manner. That is why I hired Mr. Carman, so that this matter might be resolved in a private manner."

"And if Marin is found, how do you intend to resolve it?"

"That question, Mr. Sculley, is outside the parameters of this discussion. Now, what else do you wish to know about Marin?"

Ground broken, Tommy took out his notebook and began in earnest. "Let's begin with a description; height and weight, et cetera?"

"Six-two, about two hundred and forty pounds, thick dark hair, brown eyes."

"Did you ever know him to be slimmer than two-forty?"

"He was always beefy, muscular, an athlete."

"What sports?"

"In high school he played football; maybe that's where the weight came from. Later it was tennis, swimming, golf; he played all three for Stanford. When he got out of college some of the muscle turned to fat, I guess. The only sport he played with any regularity was golf."

"What sort of personality?"

"Gregarious, charming, very smooth."

"Did he ever do any scuba diving?"

"No. He did sail, though. He kept a small sailboat at Marina del Rey."

"What was his taste in women?"

"He liked them very beautiful. His wife was,

and although he never talked about it, I suspected he played around."

"Where's his wife now?"

"Remarried. It wouldn't do any good to try and see her; she wouldn't talk about him. She believes that he took his own life."

"Any vices? Drink, gambling, drugs?"

"He drank in moderation, didn't use drugs. He never seemed to be interested in gambling."

"If he didn't kill himself, how do you think he managed to disappear so thoroughly?"

"I believe he planned it all very carefully. He knew there were times when the trust account would have a lot of money in it. It wouldn't surprise me to learn that he'd planned it for years; he was very methodical, thorough."

"How do you think he could move around such a large sum of money without attracting attention?"

"He was very clever in financial dealings. My guess is he had planned a way to move the money offshore in a hurry, probably to some place with banking secrecy laws like Switzerland or the Cayman Islands."

"Had he had a lot of experience with such transactions?"

Winfield looked at him sharply for a moment, then answered. "Yes," he said.

"Can you think of anything else that might help me? Some personal characteristic to look out for? Some weakness?"

"Nothing I haven't already told you. As for

weaknesses, he always appeared not to have any. He was a very self-confident man."

Tommy closed his notebook. "Thank you, Mr. Winfield. It's unlikely you'll hear from me directly again; if I learn anything I'll communicate it to Ms. Cortez."

Back in the car, Rita was the first to speak. "Did that help you any? Does Marin sound like your dead guy in Key West?"

Tommy shrugged. "Might be, might not. There are some similarities, but who knows?"

"Can I buy you dinner tonight?"

"I'd love to, but I've got a plane to catch."

Rita laughed ruefully. "The good ones have always got a plane to catch."

CHAPTER

34

On his first morning back in Key West Tommy picked up Daryl and headed for Dey Street, along the way explaining what he had learned in Los Angeles.

"Sounds to me like the guy *could* be Carras," Daryl said, "but what are you going to talk to Clare about?"

"I thought I'd just mention some of this stuff and see how she reacts," Tommy replied.

"Pull over a minute, Tommy."

Tommy stopped the car. "Yeah?"

"I don't think this is such a good idea."

"Why not?"

"First of all, our experience so far with this lady is that she doesn't give away much, at least she hasn't so far. She didn't bat an eye when we nearly caught her with the boyfriend, right?"

"Right."

"So, you go and lay all this Marinello stuff on her, and she'll just stare you down."

"You got a point."

"Also, she could bolt and leave us holding a very big bag."

"Not without selling the house and the yacht, she won't."

"She might, if you scare her enough. Especially if she thinks the people in L.A. know who and where she is."

Tommy thought it through. "You're right; it's not worth the risk. Maybe what we should do is to reassure her, make her more comfortable."

"I like that better," Daryl said.

"You're wise beyond your years, kid."

Clare Carras made a very good widow, Tommy thought. She seemed a little more demure today, more restrained, more dignified.

"What can I do for you, Detective?" she asked when she had arranged herself on a sofa.

216

"I just wanted to bring you up to date on our investigation, Mrs. Carras."

"I would appreciate that," she said.

"I know it won't come as a surprise to you that we have concluded that your husband's death could not have been an accident."

"I should think not. Do you have a suspect?"

"We do. In spite of my initial reservations, I now believe that Chuck Chandler murdered your husband."

She sighed. "I didn't want to believe it myself," she said, "but I'm afraid I've been drawn to that conclusion myself." Her voice was full of regret.

Tommy was impressed by her performance. "He seems to be our best bet."

"Have you arrested him yet?"

"No."

"Why not?"

"Well, the weight of evidence points to him; he certainly had a motive, and there is reason to believe he had the technical skills to accomplish it, but we don't have any physical evidence to link him to the crime. The way things are, in a trial his lawyer would certainly try to implicate you in order to get him off."

"Me?" She seemed astonished.

"Of course I don't believe it, but a clever lawyer could hang a motive on you—to further your husband's death in order to inherit his wealth—and opportunity—you were on the boat often enough. The mechanical skills involved are not that great."

"I see," she said.

Daryl was right: he couldn't read what she was thinking. Still, he could make a wild guess.

They met behind a failed, boarded-up restaurant off Highway 1, near Islamorada. Clare meant to keep this short, but he was insistent. She had to administer a quick fellating before he was satisfied, and she used all her skills to bring him off quickly. When she was done, she started in quickly with her purpose, before he could recover himself and demand more.

"We've got a problem," she said.

"What's that? I thought everything was going smoothly now, with Carman out of the way."

"That situation is resolved; you did good work, but we have another problem."

"What is it?" he sighed, zipping up his trousers.

"The police believe Chuck killed Harry, but Sculley says he doesn't have enough evidence to make it stick."

"What else could he possibly need?"

"Something conclusive, something that would wrap up the whole thing."

"Such as?"

"I was hoping you'd have a suggestion."

"Not off the top of my head."

"Maybe we should just arrange a suicide for him. You know, the weight of guilt was too much. Maybe he could blow his brains out in some secluded spot."

He shook his head. "That might just make them even more suspicious of you."

"You're right, I guess. Sculley said that a good lawyer could make a case for me having a motive."

"Not a doubt of it."

"Then we have to arrange something else, some piece of physical evidence that the D.A. can hold up to a jury and say, 'See, he did it, no doubt.'"

"That may be easier said than done."

"Oh, you can handle it, sweetie," she said, pinching his nipple.

Now he seemed impervious to her attentions, pushing her hand away.

"Why don't we just leave things the way they are? Maybe they can't convict Chandler, but they can't get you for it, either, and they don't have a clue about me. Just be patient, sell the house and the boat and let people know you're leaving. Tell them you're moving to New York or something. You could even contact a real estate agent up there, go up and look at some apartments. Then, when nobody's worrying about you anymore, I'll abandon ship and meet you someplace nice."

"No, I don't want this left unresolved. I want somebody convicted, and it's going to have to be Chuck. Otherwise, the police might one day decide they have some more questions for me and come looking."

"By that time you'll have a new identity, we both will, and we'll be long gone."

"I just don't want them looking for me, for any reason. I want this wrapped up tight. Come up with something."

He sighed again. "All right, I'll think on it." He reached for her.

"No," she said. "We can't take a chance staying here any longer. I'll go first; you wait."

Grudgingly, he got out of the car and waved good-bye.

She pulled back onto the highway, looking around to be sure she hadn't been followed. He'd come up with something, she was sure of it. In the meantime, she'd have to turn her own attention to the problem.

CHAPTER

35

Chuck stepped out of the lawyer's office into the sun, and he did not like the way he felt. He was in excellent health, an athlete, and he was accustomed to feeling perfectly well, but now there seemed to be a cold, solid object resting in his stomach, and his head hurt.

He had not liked what he heard from the lawyer. It was obvious, the man had said, that

Chuck was the chief suspect, and he might look forward to being arrested in the near future. He had the lawyer's card in his pocket, with instructions to make the first phone call to him when the ax fell. He had signed some papers that would make arranging bail easier, using his boat as collateral.

Chuck was not looking forward to being under indictment. If that happened, teaching tennis would be a thing of the past. Merk would have to let him go, and he had no other way of earning a living.

As he walked to the car he added up his assets: the boat, the car, two thousand dollars in the bank, and about sixty thousand in his retirement account, plus a few bonds. A trial could reduce the total of all that to zero; the lawyer had made that plain. Once he had been indicted, the snowball would start to roll, and it would be rolling downhill, getting bigger as it went. He could not allow himself to be arrested, it was as simple as that. But how to avoid it?

He drove slowly back to the boat, went aboard, opened himself a beer, and sat heavily down on the afterdeck to drink it. He took a few sips, then looked up and saw his colleague, Victor, standing on the deck of the Raw Bar, talking to a blonde. He waved, catching Victor's eye, and Victor waved back, then turned his attention once again to the girl.

Chuck was on his second beer when Victor appeared at the gangplank.

221

"Yo, pro!" Victor called. "Permission to come aboard?"

"Permission granted," Chuck replied. "I'll get you a cold one."

Victor settled in a deck chair and accepted a beer.

"Looked like you were doing pretty well at the Raw Bar," Chuck said. "What brings you down here?"

"You know," Victor replied, "I thought I was doing pretty well, too, but I guess she didn't share my view of our relationship. Gave me some excuse about having to rejoin her tour party. No luck tonight."

"Let's have a few, then," Chuck said.

Victor looked at him pityingly. "No luck for you, either, huh? Is Clare Carras playing the widow?"

"I wouldn't know. I'm well out of that."

"Listen, Chuck," Victor said, "there's something I want to ask you straight out, and I'll be as subtle as I can about this. Did you knock off Harry?"

"No, sir," Chuck replied. "I did not. I most definitely had not the slightest fucking thing to do with knocking him off. Not that the police, in the person of Tommy Sculley, seem to believe that."

"They giving you a hard time?"

"I think Tommy's cutting me all the slack he can, but he told me I'd better see a lawyer."

"Have you?"

222

"Half an hour ago."

"Was he encouraging?"

"He encouraged me to take steps to raise bail, just in case."

"Oh."

"Yeah."

"You look depressed, kid."

"Me? Depressed? Nah, I'm just your happy-go-lucky tennis pro, waltzing through life with a wink and a chuckle."

"Want to talk about it?"

"Yes, weirdly enough."

"Shoot."

"How the hell did I get into this, Victor?"

Victor shrugged. "You got into Clare Carras."

"Yeah, but getting laid isn't supposed to get you in trouble,

is it?"

"Is this the father in the hysterical pregnancy case that I hear talking?" Victor asked.

"Okay, okay, maybe it gets you in trouble with the odd husband, but it isn't supposed to get you a shot at the death penalty, is it?"

Victor held up a hand. "Hang on, let's analyze: *Why* do the cops even *dream* you might have done it?"

"I think their reasoning goes like this: I was screwing Harry's wife, so maybe I wanted Harry out of the way so I could cash in his chips for him."

"Sounds good to me," Victor said cheerfully. "What else?"

"Somebody put carbon monoxide into the diving tanks; I'm a diver, and I have some mechanical ability, so they reason that while I was down below fiddling with the exhaust, I pumped some of it into the tanks. Either that, or I swam over to the marina in the dark of night and screwed with the tanks."

"Impeccable logic," Victor said, beaming. "Anything else?"

"Not that I know of, and I wish you'd stop looking at this *their* way."

"Anybody see you put exhaust fumes in the tanks?"

"No. I mean, I didn't do it, so nobody could have seen me do it, right?"

"Right. Sounds to me like the cops are coming up short in the evidence department. If I've seen enough cop shows in my time—and I most certainly have—to know anything about criminal law, they ain't got enough to nail you."

"That's what the lawyer said, although he made the point that they would be doing their dead-level best to get more."

"I suppose. Still, if you're innocent, what can they get?"

Chuck brightened a little. "Now you're talking," he said. "And you're right. How could they possibly get more?"

"Well, they could invent it, I suppose."

"Victor, don't say things like that."

"Let's look at this as simply as we can," Victor

said. "You didn't do it; that's a given, as my math teacher used to say."

"Right."

"So, if you didn't do it—ergo, somebody else must have."

"Right again."

"Got any ideas?"

"Not a one. Well, Clare, of course. She gave them some answers that didn't jibe with mine, and that's what got them on my back, I think."

"Aha, the lovely Clare!" Victor crowed. "A veritable black widow! We have another suspect!"

"She's my favorite, actually."

"Do you think the possibility might have crossed the minds of the cops?"

"I suppose. They seem to be buying her version of events, though."

"Tell me, Chuck," Victor said, suddenly serious. "During your little rolls in the hay with Clare, did she, I wonder, ever propose that perhaps the two of you might do Harry in?"

Chuck shook his head. "No. Wait a minute, she did say something about how at my age I should be looking to the future."

"That seems to be a leading question, doesn't it?"

"Yeah, but it didn't lead any further. I mean, she never got around to saying that I should doctor Harry's tank."

"Pity," Victor said.

"Why?"

225

"Well, if she had, then you could mention that to Tommy Sculley and see if that causes him to tack for the other side of the bay."

"Victor, are you suggesting that I should make up something like that to divert Tommy's interest toward Clare?"

Victor shrugged. "Never, old sport; I'd never suggest that you lie to the cops. On the other hand, in your place, I'd lie like a bandit if it would get me out from under."

"Maybe you're right," Chuck said.

"Probably not," Victor replied. "I rarely am. Look here, I've got a few grand tucked away. You're welcome to as much of it as I can spare and still pay my bar bill."

"Thanks, Victor, you're a friend, but I hope it won't come to that. I'm okay for money unless I have to go to trial."

"Just let me know." Victor looked at his watch. "Well, the big hand's on the six, and that means the lovelies have begun gathering in the various watering holes. Care to join me? Might do you some good."

Chuck shook his head. "Thanks, but I think I'm done in for today."

Victor stood up. "I'm off, then. Remember, I'll help in any way I can. Just say the word."

"Thanks again, Victor. See you."

With a wave, Victor jumped ashore and ambled off toward the music down the quay.

Chuck watched him go, and he felt a little better. It was good to know he had at least one friend in all this. He drank the rest of his beer and went below to find something to heat up for dinner.

CHAPTER

36

Tommy and Daryl were back in the chief's office, and Tommy wasn't looking forward to the meeting. He watched glumly as the chief entered and arranged himself at his desk.

"Sorry I wasn't here to see you when you got back from L.A.," the chief said. "How'd it go?"

"It was interesting," Tommy said.

"*Interesting?*" the chief asked, and his face began to redden. "You've just been off on a department-paid junket to *Hollywood*, and it was only *interesting*? You'd better do better than that, boy."

"Oh, I learned quite a lot, Chief."

"Good. Tell me."

Tommy gave his boss a blow-by-blow on his trip to L.A., omitting his breaking and entering of Carman's office.

The chief blinked. "So? What does all this have to do with the murder of Harry Carras?"

"There's a pretty good chance that Carras *was* Marinello—or Marin, as he liked to be called."

"Great. How does that solve his murder?"

"It doesn't exactly solve it, but it certainly widens the pool of suspects to include the L.A. branch of the mob, whose money he stole."

"*If* Carras was Marinwhatshisname."

"Yes, sir."

"How does that help us?"

"Well, if we can establish that Carras was Marinello, then it's the mob, not Chuck Chandler or Clare Carras, who becomes the chief suspect, and that means we just might not solve this one. Those boys don't leave a lot of tracks."

The chief began blinking rapidly. "Are you trying to confuse me, Sculley?"

"No, sir; I'm just laying it out for you."

"Laying *what* out for me? Try as I might, I can't digest all this into a coherent theory of who the perpetrator is."

"I understand, Chief, and it's my first priority to bring some coherence to this case. Believe me, I'm working on it full time."

"Do I understand that you are *relieved* that there might be a Mafia connection to this murder?"

"Only to the extent that, if true, it would absolve two local citizens, Mr. Chandler and Mrs. Carras."

"*Absolve?*" the chief blurted. "We're not out to absolve anybody. We're supposed to *arrest* somebody."

"I understand, Chief."

"I wish I did, Tommy. Now come on, I want

228

you to give me—right now—your best theory for who committed this murder."

"My best theory?"

"Don't you even have one?"

"Yes, sir, but I can't back it up yet."

"Forget backing it up, for the moment. Just tell me what you *think*!"

"All right, sir." Tommy rearranged himself in his seat. "I think that Harry Carras was murdered by Clare Carras and an unknown man."

"Tell me why you believe that."

"It involves believing the story Chuck Chandler told me. If you accept his version of the events on the boat that day, then it has to be Clare."

"Explain."

"Chandler said he was in the engine room for less than ten minutes that day. That's not enough time for him to sufficiently contaminate the tanks, even if the engine had been running, which it wasn't. He also told us that Harry chose the red tank—the one that was the most contaminated—and that Clare said that Harry always used the red tank, and she used the yellow tank, which left the blue, least contaminated tank for Chuck to use. Chuck, if you believe his story, didn't know any of this until Clare explained it to him. So Harry gets hooked up to the red tank and swims away before Chuck is ready to follow him. When Chuck does follow, Clare hangs back; even Clare doesn't dispute this point. So Harry chokes on the fumes and expires. Chuck, whose tank is less contaminated, makes it back to the boat, where he finds Clare hanging on to the diving platform and puking." He stopped talking and sat back in his chair.

"So? Go on."

"Clare has all the necessary knowledge to set this up. She knows which tank Harry uses and which one Chuck is going to use. She hangs on to the boat, breathes from her tank until she gets nauseous, so she's puking when Chuck gets back. And Chuck, the putz, doesn't have a clue."

"Why do you think there's another man involved?"

"Because I don't think Clare is grease monkey enough to pull this off alone. But she does know everything necessary to help somebody else pull it off."

"Who's the other man? And why is it a man?"

"The answer to your first question is, I don't know—yet. The answer to your second question is that Clare Carras doesn't strike me as the type to want to share Harry's money with a *woman*. The lady is a human black widow spider. It's what she does best." Tommy suddenly sat up in his seat, and his eyes widened. "Holy shit," he said softly.

"What?" demanded the chief.

"What, Tommy?" Daryl asked.

"She's going to kill him."

"Kill who?" Daryl asked.

"The other guy."

230

"The one we don't know about?" the chief asked.

"Right. She's going to kill him as sure as we're sitting here."

"But why?" Daryl asked. "She thinks she's gotten away with it, so she and the boyfriend can sail off into the sunset."

"She doesn't need him anymore," Tommy said. "She's suckered in some poor schmuck to do the dirty work for her, to kill Harry and almost certainly Carman, and now she's going to blow him off—and when this lady blows you off you end up dead."

"Maybe she's in love with him," Daryl said.

Tommy shook his head. "This lady doesn't love anybody but herself, and anyway, who on this island could possibly fill her bill for a partner to share Harry's dough with? I mean, if Clark Gable was still alive, *he* might last a year or two before she sucked him dry and left him dangling in the web, but there's no guy between here and Miami she'd even be seen with. She's young, she's gorgeous, she's very rich, and she can have her pick of men. Nope, our Key West schmuck is practically dead, he just doesn't know it yet."

"So why hasn't she already killed him, then?" the chief demanded.

"Because we haven't nailed her patsy, Chuck Chandler. The minute she thinks we've got enough evidence to convict Chuck, the other schmuck's dead. What further use is he to her?

231

And he's the only one who can involve her in Harry's murder."

"Okay," the chief said, "that's a good theory *if* you buy Chandler's version of what happened. What's your theory if he's lying and Mrs. Carras is telling the truth?"

Tommy shrugged. "That would cast a different light on things, I guess. In that case, Chandler would look real good for the murder."

"Have you searched Chandler's residence for evidence?"

"No, sir."

"Why not?"

"Because, like I said, I believe the guy, and I don't think we'd find anything. We haven't searched the Carras place, either."

"Tommy," the chief said, "I want you to type out a request for a warrant, take it over to the courthouse, and find Judge Potter. The chief shook his head. "I've given you all the room to swing that I'm going to. Now, I want you to get that warrant and conduct that search without delay. Do you understand me?"

"Chief, I don't even need a warrant. Chandler would let me search if I asked him."

"Don't ask him. If he says no, then while you're getting the warrant he could dispose of any evidence. Go get the warrant and conduct the search. Is that clear? Then, if you don't find anything, we'll think about searching the Carras house."

"Yes, Chief," Tommy said wearily. He got up

232

and walked out of the office with Daryl tagging along behind.

CHAPTER

37

They were on the way to the courthouse with the warrant request before Daryl said a word.

"Tommy, why didn't you tell the chief about your conversation with Clare Carras?"

"Which conversation is that?"

"The one where you told her that we didn't have enough physical evidence to arrest Chandler."

"Oh, that one."

"Yeah, that one. Why didn't you bring it up?"

"Daryl, do you ever get the feeling that the chief has a limited capacity to digest information?"

"It never occurred to me."

"Well, I got the distinct feeling that he was full up to the gills with theories and that he couldn't absorb another one without exploding."

"You could have a point," Daryl said.

The two detectives sat on the dock next to *Choke*, waiting.

"What time do you think he'll be home?" Daryl asked.

"Soon. I don't want to embarrass him at the tennis club; it wouldn't do his prospects of staying employed much good."

"Yeah," Daryl replied, nodding. "I guess that's so."

The yellow Porsche Speedster pulled into the parking lot, and Chuck Chandler got out of the car, locked it, and walked toward the boat.

Daryl reached into his pocket for the warrant.

"Put that away," Tommy said.

"Tommy, you remember what the chief said?"

"Yeah, I remember. I just want to give Chuck the opportunity. It'll look better in court for him."

"Whatever you say."

"Evening, gentlemen," Chuck said.

"Evening, Chuck," Tommy replied. "I need to ask you something."

"Shoot."

"Would you have any objection to our searching your boat, your car, and your locker at the tennis club?"

"For what?"

"For evidence."

Chuck thought for a minute. "Maybe I should ask my lawyer about that."

"That's your right, pal, but it's not what I would do in your shoes."

"Oh, what the hell, all right; I don't have anything to hide."

"Let's go to it, then. If you'll unlock the boat and stay on the afterdeck, we'll make this as quick as possible."

Chuck unlocked the hatch and sat down in a deck chair. "Go to it."

The two detectives started in the forepeak of the boat and worked aft. They had only been at it for a few minutes when Daryl opened a locker and pulled out a twelve-gauge shotgun with a short barrel.

"Looks like a police weapon," Tommy asked. He took the shotgun and went back to the afterdeck. "What's this for, Chuck?"

"Pirates."

"Come on."

"I kid you not: pirates. There are people around who'll come aboard your boat, kill you, and take everything you own. Most of the boat owners carry something. That one's legal; it's an eighteen-and-a-quarter-inch barrel."

Tommy handed the weapon to Daryl. "Put it back, and let's get to work."

They began again, paying particular attention to the engine room and the bilges. When they'd finished they'd found nothing in the least suspicious. They went back on deck.

"You got a key to the tennis club?" Tommy asked Chuck.

"Yep."

235

"Let's take a drive over there."

"Right."

Chuck let them inside the clubhouse and opened his locker for them. "I'm afraid it's mostly dirty laundry," he said. "The hotel does it for us once a week."

"That's what's here," Daryl said.

"Okay," Tommy agreed. "Let's take a look at the car."

They walked back to the parking lot to where the Porsche was parked under a lamp. Chuck unlocked both doors, and the detectives went to work. They found nothing inside the car or in the engine bay at the rear.

"Want to open the trunk for us, Chuck?" Tommy asked.

"Sure." Chuck walked to the front of the rear-engine car and started looking for the right key, then stopped. "That's funny," he said.

"What's funny?"

"It's not locked, and I *always* keep it locked. The day I arrived in Key West some vandal broke off the antenna, so I haven't been taking any chances on getting my spare stolen."

"Let's have a look," Tommy said.

Chuck opened the trunk and stepped back.

Tommy and Daryl went to work.

"This is a pretty elaborate tool kit to have in a car, isn't it?" Daryl asked, handing it to Chuck.

"When you drive a restored car, you have to

be ready for anything. I wouldn't trust it to just any mechanic; I'd rather fix it myself if it breaks."

"Uh-oh," Tommy said.

"What?" Daryl responded.

Tommy took a Kleenex from his pocket, reached under the spare tire, and came back with a piece of clear plastic hose around eighteen inches long.

"I've never seen that before in my life," Chuck said.

"When was the last time you went into the trunk?" Tommy asked.

"I don't know, a few days ago, maybe a week."

Tommy held the hose up to the light and looked at it carefully. "Let's all go down to the station house," he said. "Chuck, you can follow us."

"All right," Chuck said.

It was quiet in the squad room when the three men walked in. "Daryl, you want to get a fingerprint kit?" he said.

"Sure, Tommy." He came back a moment later with a briefcase.

"Dust it for me, will you? I don't think you're going to find anything, but dust it anyway."

Daryl did as he was told. A couple of minutes later he said, "Nothing."

"Nothing, right," Tommy said. He handed Daryl a key. "Open our evidence locker and bring me the piece of tubing the Coast Guard found on the Carras boat."

Daryl returned after a moment with the hose, still in a plastic bag.

Tommy wiped the fingerprint powder from the tubing found in Chuck's car and laid the two pieces on his desk end to end. "Look what we got here," he said. He pushed the two hoses together. "The original piece was cut in two, and the edges are jagged. They fit together perfectly."

"Tommy," Chuck said, "I swear to God, that hose is not mine. I don't even have any on the boat right now."

"Have a seat, Chuck," Tommy said.

Chuck sat down. He looked frightened.

"You see how bad this looks," Tommy said.

Chuck nodded. "The hose isn't mine; I never saw it before."

Tommy held up the two pieces. "Chuck, I'm telling you the truth, now; this could get you the death penalty if you're not telling me the truth."

"I swear to you, Tommy."

"Chuck, this is the last chance you're going to have to tell me anything you might have forgotten, anything you might have fudged on. The very last chance. Do you understand me?"

"I understand, Tommy, but I haven't told you any lies."

"You lied about the affair with Clare Carras."

"Except that. I guess I thought I was protecting her."

Tommy nodded. "Last chance, Chuck; I can ignore anything you might have been wrong on so far, but now I've got to have the truth."

"You've already got the truth, Tommy."

"I hope you're right, Chuck," Tommy said.

CHAPTER

38

Chuck sat in the saloon of *Choke* and tried to figure out what was happening. He went to the little bar and poured himself a stiff bourbon, then sat down again and tossed back the drink. When his hands had stopped trembling he picked up the phone and dialed the number written on the card.

"Hello?" the lawyer said.

"It's Chuck Chandler. You said I could call you at home."

"Sure. What's up?"

"I don't understand what's happening."

"Tell me what's happened, and I'll see if I can help you understand it."

Chuck told him about the search, about the matching length of hose found in his car.

"And it matched the piece from Carras's boat?"

"Yes, exactly. I watched him put the two together. They fit."

"Why didn't Sculley arrest you?"

"That's what I don't understand. I asked

Tommy, but he didn't say anything. He just told me to go home and not to leave town."

"That's good advice, the part about not leaving town," the lawyer said. "I think Sculley believes you, and that's why you weren't arrested. I think that's a very encouraging sign."

"You really think so?"

"I can't think of any other reason why you're not in jail right now," the lawyer said. "They've got motive, opportunity, and physical evidence. That could put you away, unless they have some other evidence that's exculpatory. Are you aware of any evidence like that?"

"No," Chuck replied.

"Then Sculley must believe you instead of Mrs. Carras. I just hope Sculley's boss believes him."

"Me, too."

"You ever hear anything from that girlfriend of yours? What's her name? . . . "

"Meg. No, I haven't heard from her."

"It sure wouldn't hurt to have her back here telling what passed between you before you went out on the Carras boat."

"I've no idea where she is; she's been gone long enough to be almost anywhere by now."

"Well, let's hope she turns up soon. Chuck, you have a drink and get some rest. We'll just handle this as it comes, okay?"

"Okay, and thanks." Chuck hung up the phone and wiped the sweat from his forehead. He sat for a while, sipping his drink, staring into space, then he had an idea. He picked up the phone and dialed Billy Tubbs's number.

"Hello?" his star student said.

"Hi, Billy, it's Chuck; can I speak to your dad?"

"Sure, hang on."

Chuck drummed his fingers on the saloon table, not wanting to do this, but unable to think of anything else.

"Hi, Chuck, it's Norman Tubbs."

"Norman, I wonder if I can ask a very large favor of you?"

"Chuck, after Billy's performance in the Naples tournament, you can ask just about anything of me."

Chuck took a deep breath and asked.

The following morning Chuck and Norman Tubbs sat in the Tubbs airplane at the end of the runway and waited for a clearance from the tower to take off.

"Where you want to go?" Norman asked.

"I want to fly, as low as you legally can, up one side of the Keys and down the other. I want to look at every anchorage between here and Key Largo."

"You got it, Chuck," Norman said.

"Nine, two, three, five, Delta, cleared for takeoff," the tower controller said. "Say direction of flight."

"Three, five, Delta," Norman responded, "I'll be doing some low-level sightseeing, once we're past the naval air base."

"Roger," the tower said.

Norman pushed the throttles forward, and the little twin Cessna roared down the runway. He switched frequencies to ask the naval air station for clearance to cross their air space, and when he had, he pulled back on the throttle and descended to five hundred feet, then he put ten degrees of flaps in and dropped the landing gear. "That'll get some drag out, keep us slow," he said. "I don't think we should get any lower than five hundred feet, unless there's something specific you want to look at. What are we looking for, anyway?"

"A catamaran of about fifty feet, yellow hull, sloop rigged."

"At anchor?"

"That's what I'm hoping."

"This have anything to do with a girl?"

"Of course it does, Norman."

They started up the east side of the Keys, and each time they came to an anchorage they circled, looking for the catamaran. It took them nearly two hours to reach Key Largo, and, after circling the marina there, they headed down the western side of the island chain. It went faster, now, because there were fewer boats on the western side, because the water was shallower, which wouldn't matter much to a shallow-draft yacht such as a multihull.

They were nearly back to the naval air station on Boca Chica, having had no luck, when Chuck pointed east. "There, in the distance."

"Way over yonder, under sail?"

"Can we take a look at her?"

Norman banked the airplane into a steep left turn and after he cleared the eastern shore, started a descent. "I'll get you down good and low," he said. A minute later he said, "There, we're at about fifty feet. That do?"

"That'll do fine," Chuck said, keeping his eyes glued to the yacht. "Can you go any slower?"

"I'll bring her back to ninety knots; that's the best I can do without risking a stall, and I don't want that at this altitude."

The airplane's flight became mushy, now, and Norman seemed to be making very large movements with the yoke to keep the airplane steady on course.

"Go astern of her," Chuck said.

Norman made a correction.

Chuck watched as they neared the yacht. Her color was yellow, and she was sloop-rigged. In a moment he was sure it was the Haileys' catamaran. "That's the boat, Norman! Can you circle her?"

"Sure, but I'm going to put the gear up and gain some speed; I don't want to dump us into the drink." Norman banked the airplane to the right, and Chuck strained to see who was at the wheel. There was no one.

"She's under self-steering," Chuck said. "Can you make a low pass right over her cockpit? Let's see if we can scare up somebody."

Norman did as he was asked, and as they

passed over the yacht, a woman's head popped up through the hatch.

"There she is! It's Meg!" Chuck shouted.

"Looks like she's headed toward Little Palm Island," Norman said. He maneuvered the airplane astern of the yacht and checked his heading. "Yeah, she'll make it on this tack. There are always a few boats anchored inside Little Palm."

Chuck winced as he remembered his night on Little Palm with Clare. He would never feel the same about the place again. "Okay, that's it," he said to Norman. "We can go home now."

"Home it is," Norman said. He switched to the Boca Chica frequency and announced his intentions.

Back on the ground, Chuck ran for a pay phone and called the club.

"Olde Island Racquet Club," Merk's voice said.

"Merk, it's Chuck. I know I was supposed to be there in ten minutes, but something important's come up. Can Victor take my lessons this morning—maybe this afternoon, too?"

"I'll check," Merk said, and there was the sound of rustling pages. "I'll have to cancel at least two," Merk said.

"Can you put somebody on the ball machine instead of a lesson?"

"Okay, I can put one of them on the machine. Maybe I'll take the other one myself."

"You're a good guy, Merk; I'll make it up to

you." Chuck hung up the phone and ran for his car.

He was nearly to the bridge to Stock Island and U.S. 1 before he remembered he'd been told not to leave town.

CHAPTER

39

Tommy rang the bell. When Clare Carras came to the door, she no longer looked the grieving widow. She was dressed, if one could call it that, in the smallest excuse for a bikini he had ever seen. It was composed mostly of string, and it concealed so little as to be very nearly invisible. Her skin was rubbed with oil, and she positively glowed from the sun.

"Good morning, Mrs. Carras," Tommy said, trying not to gulp.

"Good morning, Detective," she replied. "What can I do for you?" She did not move to let him into the house.

"Mrs. Carras, it might be very useful to our investigation if you would give us permission to search your house."

"Search my *house?*"

"Yes, ma'am."

"Are you out of your *mind?*"

"I don't believe so, ma'am. As I said, it would be helpful to our investigation if you would consent to a search."

"Absolutely not," she said firmly.

Tommy produced the paper. "In that case, ma'am, I'm serving you with a search warrant." He opened the screen door and handed it to her, and he did not let the door close again.

She unfolded the document and read it carefully while Tommy waited. "Well," she said, finally, "when do you want to do this?"

"Immediately," Tommy replied.

"Do you mean *right now*?"

"Yes, ma'am, that's what immediately means."

She reached for the screen door as if to close it. "If you'll allow me a few minutes to get dressed."

Tommy held on to the door and stepped into the hallway, closely followed by Daryl. "I'm sorry, ma'am, but I can't wait. Of course, you can get a robe if you like."

She turned and padded down the hall in her bare feet. "Do whatever you want," she said. "I'll be out by the pool."

"Yes, ma'am," Tommy called after her. He turned to Daryl. "Her bedroom seems to be on this floor, straight ahead. You get to go through her underwear; I'll be upstairs."

"Right," Daryl replied. He went into the bedroom.

Upstairs, Tommy went straight for the desk where he had previously looked at Harry Carras's checkbook. He opened the middle drawer, extracted the checkbook, and began examining it. The balance, which had been over eighty thousand dollars at his last inspection, was now down to around thirty thousand. He flipped backward through the ledger, looking for anything unusual. There were steady weekly deposits ranging from ten to twenty thousand dollars, probably income from investments, Tommy thought. There were also a number of large checks written to cash, and that interested him.

He examined the drawer carefully for anything else, then began methodically going through the other drawers. He found a stack of statements from the Miami office of a well-known brokerage firm, and he went through them. During the past twelve months, he saw, the balance had risen from a little more than nine million dollars to just under twelve million, and there had been no fresh infusions of cash. Harry had done very well for himself in the market.

In another drawer he found a contract with a Fort Lauderdale yacht broker, giving him the exclusive right to sell *Fugitive.* There were rubber-banded stacks of household bills, but none from credit card companies or department stores. It seemed the only credit Harry had wanted was the kind that could be secured with a cash deposit. No wonder the guy didn't have a credit record to speak of.

In the bottom drawer he found a legal document titled "Revocable Trust." He read quickly through the list of assets, which included Carras's house, yacht, airplane, and brokerage account. He returned it to the drawer.

He finished with the desk and turned his attention to the rest of the room. He took down every book in the bookcase, flipping through it before replacing it, then moved all the furniture, looking under it before returning it to its original position. He felt in the crevice under the cushions, then unzipped each cushion and probed it for concealed objects. He rolled back the rug and looked for hidden compartments, then he went to the kitchen and began work there.

He opened every cabinet and took out the contents, inspecting each item before replacing it. He opened the refrigerator and freezer and checked each item carefully, then he looked inside the ovens, the dishwasher, and the trash compactor. He opened each spice bottle on the rack and probed its contents with a pen. He then went to the powder room off the living room and looked inside the toilet tank.

He went up another floor and found an attic space that had been finished, but seemed unused. A ladder ran up to the roof; he climbed it and found himself on a widow's walk. He looked down toward the pool and saw Clare Carras lying on her back, her legs slightly spread, her bikini top gone. Transfixed, he took all of her in for a full minute before he forced himself to return to the living room.

"Tommy, you want to come down here a minute?" Daryl called from downstairs.

"Right with you," Tommy called back. He walked downstairs and into Clare Carras's bedroom. "How's it coming?"

"I've been through everything," Daryl said, "and all I found was this." He pulled back a group of hanging dresses and on the floor under them was an expensive-looking safe.

"Oh, boy," Tommy said. "Daryl, would you mind going out to the pool and asking Mrs. Carras to come in here? Don't yell at the lady, that wouldn't be polite; go to her." Grinning, he watched Daryl disappear through the side door. A minute later, Clare Carras came into the room, fastening the tiny top to her bikini. Daryl was close behind her, blushing.

"Mrs. Carras, would you please open this safe?" Tommy asked.

"I'm afraid I can't help you," she replied.

"Mrs. Carras, I have to warn you that to impede this search in any way is contempt of court, and Judge Potter is harsh with people who don't obey his court's orders."

"I'm sorry, but I don't have the combination," she said. "Harry never gave it to me."

"What's inside it?"

"Some of my jewelry, but he always got it out and put it away for me. I doubt if there's much else."

"Daryl," Tommy said, "do you know a good locksmith?"

"Yeah," Daryl said. "There's one just down the block."

"Go down there and see if they got anybody who can crack a safe."

"Right."

"Mrs. Carras, you can go back to your sunbathing, if you like. We'll make this as fast as we can."

Clare Carras headed out the door to the pool, untying her bra as she went.

Tommy and Daryl had been waiting for more than an hour while the locksmith repeatedly attacked the safe and failed. He was on the phone with the manufacturer now, taking notes. Finally, he hung up.

"Okay," he said. "I've got the combination."

"Thank you," Tommy said. "Let's see what's inside."

The man expertly twirled the knob, and the safe came open.

"Stand back," Tommy said. He knelt before the safe and examined the interior. On the top shelf was a velvet box. There was nothing else in the safe. He opened the box and found a dozen pieces of gold and diamond jewelry. "Here you are," he said, handing Clare the box.

"And here's the combination," the locksmith said, addressing her breasts.

"Thank you," she said, beaming at him. "And thank you, Detective."

"Don't mention it," Tommy said.

She put the box back into the safe, closed the door, twirled the knob, and went back to the pool.

"She knew the combination all along, didn't she?" Daryl asked.

"You bet your ass she did," Tommy replied. "Let's have a look around outside.

They walked around the house, looking under shrubs and inspecting a shed full of gardening tools. Before they rounded the house on the pool side, Tommy called out, "Mrs. Carras, could I have just one more moment of your time?"

"Come ahead," she called back. She was sitting up and had her bra on again when they arrived. "What is it, Detective?"

"In going over your checkbook I saw that someone had made a number of large cash withdrawals over the last few weeks, usually ten to twenty-five thousand dollars at a time. Can you tell me what the money was for?"

"I haven't the faintest idea," she said. "Harry liked having cash on hand; he wouldn't use credit cards."

Tommy nodded. "Thank you, ma'am," he said. "And thank you for your cooperation. We'll be going now."

"Bye-bye," she said, and reached behind her to untie her bra.

Tommy and Daryl beat a hasty retreat.

"Jesus Christ!" Daryl said when they were in the car again. "You should have warned me."

Tommy grinned. "I thought I'd let you enjoy yourself."

Daryl took a deep breath and let it out. "Did you find anything at all?"

"Not much," Tommy replied. "Just the record of withdrawals and a trust document signed by Harry Carras."

"What kind of trust?"

"It means that Clare Carras doesn't have to go through probate; Harry's estate is hers right now."

"Which means she could take off at any time?"

"Right. Any time at all."

"Then why hasn't she already?"

"Like I told you before, she's waiting for us to convict Chuck Chandler, the designated putz, of her husband's murder. Then she can sail away, leaving no loose ends behind her for us to follow up."

"Swell," Daryl said.

"Except for the secret lover. She'll have to tie up that loose end, and it'll be interesting to see how she does it."

"And who she does it to," Daryl said.

CHAPTER

40

Chuck pulled to a stop at the marina that served Little Palm Island. He went around to the marina office and, after a brief negotiation, rented a small Boston Whaler, and in a few minutes he was headed down the little canal toward open water.

He kept his speed down, so as not to cause a wake, until he was past the houses on the beach; then he opened the throttle and felt the breeze in his face. A couple of miles down the little bay were half a dozen yachts at anchor, and soon he could make out the outline of the Haileys' catamaran. As he approached he slowed to idle, not wishing to disturb those on board the boats, then cut the engine and drifted alongside the yellow cat. There was no one in the cockpit, but the hatch was open.

"Meg!" he called out.

There was a muffled sound of someone moving below, and a female head emerged from the hatch. It was not Meg.

"Yeah, what is it?" the woman asked. She was a thirtyish brunette.

"I'm looking for Meg Hailey," he said. "Is she aboard?"

"Who wants to know?" the woman asked.

"Chuck Chandler."

The woman looked below. "Chuck Chandler," she said to somebody.

There was a muffled cry from below. "Tell him to go to hell!"

"Meg!" Chuck shouted. "Please come up here and talk to me! It's very important!"

"Get out of here, Chuck!"

"Meg, the police want to talk to you!"

A short silence. "What?"

"Haven't you heard what's happened?"

"Is this some kind of trick?"

"Meg, please come up here, I've got to talk to you!"

The brunette's head vanished and was replaced by Meg's. She looked sleepy and tousled. "All right, *what*?" she groused.

"Haven't you heard what's happened?"

"We've been in the Bahamas, and we haven't heard about anything. What are you talking about?"

"Can I come aboard?"

She picked up a heavy winch handle. "Don't even think about it."

"Meg, Harry Carras has been murdered."

She stared at him uncomprehendingly for a moment, then the penny dropped. "You mean the witch's husband?"

"That's the one."

"Who killed him?"

"There's a fairly large body of opinion that holds that I did."

"Did you?"

"Of course not."

"Chuck, if this is some kind of trick to get next to me again I . . ." She raised the winch handle.

"It's not a trick, it's what happened. It happened the day I went out on the boat with them, the day you packed up and left."

"I told you not to go, didn't I?"

"Yes, and that's what you've got to tell the police."

She looked around. "Where are the police?"

"In Key West. I'll take you to the detective in charge right now, if you'll let me."

She stared at him for a moment. "Chuck, if you're just trying to get 'round me, I swear . . ."

"Come on, Meg; get some clothes on, and I'll drive you to Key West. I'll have you back here by sunset."

Her shoulders slumped. "Oh, what the hell." She disappeared below.

Chuck sat in the boat, holding on to the gunwale of the cat, and waited. Ten minutes later she came up, dressed in jeans and a cotton sweater. It was the most clothing he had ever seen her wear. She handed him a large handbag and got into the Whaler. He started the engine and headed back to the marina.

"Who's the girl?" he asked.

"Dan picked her up in Eleuthera; she was

stranded. And that's all I've got to say to you." She set her jaw and refused to look at him.

Ashore, Chuck went to a pay phone and called his lawyer.

"I've found Meg Hailey," he said.

"That's good news," the lawyer replied.

"What should I do with her?"

"I'll meet you at police headquarters, in . . . wait a minute. It would look better if you just showed up there and handed her over."

"Okay, I'll do that."

"Have you discussed with her anything she's going to tell the police?"

"No. She's not speaking to me."

"Just as well. Don't rehearse anything, just let her tell her story. Call me later if there's anything I can do."

"Okay." Chuck hung up and went to the car. Meg, having produced a large straw hat from somewhere, was sitting in the passenger seat. He got in, started the car, and drove onto the highway.

"What am I supposed to tell the police?" Meg asked sullenly.

"Just answer their questions truthfully."

"*What* questions?"

"I'm not supposed to rehearse you."

"I don't get it."

"You don't have to. When the police are through questioning you, I'll explain everything." He drove on toward Key West. He wanted in the worst way to touch her, kiss her, but he restrained himself.

At police headquarters he asked for Tommy Sculley, and after a moment Tommy appeared.

"Tommy, this is Meg Hailey," Chuck said.

"How do you do, Ms. Hailey," Tommy said, then he turned back to Chuck questioningly.

"The young lady I told you about."

Tommy looked at him blankly.

"I knew it," Meg said. "This is some scam of yours."

"Shut up, Meg. Tommy, this is the girl on the boat next to mine, the one you wanted to talk to."

"Oh, *that* girl," Tommy said. "Yes, Ms. Hailey, we would like to ask you some questions. Would you come with me, please?"

"I'll wait," Chuck said.

"Nah, we'll be a while. Why don't you go home, and I'll call you when we're done."

"Okay," Chuck said.

He drove back to Key West Bight, made some iced tea, and sat on the afterdeck next to the phone, waiting.

The sun was nearly down when Tommy Sculley and his partner pulled into the parking lot and got out, followed by Meg. The three walked toward the boat, and Chuck stood up to meet them.

"Here she is, Chuck," Tommy said. "That's quite a girl you've got there."

"I'm afraid I don't have her," Chuck said. "I wish I did."

"Oh," Tommy said. "Well, we'll be going. She was very helpful to your case, Chuck." He walked away, followed by Daryl.

"Would you like some iced tea?" he asked.

"Was that you in the airplane this morning?"

"Yes, a friend flew me out to look for you."

"Had you looked for me before?"

"I didn't know where to look. Finally I got desperate, and my friend agreed to fly me up the Keys."

"Desperate because you needed me to back up your story?"

"That too," he said.

She placed a hand on his cheek. "You really have been in a lot of trouble, haven't you?"

He nodded.

She reached up and kissed him lightly on the lips. "Don't ever leave me again to spend a day with another woman," she said.

"I won't," he replied. "I promise." It occurred to him that he had never before promised anything like that to any woman.

CHAPTER

41

Tommy strode along the pontoons of the Treasure Island marina, looking idly around.

"I don't get it," Daryl said, ambling alongside him. "Why are we looking at boats?"

"We're not looking at boats," Tommy replied. "We're looking at hunks."

"Tommy, is there something about your preferences you haven't told me?"

Tommy looked at him. "Kid, I haven't told you *anything* about my preferences. What we're doing is trying to figure out Clare Carras's preferences."

"Her other guy? Gotcha."

Tommy stopped. They were standing alongside Harry Carras's yacht, *Fugitive,* and there were three young men aboard. One of them, a tall, blond beach bum type, hopped down to the pontoon and began undoing the yacht's lines.

"Where you headed, guys?" Tommy called out.

Another suntanned boat bum on deck, who seemed to be giving the orders, looked down at Tommy and his street clothes, his leather shoes, with utter contempt. "The South Seas, *guy*," he said witheringly.

Tommy held up his badge and grinned. "Permission to come aboard?"

The boat bum's face fell. "Okay." He turned to the man on the pontoon. "Make those lines fast again."

Tommy and Daryl climbed aboard. "Who are you?" he asked, "and what are you doing aboard the Carras yacht?"

"I'm Jim Bowles; we're moving the yacht to Fort Lauderdale to sell her. I do ferry work for the broker."

"Mind if I have a look around?"

"Not at all," the man said, anxious to be cooperative now.

Tommy walked down into the saloon and looked around him at the mahogany paneling and the expensive furniture. "This is some way to travel, isn't it?"

"I'll say," Daryl replied.

"Follow me." Tommy walked aft to the engine room and looked around.

"This is where the deed was done, huh?" Daryl asked.

"Yeah, it is." He walked further aft to the rear of the engines. "And this is where the exhaust was connected to the diving tanks."

"Tommy, would the exhaust from the engine have enough pressure to pack fumes into a tank of compressed air?"

"I don't know," Tommy said, "but look here."

He pointed to the compressor. "If he connected the exhaust hose directly to the compressor intake, the compressor would do the work. That's how it had to be done."

"Right," Daryl said quietly. He placed a hand on the exhaust pipe. "So the tubing we've got would fit inside this hose, and the other end would go over the intake for the compressor?" He placed a hand on the compressor's intake hose.

"That's the drill."

Daryl nodded. "Makes sense; I guess I was hoping to find something new about all this."

"Well," Tommy said, pointing to the two hose clips holding the exhaust tubing to the overboard pipe, "if all Chuck had to do was to put this back onto that exhaust pipe, it certainly couldn't have taken him forty-five minutes to do the job, as Clare swore. It didn't take that long to do the time when I was on board, and it didn't the second time."

"Anyway, the engine wouldn't be running when he was making that kind of repair," Daryl observed.

"Let's take a look around this tub," Tommy said.

The two detectives went forward again to the saloon.

"You guys going to be much longer?" the ferry skipper called from on deck.

"Yeah, we are," Tommy called back. "We'll let you know when we're done."

261

They went to the forward cabin and began a search, working aft, just as they had on Chuck Chandler's boat. Half an hour later, Daryl called Tommy over to look at something in the aft owner's cabin. "Look at this," he said, pointing to what seemed to be a cupboard opening. "There's no knob or pull on it."

Tommy reached down and pushed the panel; it sprang open. There was nothing inside the exposed locker, but there were spring clips fixed to the inside of the cupboard door. "What do you make of that?" Tommy asked.

Daryl reached inside his jacket, produced his nine-millimeter automatic, and pressed the pistol into the spring clips. "I think that's what it's for," he said.

Tommy looked at the king-size berth. "If Harry slept on this side, that would put a weapon right at hand for him, wouldn't it?"

"Yeah, but where's the weapon?" Daryl asked. "You see any when we searched the Carras house?"

"Nope." Tommy began going through the lockers in the cabin, and he came across one containing wet suits and diving gear, including spare tanks of various sizes. "Guess Harry was an enthusiastic diver, huh? He was ready for anything, except breathing carbon monoxide." He picked up a compressed-air spear gun and felt the tip. "I wouldn't like to take one of these in the gut."

"I get your point," Daryl said.

Tommy groaned. "Let's get out of here."

Back in the car, Tommy said, "Let's go down to the Olde Island Racquet Club. I'd like to talk to Victor."

"How come?"

"Remember, when we were searching Chuck's car, he said he'd left the trunk locked, but it had been unlocked?"

"Yeah."

"I was just wondering how somebody else might have had access to Chuck's car keys, and . . ."

"Chuck's locker in the clubhouse, right?"

"Right."

Victor finished a lesson, got a Coke from the machine, and headed to where Tommy and Daryl were sitting at a table at courtside.

"Let me talk to Victor alone, okay?" Tommy said.

"Sure; I'll go over to the hotel and pick up a paper," Daryl replied.

"Take your time."

Victor sat down as Daryl left. "How's it going, Tommy? Haven't seen you on the courts lately; don't want you to get rusty."

"Been busy as hell, Victor, until this morning. Daryl wanted a paper, so I thought I'd take a load off for a few minutes. You teaching a lot lately?"

"Yeah, especially since Chuck has been taking some time off. I hope you guys are making some headway toward clearing him. I don't believe for a minute he could have had anything to do with Harry's death."

"That's good," Tommy replied. "You know Chuck well?"

"Not intimately, but we have a beer now and then."

"How about the Carrases?"

"I knew them from here." He nodded toward the courts. "Chuck and I had dinner with them once, and of course, we were all out together snorkling that day."

"Yeah, we were. What kind of a life do you have in Key West, Victor?"

"Not bad, I guess. Merk and I get the best of the weather here in winter, then we head to Santa Fe for the summers. It's a nice combination."

"Got a girl in Key West?"

"Nobody special. I sort of like cruising the tourists. You have a few nice nights together, then they're gone until next year. I got a little black book that would stand me in good stead in just about any major city in the United States, I guess."

"They come from all over, huh?"

"Yep."

"Victor, did you ever see Clare Carras alone? Without Harry, I mean."

"I gave her a couple of lessons, but when Chuck came he took over the better players."

"No, I mean alone like at her house."

"Nope." He looked at Tommy appraisingly. "Hey, wait a minute, Tommy; she's way out of my league. The Chuck Chandlers of this world service the Clare Carrases; ol' Victor has to be content with the secretaries on vacation. That woman would chew me up and spit me out in five minutes."

"You're a good judge of character, Victor," Tommy said.

"Once, in my youth, I got mixed up with somebody like that. It cost me a good job at a great tennis club. If I hadn't blown that I'd be knocking down a hundred and fifty grand a year."

"Do you regret that, Victor?"

Victor smiled. "Not really." He waved a hand at the three courts. "This is more my speed."

"No ambition?"

Victor shook his head. "Merk is the one with the ambition. He's always dreaming about opening up a chain of these places—a hundred, hundred and fifty."

Tommy looked at Victor with interest. "Merk's ambitious, huh? Does he have any hope of pulling it off?"

"Not without a major investor, and so far, he hasn't been able to come up with one. Tell you the truth, I keep hoping he'll sell me this club. It would suit me, I think; keep me going in my old age, which ain't all that far away."

"Merk's a good-looking guy; what sort of social life does he have?"

"Merk seems to read a lot," Victor said. "We have a beer now and again, but he's always home early."

"Married?"

"Divorced. She took him pretty good, or he might have had that chain of tennis clubs by now."

"Does he have any friends?"

"Just me, I guess. He's the quiet type."

"Yeah. How much time do you spend in the clubhouse, Victor?"

"Hardly any," Victor replied. "I'm out here all day, then I head for home or the bars when the day's over. Merk's the office guy; he's in there all day, keeping the books and selling equipment. Once in a while he'll do a lesson, if we're short-handed, but mostly he's in there bent over a desk."

Tommy looked toward the club. "He in there now?"

"He went to the post office, I think. Oops, here comes my next lesson. See you later."

"Victor," Tommy said.

Victor stopped and turned. "You were smart to stay away from Clare Carras. Look what's happened to Chuck."

Victor grinned. "The secret to happiness, I think, is knowing your limitations."

Tommy watched Victor trot on court to meet his client, an elderly man in whites, then got up and walked into the clubhouse. The place was deserted. He walked into Merk's office and

266

looked around. Nothing but a desk, a computer, and a telephone. He opened another door, and it led to the small locker room where he'd searched Chuck's locker. On one wall of the office was a small key safe. Tommy opened it and browsed. He came up with one labeled "Master, lockers." He put the key back and left the club. Daryl was waiting for him in the parking lot.

"What do you think?" Daryl asked. "Is Victor in this somehow?"

"I don't think so," Tommy said. "Like Chuck Chandler, he doesn't strike me as the type. What do you know about Merk, the guy who runs the place?"

"Not much."

"Neither does anybody else."

CHAPTER

42

Daryl shifted his weight and switched radio stations for something that would keep him awake. He had followed Merk Connor home from the tennis club three hours before, and Merk was still inside. Daryl could see him occasionally as he moved around the little shotgun Conch house. A little legwork had told him that after his divorce, Merk had moved here from a larger house in a better neighborhood.

Daryl glanced at his watch; another forty-five minutes before he was relieved by Tommy. When he looked back at the house, all the lights were off. It was a little early for bedtime, he thought. Then, as he watched, there was the movement of a shadow behind the house, and a figure vaulting over a low fence and disappearing toward the next street. Daryl got the car started and quickly drove around the block. At the next intersection he got out of the car, ran to the corner, and looked around a building. The street was nearly deserted, but he saw a familiar figure turn another corner ahead, toward Duval Street.

Daryl got back into the car, drove straight ahead until he came to Duval, turned the corner, and pulled up at the curb, leaving the engine running. Half a minute later, Merk walked into Duval and started down the street at a rapid pace, headed toward the western end of the island. Daryl followed slowly, just close enough to see that sometime after arriving home from work, Merk had changed into fresh clothes.

Daryl was holding up traffic now, so he pulled over, flipped down the sun visor to expose the car's ID to the foot patrolmen handing out parking tickets, and continued to follow Merk on foot. Merk never window-shopped or slowed down; he seemed to know exactly where he was going and was in a hurry to get there. He was getting closer and closer to Dey Street and Clare Carras.

From a block back, Daryl saw Merk suddenly turn into a building, and he resisted the temptation to run to catch up. It took him a full minute to make up the distance and find that Merk had turned into a bar. Daryl pushed open the door and walked in.

People turned and looked at him as if they'd been expecting him to arrive. He tried not to appear to be looking for anybody; instead, he ambled up to the bar and ordered a beer. When the bartender had poured it, he allowed himself to lean on the bar and take a good look around for Merk. Suddenly it came to him that he was in a gay bar, and that Merk was not present. At the other end of the bar, he spotted another door to the side street. Cursing under his breath, he left and headed toward the door.

"Don't rush off," a man at the bar said as he passed.

Rushing was all Daryl felt like doing. He pushed open the door and emerged into the side street, looking both ways. Merk was nowhere in sight. Had he noticed Daryl following him and deliberately lost him, or had he just taken a short-cut?

Daryl ran back to the corner and back down Duval Street to his car. He got it started and turned right at the next intersection, heading for Dey Street. The bar had been only a block and a half from Clare Carras's house.

He cruised slowly down Dey Street, waiting for her house to come into view. Just as it did, the living room lights upstairs went off. A moment later there was a glow from behind the fence from approximately where Clare's bedroom was located. Daryl drove around the corner into Elizabeth Street, parked, and called Tommy on his portable phone.

"Hello?"

"Tommy, it's Daryl. Merk stayed home for better than three hours, then suddenly left the house by the back door and walked over to Duval Street."

"Did you follow him?"

"Yeah, to a bar that turned out to be full of extremely graceful young men, but he wasn't there. There was a back door, and by the time I figured it out, he had disappeared."

"How far was the place from the Carras house?"

"A little more than a block. I drove around there just in time to see the living room lights go off and what looked like her bedroom light go on."

"Bingo!" Tommy said. "I think we've found our man."

"I'm around the corner from the house now; are you going to relieve me?"

"I think we'll let it go for tonight," Tommy said. "No telling what time he'll come out of there, and it would take more than the two of us to watch all four sides of the house. I'll see you at the station tomorrow morning, okay? We'll do some checking on Merk."

"See you tomorrow," Daryl said. He started the car and headed for home.

Tommy arrived at the station the following morning to find Daryl there ahead of him, working at a computer terminal.

"Hi," the younger man said. "I'm logged on to the state crime computer right now; it's doing a search on Merk."

"You're sure he left the bar before you did last night?"

"I'm sure; the place wasn't all that crowded, and I looked at every face."

"Okay."

"Oops, looks like we came up empty," Daryl said.

"No record," the computer screen read.

"Try the FBI computer," Tommy said. "I'm going to get some coffee."

"Right. Bring me some, will you?"

Tommy walked into the little kitchenette and poured two cups of coffee, black for himself, milk and two sugars for Daryl. One day the kid would learn about coffee, Tommy thought, about how much better it was without all that stuff in it. He returned to the squad room and looked over Daryl's shoulder.

"Bingo," Daryl said, hitting the keystrokes for a printout.

Tommy grabbed the sheet as it came out of the

printer. "Well, well," he said. "Mild-mannered Merk wasn't always so mild-mannered. He had two arrests for assault with a deadly weapon in 1970, in California, no convictions, and lookahere, he got a year for battery in L.A. a few months later and served four months on the county farm. He was picked up on a parole violation, what looks like a barroom brawl a couple of months after that. Then nothing; I guess he's been clean since then."

"How old is the guy?" Daryl asked.

Tommy looked at the sheet for Merk's date of birth. "Fifty-one, why?"

"That would make him the right age for military service during the Vietnam War, wouldn't it?"

"Daryl, you amaze and astound me. Get off a request to the Department of Defense; let's see if he has a service record."

Daryl began typing out the request on the computer. "This'll take a while," he said. "We'll be lucky if we get a reply today."

"Mark it urgent," Tommy said. "Say it's for an investigation of a serious crime."

Daryl finished the request and sent it out by modem. "Maybe that'll move them a little quicker."

"Maybe, but let's not count on it." Tommy thought for a minute. "While we're at it, why don't we run the record checks on Victor and Chuck. You never know."

"Okay," Daryl said, and began typing.

Tommy sat down and sipped his coffee, drumming his fingers on the desk, trying not to think of anything in particular. Sometimes his mind came up with stuff when it was just idling.

After a few minutes, Daryl swiveled around in his chair. "Nothing on either the FBI or Florida state computers. They're squeaky clean, both of 'em."

"I'm glad to hear it," Tommy said.

"Tommy," Daryl said, "do you always think that people you like wouldn't commit a crime?"

Tommy shook his head. "As a matter of fact, I'm in the habit of thinking the worst of everybody, until they prove me wrong."

"Even me?"

Tommy grinned. "Especially you, kid."

CHAPTER

43

When Tommy arrived in the squad room the next morning a secretary handed him an envelope. "This came in late yesterday," she said.

Daryl arrived while Tommy was opening the envelope. "What's that?" he asked.

Tommy looked at the sheaf of papers. "It's a digest of Merk Connor's service record."

"Read me the juicy parts," Daryl said.

Tommy started through the document. "He was drafted in '66, right out of college; he went to OCS and got into Special Services."

"You mean like the Green Berets? Was he in Vietnam?"

"No, like the entertainment and sports services. Yeah, he was in Vietnam, running a tennis program at an officer's club in Saigon."

"Not bad duty."

"Sounds like pretty good duty to me, in the middle of a war and all. Still, he managed to get himself court-martialed."

"What for?"

"Conduct unbecoming an officer and a gentleman," Tommy read. "I wonder what that means? Sounds like a catchall charge that could cover just about anything."

"Was he convicted?"

"No, the charges were dropped, and he was, I quote, 'transferred at the request of his commanding officer.' "

"Sounds like he was told to get the hell out, doesn't it?"

"Sure does, but that's all the record says. Wait a minute, he was discharged as a second lieutenant; he didn't get promoted in three years of service. Now *that* ought to tell us something. I mean, shavetails get promoted to first lieutenant automatically if they keep their noses clean. He also got a general discharge under honorable circumstances. That's a peg down from a regular honorable discharge."

"If you say so. Does it say who his commanding officer was? Maybe we could run him down."

"Lieutenant Colonel Jacob Morrell, it says here."

"I'll get some e-mail off to the DOD and see if we can get an address," Daryl said.

"Let me phone instead, see if I can press them for an immediate answer; it's all in their computer." Tommy picked up the phone, consulted a directory, and called the Pentagon, asking for personnel records.

"Active or retired?" the sergeant asked.

"I'm not sure; try retired." He gave the officer's name and listened to the keystrokes on the other end.

"Here we go, got a pencil?"

"Shoot." Tommy scribbled down the information, thanked the sergeant, hung up, and handed the results to Daryl. He lives in Fort Myers," Tommy said. "How far is that?"

"It's just up the west coast of Florida; there's a direct flight, I think. If not, there's one to Naples, and it's not much of a drive from there."

Tommy grinned. "I got to go to L.A.; you can have this one."

"Thanks a lot," Daryl said.

Daryl flew to Naples, rented a car, and was in Fort Myers by noon. He grabbed a hamburger, then found the colonel's address, which turned out to be one of an attractive group of condominiums across the road from the beachfront hotels. He found the apartment and knocked.

A gray-haired but very attractive woman answered the door. "Yes?" she said.

Daryl thought she must have been a knockout when she was twenty-one. "Good morning, ma'am," Daryl said, "I'm looking for Colonel Morrell."

"He isn't in right now," she said. "I'm Mrs. Morrell; may I help you?"

"I'm afraid not, ma'am; I'll have to talk to the colonel himself."

"With regard to what?" she asked.

Daryl produced his badge. "It's a police matter," he said.

The woman's face fell. "Police?"

"It's a routine inquiry, ma'am, in connection to somebody he served with."

"Oh," she said, looking relieved. "Well, he's playing golf." She looked at her watch. "He should be finishing his round soon, and he'll have lunch at the clubhouse." She gave Daryl directions. "By the way," she said, "it's *General* Morrell; he retired as a brigadier. You won't get a thing out of him if you call him Colonel."

Daryl thanked her and returned to his car.

The golf club was less than five miles away, and, after identifying himself to a security guard, he was directed to the clubhouse. He asked for General Morrell at the pro shop, and the young man pointed outside to two men who were sitting on a bench, removing their golf shoes.

Daryl went outside. "Excuse me, gentlemen, is one of you General Jacob Morrell?"

The older of the two men removed his cap and wiped his head with a towel. He still had a whitewall haircut, even in his mid- sixties. "I'm Jack Morrell," he said. "Let's not bother with rank."

"I wonder if I could speak to you in private, Gen . . . Mr. Morrell."

"This is Mark Haber, an old comrade-in-arms," the general said, nodding to the slightly younger man on the bench beside him. "I don't have anything to hide from him."

Daryl produced his badge. "My name is Daryl Haynes; I'm a police officer. I'm looking for information about a man who served under you."

"I served with thousands of men," the general said. "Might not remember him."

"His name is Merkle Connor."

The general's face darkened. "Good God, he's not living in Fort Myers, is he?"

"No, sir, I'm with the Key West department."

"Is the sonofabitch in trouble with the law?" he asked. "I hope so."

"I can't go into that, sir; I just want to ask you some questions about him."

"What sort of questions?" The general was becoming more and more uncomfortable as they talked.

"Well, sir, Mr. Connor's service record shows

that he was court-martialed in Vietnam, but the charges were dropped and he was transferred. Will you tell me what that was about?"

The general suddenly stood up. "No, sir, I will not. This conversation is at an end." He turned to his companion. "Mark, I'm going to have a piss; I'll meet you in the grill." With that, he turned and strode into the clubhouse.

Daryl stood, gaping, looking after him. "What happened?" he asked the other man.

"Don't mind Jack," he said. "He gets wound up about certain things. Sit down, and I'll tell you what you want to know."

Daryl sat down and turned his attention to the man. "I'm sorry, sir, your name is Haber?"

"That's right; I was Jack's executive officer in Saigon and at two other posts."

"Did you know Merkle Connor?"

"I did; he worked directly for me, operating a tennis instruction program at the club there."

"Can you tell me what sort of an officer he was?"

"Lousy. He angled his way into Special Services, and he was okay with the tennis program, but that was it. He had a real problem with authority of any kind, and he was always in trouble, always just on the edge of insubordination."

"What led to his being court-martialed?"

"He was screwing Jack Morrell's wife," the man said.

Daryl's mouth dropped open. "I met her half an hour ago."

"Then you can see that she was quite something when she was younger. She still is, in fact."

"Yes, sir, she certainly is."

"Connor had been screwing everything in skirts, and Jack had always thought it was funny, until he caught him in bed with Nadia. He would have shot Connor if the lieutenant hadn't been quick on his feet. As it was, Jack brought charges the next morning—conduct unbecoming."

"Why were the charges dropped?"

"I talked Jack out of it, convinced him that a court-martial would be an enormous embarrassment. He finally agreed, then did his best to get Connor transferred to a combat assignment. Nobody would have him; he didn't have any real combat training. I finally got him sent to the Aleutians—it was September, and winter was coming—and I saw to it that he served out his hitch there in an engineering company." Haber grinned. "His CO, who was an old friend of mine from the Academy, put him to work setting explosive charges on a road they were blasting out of rock. For two years, he never knew if he would live through the working day. I sort of liked that. Jack and Nadia made their peace, and I don't think he's heard Connor's name mentioned since then, until you came along."

"I'm sorry I upset him," Daryl said, "and I thank you for the information. Is there anything else you can tell me about Connor's character?"

Haber thought for a minute. "He was always getting into fights—you know, barroom stuff, the sort of thing you would expect of a combat enlisted man. I got him off with the MPs twice. I'd say, on the whole, he was a very screwed-up young man."

Daryl stood up. "Thank you, sir; I appreciate your help. Please apologize to the general for me."

"I'll buy him a couple of drinks, and he'll get over it," Haber said.

The two men shook hands, and Daryl was on his way back to Key West.

CHAPTER

44

When Chuck got home from work the yellow catamaran was once again moored next to *Choke*, and Meg, her brother, Dan, and his new girlfriend were seated in the cockpit, drinking margaritas.

"Come aboard," Meg called, with a wave. "Dan, get another glass for Chuck."

Chuck hopped aboard and flopped down in the cockpit, gratefully accepting the frosty glass. "I'm whipped," he said. "I've got this kid, Billy Tubbs, who wants to be a pro, and he's gotten to the point where he beats me half the time, and the other half it nearly kills me to win."

"Chuck," Meg said, "you haven't met Charlie."

Chuck turned to the girl and stuck out his hand. "Charlie what?"

"Just Charlie," she said, shaking his hand. She was petite and dark-haired, with a gamine figure that looked wonderful in the bikini. "I never saw the need for last names."

"I guess you have a point," Chuck said, "but how do you differentiate yourself from all the other Charlies?"

She smiled. "I've never had that problem."

Everybody laughed.

"I guess not," Chuck conceded.

"Present company excepted," Meg said, snuggling up to Chuck.

"Where you from, Charlie?" Chuck asked.

"Grew up in the San Fernando Valley; lived in L.A. and Las Vegas for a while after school. Recently I've just been traveling."

"Where'd you travel?"

"From Vegas I worked my way east, stopped in Santa Fe and New Orleans, then went down to Miami. I was in the Bahamas when I met Dan and Meg. Not a moment too soon, either; I was broke."

"It's just as well I'm back on *Choke*," Meg said. "It was getting a little crowded, anyway, and it wouldn't have been long before Dan and

Charlie would have ditched me on a beach somewhere."

"Damn right," Dan said. He held up the empty margarita pitcher. "Shit, and I'm out of lime juice."

"I've got to go to the Waterfront Market for a few things anyway, so I'll get you some," Chuck said. "Meg, why don't we invite this lovely couple aboard *Choke* for dinner?"

"Suits me."

"I'll pick up some steaks at the market, and you go rustle up a salad; the fixings are in the fridge."

"I'll take a shower, if we're going out," Dan said. "Charlie, we need a few things, too. Why don't you go along with Chuck?" He handed her some money, which Charlie tucked into her bikini bra.

Chuck and Charlie strolled along the quay to the Waterfront Market, chatting idly.

"What do you think of Key West?" Chuck asked.

"It has more character than most places on the water," Charlie replied. "Places on the water always remind me of Vegas."

"But Las Vegas is in the desert," Chuck said.

"The ocean is a desert; hadn't you ever noticed?"

Chuck shrugged. "I guess maybe it is, in a way. The sea is full of life, like the desert, but the life is hidden, as in the desert."

"Key West isn't Florida, either," Charlie said. "It hasn't been paved over yet."

"They're working on it," Chuck replied. "But at least there are others trying to keep it the way it is. If I stay here long enough, maybe I'll try to help."

In the market they each got a basket and went their separate ways, stocking up. Chuck had chosen the steaks and selected a couple of bottles of wine and was headed for the register when Charlie appeared from behind a shelf, looking flustered.

"Something wrong?" Chuck asked.

"I just saw somebody I used to know and don't want to know anymore. Let's just stay here for a minute until the coast is clear."

"You wait here; I want to get some bread." Chuck left her with her cart and went toward the baked goods counter. He was nearly there when Clare Carras passed in front of him, heading for the checkout and looking neither to her left or right. Chuck was happy she hadn't seen him; he had no desire to talk to her. He got the bread and went back for Charlie.

"Was it a woman you were avoiding?" he asked the girl.

"You could say that," Charlie replied. "You could also call her a snake."

"Is her name Clare Carras?"

"It was Clare Connor when I knew her."

"She's checked out by now; the coast is clear."

They paid for their groceries and started back to the boat.

"Where did you know her?" Chuck asked.

"In Vegas; she was a pro."

It took Chuck a moment to figure out that she wasn't talking about tennis. "You mean she was a hooker?"

"No, *I* was a hooker; she was my boss."

"Oh?" Chuck said, his eyebrows going up.

"Don't be so shocked," Charlie said. "Dan knows about it; it's okay with him."

"I didn't mean to seem shocked," Chuck replied. "It's just that I was . . . "

"Shocked," Charlie said.

"Okay, shocked."

"Clare was running a string out of the Empress Hotel, and she was married to the tennis pro at the hotel. She was an absolute bitch."

Chuck stopped and looked at her. "What was the tennis pro's name?"

"Connor, I guess. I never knew his first name."

"That is really strange," Chuck said. "The guy I work for here is named Connor, and he's a tennis pro."

"Probably not the same guy," she said.

"Probably not." Chuck was thinking about that.

"Go ahead, ask me," Charlie said.

"What?"

"Ask me the question."

"What question?"

"The one every man asks me: What was it like being a pro?"

"Okay, what was it like being a pro?"

"It was fun."

"*Fun?* I always thought it would be damned hard work."

"Well, the hours could be long, but the money was great, and the sex was good."

Chuck stopped in his tracks. "The sex was good? Even when you were . . . "

"Doing it all the time? Sure it was. Most of the girls I knew—those who weren't dykes—were in it for the sex."

"Not for the money?"

"Sure, for the money, too, but think about it: If you like sex, and I sure do, then you can have all you want by turning pro. People are always saying—if they like their work—that they would do it even if they weren't being paid for it."

"I guess I've always thought about my work that way," Chuck admitted. "I've always enjoyed it."

"So did I," Charlie said. "Do you think that makes me a bad person?"

"No, I guess I don't."

"Good," she said, apparently satisfied.

"Clare was your madam, huh?"

"That's right."

"Did she ever . . . "

"Turn tricks? I'm not sure I would call it that—not for the kind of money she got for it."

"What kind of money?"

"Well, most of us were in the two-to-five-hundred bracket," Charlie said. "Then there were a few absolute knockouts who got a thousand to fifteen hundred, but Clare, rumor had it, got five grand a pop."

"*Five thousand dollars?*"

"For an hour."

Chuck wondered what his tab would have been if he had been paying. "That's astonishing."

"Well, it was just a rumor among the girls. We never knew for sure, but once in a while—every couple of weeks or so—some dandy john would turn up, and Clare would disappear with him—always for a drink, she would say."

They had reached *Choke* and were ready to go aboard.

"Charlie," Chuck said, "would you do me a favor?"

"What kind of favor?"

"There's a guy I know I'd like you to meet."

"No thanks, Chuck, I'm out of the game," she said.

"No, you don't understand; he's a cop, not a potential client."

"Is this connected with the trouble you're supposed to be in?"

"Yes."

"Well, if I can help, sure."

"Thanks, Charlie; I appreciate it very much."

"No problem."

They went aboard and Chuck surrendered the steaks to Meg. All through dinner he thought about what Charlie had told him, but he couldn't make any sense of it. Maybe Tommy Sculley could.

CHAPTER

45

Tommy and Daryl had just taken seats in the chief's office when the chief's secretary came in. "There's a Chuck Chandler to see you," she said to Tommy.

"Chief," Tommy said, "do you mind if we see Chandler before we bring you up to date?"

The chief leafed through his calendar. "In an hour and a half," he said.

"Yes, sir," Tommy said, and led the way from the room. Chuck was in the foyer with a very pretty woman. "What's up?" Tommy asked.

"There's some new information you ought to know about," Chuck replied. "Can we talk somewhere?"

"Sure, follow me." Tommy led them to an interrogation room, and everybody took a seat.

"This is Charlie," Chuck said. "Detectives Sculley and Haynes."

"How do you do?" Tommy said.

"Tommy, Charlie is living aboard the boat next to mine, and yesterday we were in the Waterfront

Market when we saw Clare Carras. Charlie, tell him what you told me."

Tommy listened, rapt, as Charlie told her story, not interrupting her. When she had finished he sat there grinning.

"Is this helpful?" Chuck asked.

"Very possibly," Tommy replied. "Folks, I thank you for the information, and I'll be in touch." He stood up and shook Charlie's hand.

"Aren't you going to ask Charlie any questions?" Chuck asked.

"Charlie is a very thorough young lady," Tommy said. "If we need to know more we'll get ahold of her. And Charlie, I'd appreciate it if you'd let me know if you should decide to leave town."

"Sure," Charlie said.

"Let's start again," Tommy said to the chief. "We've just had some new information that's very interesting."

"I'm glad to hear it," the chief said. "Tell me."

"At our last meeting I told you my theory of another man who helped Clare Carras murder her husband."

"I remember," the chief replied.

"Now we think we may know who the man is."

"I'm all ears."

"Listen to this: the Olde Island Racquet Club is run by a man named Merkle Connor, called Merk. We looked into his background and learned that he has a history of playing around with other men's wives. In fact, it almost got him court-martialed when he was in the army. He was having it off with his commanding officer's wife."

"Interesting parallel," the chief said.

"Right, and there's more. As a result of his philandering, Merk got shipped up to the Aleutians, where his daily work was setting explosive charges on a road they were building."

"Ties in nicely with the exploding yacht, doesn't it?"

"Right. And remember, when the yacht went up, both Chuck Chandler and the other instructor, Victor Brennan, were having dinner with the Carrases at Louie's."

"But not Merk."

"Not Merk."

"I like this, Tommy."

"There's more, Chief. We've just had the most enormous break in tying this all together. A girl who's visiting on the island recognized Clare Carras in the grocery store. She knew Clare from Las Vegas and said that the lady was a high-class madam there, and get this, she was married to a tennis pro named Connor."

"Our boy Merk?"

"That's my guess, Chief."

"They're divorced now?"

"Right. We knew that Merk had gotten clobbered financially in a divorce, but we had no idea it was a divorce from Clare."

"So they got back together?"

"It's happened before. How many guys get divorced, then marry their ex-wives again? Happens all the time."

"Except this time, the lady already had a husband."

"A very rich one. From the fruits of our search of the Carras place, we know he was worth at least fifteen million, and I suspect he had a lot more hidden."

"You going to pull in Merk Connor, then?"

"I don't think we're ready for that, Chief."

"Why not?"

"The usual: no material evidence."

"Bring him in and sweat him, then, see what he has to say for himself."

Tommy shook his head. "If we do that he'll just deny everything, and we're in no position to prove he's done anything. Right now, our strongest card is that Clare Carras and Merk Connor don't know that we know about their connection. I think we're better off keeping an eye on both of them and waiting for something to happen."

"Wait for *what* to happen?" the chief demanded.

"For them to make a mistake of some kind."

"*A mistake of some kind?* Tommy, you're driving me nuts."

"I'm sorry, Chief, but we have to play this game with the cards we're dealt, and right now our hand just isn't strong enough."

"Okay," the chief said, "then it's my deal.

Here's what you're going to do, and I don't want to hear a word of objection from either of you, understand?"

"Yes, sir," the two detectives said simultaneously.

The sun was low in the sky as Tommy and Daryl pulled up to the Olde Island Racquet Club. They could see Chuck Chandler as he ended a lesson and walked from the court toward the clubhouse.

"Come on," Tommy said.

"I wish I knew this was the right thing to do," Daryl replied.

"We've got our orders; let's make it look good."

"Is Merk in the office, do you think?"

"He usually is."

Tommy led the way past the courts and into the clubhouse. Chuck was talking to his student about a racket and how it should be strung. Merk was in his office working at the computer.

"Let's wait 'til he's done," Tommy said in a low voice. He pretended to be interested in some sweat socks on a display.

Merk turned at his desk and saw Tommy; he got up and came out from behind the counter. "Hi, can I help you guys?"

"We just want a word with Chuck," Tommy said. "When he's finished." He watched Merk go back to his desk.

The student thanked Chuck for his advice and left the clubhouse.

Chuck turned and saw the two detectives. "Hi, Tommy," he said. "What's happening?"

Tommy stepped up to the counter. "Chuck, you're under arrest for the murder of Harry Carras."

"What?" Chuck said weakly.

"You have the right to remain silent; you have the right to an attorney; if you can't afford an attorney, one will be appointed by the court to defend you; if you choose to talk to us, anything you say may be used against you in a court of law. Do you understand these rights?"

"Tommy, you can't believe . . . "

"Do you understand these rights?"

"Yes, I understand."

"Chuck, let's do this quietly. Now, I'll forgo the handcuffs if you'll give me your word not to make a disturbance."

"Well, sure I will, but . . . "

"You want to get some street clothes on?"

"Yes, thanks."

"Daryl, go to the locker room with Chuck." Tommy watched the two men leave the room. He leaned against the counter and waited. After a moment, Merk, who had heard everything, got up from his desk and walked over to the counter.

"Tommy, did I just hear right?" Merk asked.

"You did, Merk."

"You really think he did it?"

"That's where new evidence leads us. I can't comment further than that."

"Jesus," Merk said under his breath.

"What?"

"I was just wondering where I'm going to get somebody on short notice to take his classes."

Merk, Tommy thought, *you're a sweet guy.*

CHAPTER

46

Tommy looked at Chuck in the rearview mirror. He was wiping sweat from his face with a towel. "Chuck, listen to me," he said.

Chuck looked up, and his face was haggard.

Tommy pulled over. "You drive," he said to Daryl. He got out of the car, then into the back seat with Chuck. "This is not as bad as it seems," he said. Daryl drove off.

"What do you mean?" Chuck asked. "It's hard to see how it could get any worse."

"We're not going to the station; we're going directly to the courthouse. Your lawyer is meeting us there."

"I don't understand," Chuck said.

"The chief has spoken to the D.A. and the judge. You're going to be arraigned in chambers and released on bail. You'll spend the night at my house, then you'll go back to work tomorrow morning."

"Now I really don't understand," Chuck said.

The judge did not seem at all happy about the proceedings. "This is the damnedest thing anybody has ever asked me to do," he said. "Do you people think a murder charge is some kind of game?"

"No, sir," the D.A. said. "I'm acting at the request of the chief."

"Chief, do you want to tell me what is going on here?" the judge demanded. "You come in here wanting an arraignment in chambers for a first-degree murder charge, and you want the suspect released immediately on bail of a hundred thousand dollars? For a capital charge?"

"Judge, we don't believe that Mr. Chandler committed this murder."

"Then why the hell did you arrest him? What the hell is he doing in my court?"

"I'll let Detective Sculley explain," the chief said.

Tommy stepped forward. "Your Honor, we're at an impasse in this case. There is circumstantial evidence weighing against Mr. Chandler, but we believe the murder to have been done by other parties. We believe that these parties have caused it to seem that Mr. Chandler is guilty and that they are waiting for his arrest before making their next move."

"And what is their next move?" the judge asked, clearly very interested now.

"We don't know, Your Honor, but we believe they may do something that might incriminate them."

"So this isn't really an arrest?"

"Officially, it is; unofficially, Mr. Chandler will only appear to be booked for the crime. Nothing will go on his record, which is exemplary, as far as we are concerned."

"Is there any material evidence against Mr. Chandler?"

"There is, but we believe it to have been planted by the other parties."

The judge turned to the D.A. "Is it your intention to *try* Mr. Chandler?"

"Oh, no, sir," the D.A. responded. "It won't go that far; we'll just drop the charges and issue a statement vindicating Mr. Chandler—once we have the real culprits."

"The real culprits," the judge repeated tonelessly.

"Yes, sir," the D.A. replied.

"Well, I've certainly never been involved in anything like this," the judge said, "but I'm looking forward to seeing how it's all resolved."

"So am I, Judge," the D.A. said.

"All right, Mr. Chandler, you've been duly arrested and charged with murder in the first degree. How do you plead?"

Chuck looked at his lawyer.

"Not guilty, Your Honor," the lawyer said. "Request bail."

"Mr. Chandler, you are hereby released on

one hundred thousand dollars bond." He looked around at the others. "Is that what you all want, gentlemen?"

There was a murmur of assent from the group.

"That's correct, Your Honor," Chuck's lawyer said. "We've completed the paperwork for a property bond." He laid the documents on the judge's desk.

"Wonderful," the judge said, signing the documents, "just wonderful."

Chuck sat at the dinner table in Tommy and Rosie's new house and ate pasta.

"So, Chuck," Rosie said, "how you been?"

"Okay, until tonight," Chuck replied, twirling spaghettini on his fork. "Let me tell you something, you haven't experienced life until you've been arrested on a capital murder charge."

"I'm sorry I had to put you through that, Chuck," Tommy said, pouring him some more wine, "but we had to make it look good for Merk. Nothing I could have said would have been as effective as the look on your face when I read you your rights. If you had known what we were up to, it wouldn't have worked."

"And now you want me to go back to work tomorrow morning?"

"Right. There'll be a story in tomorrow morning's *Key West Citizen* announcing an arrest, but withholding your name."

"You think Merk will take me back?"

"Why not? No one knows but him. And

anyway, the last thing he said to me had to do with finding your replacement." Tommy looked at Chuck's plate. "You finished?"

"I couldn't eat another bite," Chuck said.

"Then why don't you call Merk now and tell him you'll be at work tomorrow? After all, we wouldn't want him to replace you."

"Okay. How will I explain being out of jail?"

"Tell him you're calling from the jail, that your lawyer has arranged bail and that you're being released early tomorrow morning," Tommy said. "I'll get on the extension."

Chuck dialed the number and waited for three rings.

"Hello?"

"Merk? It's Chuck."

"Chuck? Where are you?"

"I'm at the jail on Stock Island, but I'm being released tomorrow morning, so I wanted to let you know I'll be at work at nine, as usual."

"As usual?" Merk said. "Chuck, when the papers get hold of this, nobody is going to want to take lessons from you."

"Tommy is doing me a favor; he's not releasing my name to the papers, so nobody will know. Except you, of course. I'd appreciate it if you'd keep all this under your hat."

"Well, sure, Chuck; I guess you can keep on teaching, as long as it's kept quiet. When will the trial be?"

"Not for months."

"You can get through the season, then?"

297

"Through the summer, if you want me."

"Well, sure. I was already looking for somebody; I'll stop, though."

"Thanks, Merk; I'll see you in the morning." Chuck hung up.

Tommy came back into the room. "You know him better than I: how'd he sound to you?"

"Perplexed," Chuck said.

"That's what I thought," Tommy replied. "One more call to make; this one's mine." He looked up the number, held a finger to his lips, and dialed the number.

"Hello?"

"Mrs. Carras? This is Tommy Sculley; how are you?"

"I'm all right, Detective."

"I hope you'll feel better after what I have to tell you."

"I hope so, too," she said. "What is it?"

"We've arrested your husband's murderer."

"Well, that is good news," she said. "It's Chuck Chandler, of course."

"Yes, ma'am."

"I'm so relieved," she said. "I don't know what took you so long; I thought you would never arrest him."

"It's only recently that some physical evidence came into our hands; we had to have that before we could move," Tommy said.

"I suppose you'll want me to testify," she said.

"Yes, ma'am. The trial is probably going to be

some months away, though. His lawyer will do all the maneuvering he can."

"But there's no reason for me to stay in Key West, is there?"

"Oh, no, ma'am; not as long as we know where to reach you. Were you planning to leave?"

"As soon as I sell the house, maybe sooner; I've been thinking of doing some traveling."

"You go right ahead, ma'am; just leave us your itinerary."

"I'll do that, Detective. Thank you for letting me know." She hung up.

Tommy put the phone down and held up a thumb. "Now let's see what she does."

Clare dialed the number on her portable phone.

"Yeah?"

"They've arrested him," she said.

"I heard," he replied.

"The length of hose apparently did it."

"There was a mention of new evidence."

"We'll make our move soon."

"I'll look forward to it."

She hung up, took a deep breath, and sighed. "At last," she said aloud to herself.

CHAPTER

47

Chuck stood in front of the jail building on Stock Island and waited. He had been smuggled there earlier that morning in the back of Tommy's car, walked in one door and out another of the facility, and allowed to telephone for a ride. After a few minutes Meg drove up in the Porsche, and he got in.

"What's happened?" she said, kissing him.

"They arrested me for murder," Chuck said, "but there's nothing to worry about."

"*Nothing to worry about!*" she cried.

"Please, Meg, just drive back to Key West Bight; I'll try and explain on the way."

"I rode my bicycle to the tennis club and got the car. I'll have to ride back with you to get the bike."

"Fine, I appreciate your doing this."

"I don't understand how you can be so calm," she said, thrusting the morning paper at him. The headline read:

ARREST IN CARRAS MURDER

Chuck quickly scanned the story to make sure his name wasn't mentioned. "Whew!" he said when he had finished. "I'm not calm, believe me. I'm more than a little scared."

"Start explaining," she said.

Chuck explained. While doing so he made a great effort to follow Tommy's instructions and not look over his shoulder to see if anyone had taken note of his leaving the jail.

He was at the tennis club on time, showered and ready to teach. Merk was at his desk as usual.

"Everything okay?" Merk asked.

"I think so," Chuck replied.

"I don't know how you can be so calm about this. I'd be a nervous wreck."

"I'm not calm, but I'm glad you thought so. If I can just get through the day with my students, I'll be all right."

Victor walked into the clubhouse. "Hey, Merk told me what happened. I'm sorry; anything I can do?"

"I don't think so. I made bail, and I'm out until the trial rolls around."

"What's your lawyer saying about your chances?"

"He's not telling me a lot, just not to worry. Fat chance of that."

"He's right, though; you've got to get through this somehow, and worrying isn't going to help," Victor said. "Well, my clinic is gathering on the court. You let me know if I can do anything— and I mean *anything*—to help."

"Thanks, Victor," Chuck said. He got his

racquet and went out to his lesson. He noticed that in spite of hearing what Victor had said, Merk had made no offer of help.

At the end of the day, Victor approached Chuck. "Can I buy you a beer, buddy?"

"Tell you what, Meg is back; why don't you come aboard *Choke* for dinner? You can bring the wine, and a girl, if you can find one."

"Love to, and I'll bring the wine, but it's a little short notice for a girl."

"We'll have you all to ourselves, then," Chuck said. "Seven o'clock?"

"Seven it is," Victor replied. "Red or white?"

"Both; why take chances?"

At seven, Victor rapped on *Choke's* hull with a wine bottle. "Prepare to repel boarders!" he shouted.

"Did you bring the wine?" Chuck called from below.

"Yep."

"Come aboard, then."

The three of them dined on pasta and pork chops, and both bottles of wine vanished in due course.

"What did Merk have to say to you?" Victor asked, draining the last of his red.

"Not much; his principal concern seemed to be that none of the customers find out that I got busted."

"Well, he's got a business to run, I guess," Victor said, "whereas all you and I do is show up."

Meg found another bottle of wine and refilled their glasses. "I think Merk's a shit."

"He's not so bad," Victor said.

"Oh, Victor," Chuck said, "you never speak ill of anybody."

"Well, not while they're around, anyway. Merk's been okay to me, though, and I know him pretty well by now."

Chuck drew on his new glass of wine. Much of the stress of an awful twenty-four hours had drained from him, and he was feeling loose. "I'll bet I can tell you something about Merk you don't know," Chuck said.

"I don't see how you could," Victor said. "After all, I've been around here for a couple of years, and you're the new boy."

"Still," Chuck replied.

"You got any brandy?" Victor asked.

"Would you get some cognac, please, Meg? The cheap stuff; it's for Victor."

Meg brought a bottle of Courvoisier and three glasses to the table and poured them all a slug.

"So, Chuckster," Victor said, "what could you possibly know about Merk that I don't? You been sleeping with him?"

"Not likely," Meg said, resting her head on Chuck's shoulder. "I've been taking up all his time and talent."

"You told me once that Merk's ex-wife had

stripped him of most of his worldly goods," Chuck said, sampling the brandy.

"I told you, and it's true," Victor said.

"Do you know who the ex-wife, the holder of his former goods, is?"

Victor blinked and had some brandy. "It was before he came to Key West," he said. "Before I won his confidence. A lady in another part of the world."

Chuck shook his head slowly. "Nope," he said, grinning. He sipped his brandy.

"Nope, what?" Victor asked, his eyes half closed. "Jesus, this is good cognac."

"I brought it from the Bahamas," Meg said. "Duty free."

"Free is all that matters," Victor said. "Was I saying something?"

"No," Chuck said.

"Yes, I was; I just can't remember what."

"You were asking about Merk's ex-wife," Meg said helpfully.

"No," Victor said, wagging a forefinger at her, "*Chuck* was asking about Merk's ex."

"No, Chuck was *telling.*"

"Telling what?"

"About Victor's ex-wife."

"*I'm* Victor, last time I checked." He pulled out the waistband of his trousers and regarded his crotch. "Yup, I'm Victor. Who's the ex-wife?"

"Clare," Chuck said.

Victor squinted at him. "Clare?"

"Clare."

"She's *Harry's* ex-wife. Sorry, ex-widow. Widow."

Chuck shook his head. "Nope. Merk's."

"Merk's widow?"

"Ex-wife."

Having exhausted all the possibilities, Victor finally got it right. "Merk's ex-wife?"

"Right."

"Who?"

"Clare."

"Clare is Merk's ex-wife?"

"Now you've got it," Chuck said.

Victor grinned and looked at Chuck suspiciously. "You're shittin' me."

"I shit you not."

"*Merk and Clare?*"

Chuck nodded slowly.

Victor's eyes narrowed. "How do you know this?"

"Meg and I know somebody who knew them both when they were married, in Las Vegas."

"*Clare and Merk?*"

"Man and wife. Ex."

"Do you mean . . ." Victor paused and belched. ". . . that I am the *only* employee of the Olde Island Racquet Club who has not fucked the lovely Clare?"

"Only you can accurately draw that conclusion, Victor," Chuck said, enjoying Victor's astonishment.

"The story of my fucking life," Victor said. "Even in high school, the other guys got the beauties. I got the girl jocks. Is there any more brandy?''

Meg poured him some more, but withheld the glass. "Only if you stay here tonight," she said.

Victor drew himself up to his full height. "You think I can't drive?''

"That's what I think," Meg said. "You're sleeping in the saloon."

"If you insist," Victor said. "About the brandy, I mean."

"About sleeping in the saloon," Meg said firmly.

"Oh, all right. I'm very sure I could drive, but I'm not sure I could walk to the car." He turned and looked at Chuck again. "You really mean I'm the only one who hasn't fucked Clare?''

"Life is unjust," Chuck replied, sipping his brandy.

"It's unfair, too," Victor said glumly.

CHAPTER

48

Chuck was shaken awake at eight o'clock by Meg. "Come on," she said, "you'll be late for work."

He blinked in the morning light; his head felt very large. "Boy, did I overdo it last night," he said. "Is Victor still here?''

"He's trying to drink some coffee; I suggest you do the same," Meg said. "I'll make you some breakfast."

When Chuck emerged into the saloon Victor was holding a mug of coffee in both hands and staring at a plate of bacon and scrambled eggs.

"Eat it, Victor," Meg was saying, "it'll do you good."

"It'll do me *in*," Victor moaned.

"Eat."

He picked up a fork and tried.

Chuck sat down next to him, feigning good health. "So, pal, you tied one on last night, did you?"

"You could say that," Victor replied, gulping down some egg. "My best recollection is that you had a few, too."

"I guess," Chuck replied, downing some orange juice and trying to keep it there. And when Meg put down the plate of bacon and eggs, he couldn't look at it. "Okay, I guess I'm a tad hung over," he admitted.

"That makes me feel so much better," Victor said.

They arrived together fifteen minutes before the first student was due. After they were dressed, Merk called them into his little office. Chuck had to stand.

"I wanted to talk to both of you," he said.

"Does it have to be now, Merk?" Victor asked.

"It may as well be."

"What's up?" Chuck asked.

"I've decided to give up the Key West club and concentrate on Santa Fe. I've got a local investor out there who will finance fixing up the facilities, and I think by concentrating on the one place I can do better. Which leaves the Olde Island Racquet Club up for sale—the remainder of my lease, which runs another four years, the computer and office equipment, and the stock in the shop. You guys interested?"

Chuck and Victor looked at each other. "Yes," they said simultaneously.

"Okay, here's the deal, and I'm afraid there's no room for negotiation, it's take it or leave it. I want twenty-five grand for my lease and goodwill, plus fifty percent of the retail value of the shop goods—I reckon that comes to another fifteen grand. So it's twenty thousand apiece, and it's yours. I reckon if you both go on teaching and hire somebody to run the shop and keep the schedule and the books, you can make out okay. When the lease is up in four years, you'll have to renegotiate with the hotel, but I doubt if there'll be any competition for the lease. I'll stay on for a week and teach the computer program to whoever you hire to do the bookkeeping. What do you say?"

"You mind if we talk about it for a minute?" Chuck asked.

"Go right ahead."

Chuck pulled Victor into the locker room. "What do you think?"

"I've been expecting this, so I've already run the numbers, and it sounds good to me. Do you think Meg would do the inside job?"

"Probably. You want to do this?"

"Okay with me."

"I'm assuming you've got twenty grand," Chuck said, grinning.

"I can manage a check today."

"I can write a check on my brokerage account."

"That didn't get tied up for bail?"

"No, just the boat."

"One other thing, Chuck; are you going to beat the murder rap?"

"I didn't do it, so I'm going to beat it. Trust me on that, Victor."

They went back into the office. "You've got a deal," Chuck said, and they all shook hands on it.

Merk produced three copies of a short document. "This outlines what we've agreed. Please look it over."

The two pros both read the document. "Suits me," Chuck said, and Victor nodded. Everybody signed.

The two new partners took the court feeling their hangovers much less. During their lunch break they paid Merk, sealing the deal.

At the end of the day, Victor said, "How you feeling?"

"Pretty good, considering," Chuck replied. "I think I've sweated out my hangover."

"Me, too," Victor said. "Why don't you go get Meg, let's go to Louie's for dinner and do it all over again? I think we're due a celebration."

"You're on, partner."

The three of them sat on the rear deck at Louie's Backyard sipping vodka gimlets and perusing the menu.

"You know," Victor said, "I knew Merk was thinking about this, but I was worried about handling it on my own. I'm glad to have a partner; if the truth be told, I'm not a businessman."

"Bad news," Chuck said, "neither am I."

Meg looked up from her menu. "I am," she said, "and I've got some money to invest. I can run the shop and keep the books, and it seems to me there ought to be a kids' program. I could handle that; I used to teach tennis at a summer camp."

The two pros looked at each other, then Victor put his hand on hers. "Sweetie," he said, "I have the feeling you know a lot more about what you're talking about than either of us. Why don't we make it a three-way partnership?"

Meg beamed. "I think I can handle that," she said.

"Waiter," Chuck called, "three more vodka gimlets!"

When they left the restaurant they found themselves in possession of two cars and only one person, Meg, sober enough to drive.

"All right," she said, "pile into the Speedster; Victor, you're sleeping aboard *Choke* again."

"Your wish . . . et cetera, madam," Victor said, squeezing into the small space behind the two seats.

"We're not going to make a habit of this, though," she said, "partners or no partners."

"Yes, ma'am," Victor muttered, then began snoring.

Half an hour later, the three of them were in the same beds they had occupied the night before.

CHAPTER

49

Merk Connor left the tennis club later than usual and drove home. He unlocked the door of the little Conch house and picked up the mail, which had come through the slot in the door and was now scattered on the hall floor. He poured himself a rum and tonic and sat down to open what he expected would be nothing but bills.

Then, at the bottom of the stack, he found an envelope with no stamp and his name written in a flowing hand. He thought he recognized the handwriting, and anxiously he tore open the envelope. Inside he found a note and a check made out in his name in the amount of twenty-five thousand dollars, unsigned. He read the note; it was brief:

Bring this note to the Gulfstream marina on Stock Island at three A.M. sharp tomorrow morning, and I'll sign the check. Be sure you're not followed. I'll be in slip 19.

Merk looked at the check and thought about how far it would go to solve his financial problems. He put it back into the envelope and laid it on the end table, then went to change clothes.

Daryl was on his second night of watching Merk Connor, and he couldn't say he was enjoying the stakeout. He had a magazine, but he couldn't turn on the dome light to read it without attracting attention to himself, and the batteries were getting weak in his portable radio. He and Tommy were spread thin, what with watching both Merk and Clare Carras, so he had a long night to look forward to.

Then he saw, as he had the last time, a figure leave the back door of the house and vault over the fence. He got the car started, drove around the block to Duval, and, just as he had before, Merk emerged into the street and walked briskly west.

This time, Daryl stayed in the car. He followed Merk down the street, stopping from time to time and waving traffic around him, and when Merk turned into the same bar, Daryl drove to the corner and stopped, watching both entrances. When Merk did not emerge from either, Daryl parked the car, walked across the street, sat down in an outdoor cafe, and ordered coffee. Nobody was getting out of that bar whom he wouldn't see.

Two and a half hours later, Merk emerged from the door he had entered and walked back toward his house. Daryl followed him all the way, watching as he let himself in the back door. Twenty minutes later, one by one, all the lights in the house went off. Daryl settled in for the night watch.

At two-thirty A.M. the alarm went off, and Merk sat up in bed. He was hung over and sleepy, but he forced himself to get dressed. He was about to go out the front door when he remembered that he had been warned against being followed. With the lights still off he peeped through the venetian blinds in the living room and saw the car that had followed him earlier in the evening. It was strategically parked so as to cover both the front and rear entrances.

Merk thought for a moment, then picked up the envelope on the end table, put it into his pocket, and went into the kitchen. He opened a window on the side of the house opposite the car and stepped out into the night, leaving the window open so that he could reenter the same way. His motor scooter was in the garage with his car. He backed out the scooter and pushed it a block from the house before kicking the starter, then he headed toward Stock Island. The streets of Key West were eerily empty at this time of night, and he headed for the eastern end of the island, past the tennis club, toward the airport. From there he continued northward, over the bridge and onto Stock Island. He turned right at the first traffic signal, remembering that the marinas were at the end of this road.

He wasn't sure which one was the Gulfstream, but there was a large sign. He remembered then that this was an older marina that had silted over and was no longer useful for larger boats. He parked the scooter in the deserted parking lot and headed toward the pontoons, passing a sign that read NO LIVEABOARDS. A single bulb illuminated the entrance to the slips; after that it was dark, with no lighting for the pontoons, and he took care not to fall into the water. He could barely see the slip numbers painted on the pontoons.

Near the end of the pontoons, not far from the entrance to the marina, he came to number nineteen, which was occupied by a small cabin cruiser. Through drawn curtains, he could see a glimmer of light from inside. Not wanting to call out, he rapped sharply on the hull. There was no response. The boat was moored stern to, and he stepped lightly aboard. The cabin door was closed, and as he was about to knock on it a familiar voice said, "Come in."

Merk opened the door and stepped down into

the cabin. At first it appeared that there was no one inside. Straight ahead of him was a table on which there were a small lamp providing the only light, a bottle of Myers's rum, and a glass. Then Merk felt something cold and metallic on the back of his neck.

"Sit down, Merk," the familiar voice said, "and have a drink."

Merk was afraid for the first time, and he didn't move.

"No need to be worried," the voice said. "After we've talked for a while I'll sign the check, and you can go. Now sit down."

Merk seated himself at the table, his back to his host.

"Pour yourself a drink," the voice said. "A large one."

Merk picked up the bottle of rum and poured a stiff drink.

"More."

He poured until the glass was half full.

"Fill the glass to the brim."

Merk did as he was told.

"Now drink it."

"*All* of it?" Merk asked.

"Every drop. Get it down."

Merk began to drink, and it was not as hard to swallow as he had feared.

"Go on," the voice said. "It's your favorite, isn't it?"

Merk took a deep breath and finished off the glass.

"Now put the check on the table, and I'll sign it."

Merk reached into his pocket, produced the envelope, and placed it on the cabin table.

"Take it out of the envelope; the note, too."

Merk did as he was told. Then something heavy smashed into the back of his neck, and he fell into unconsciousness.

Daryl sipped coffee from his Thermos and waited for Merk to leave the house for the tennis club. At ten past nine he began to wonder what was wrong. The club opened at nine, and it was his information that Merk was always there first. He picked up his phone and called Tommy.

"It's Daryl. Merk is late leaving for work."

"Give it half an hour and call me back," Tommy said.

Daryl waited the half hour, sipping his coffee, then called back. "He's still in the house."

"Hang on, I'll call the number."

Daryl waited patiently until Tommy came back.

"No answer. I called the tennis club and got an answering machine."

"What do you want me to do?"

"Knock on the door; if there's no answer go in, if it's unlocked. Call me back."

Daryl got out of the car, walked down the street to the little house, and knocked loudly on the front door, trying to think of something to say if Merk answered. No answer. He tried the door and it was unlocked, so he stepped inside. "Merk?" he called out. No reply. He walked around the house, looked into the bedroom with its unmade bed, saw the mail on the end table, checked the kitchen. He got out his phone.

"Tommy?"

"Yeah?"

"He's not here, and there's an open window in the kitchen, on the opposite side of the house from where I was."

"Shit," Tommy said.

"What do you think?"

"I'm afraid to think," Tommy said, "because I think I've made a big mistake. Meet me at the tennis club *now.*"

Daryl hung up the phone and got going.

CHAPTER

50

Tommy and Daryl met in the parking lot of the tennis club at a quarter to ten, then went inside. The place was empty. They walked outside where both Chuck and Victor were conducting lessons and sat down at the courtside table. Shortly the two pros came over.

"Morning, Tommy, Daryl," Chuck said. "What's up?"

"You guys seen Merk this morning?" Tommy asked.

"No, he didn't show up," Victor said, grinning at Chuck. "Actually, I'm not surprised he took the morning off."

"Why?" Tommy asked.

"Because Chuck and I bought him out yesterday," Victor replied.

"Out of the club?"

"Yep. Merk said he wanted to devote full time to the Santa Fe operation. He offered us a deal, and we took it."

"Santa Fe?"

"Merk has an operation there, too. In fact, he told Chuck and me yesterday that he had an investor who would back a revamping of that club, and he had decided to spend all his time there. That's why he sold out to us."

Tommy looked at Daryl. "So Merk is leaving Key West, huh? What a surprise."

"What do you mean?" Chuck asked.

"Merk's not at home this morning. He went to bed last night, but he wasn't there this morning."

"I don't get it," Victor said.

"Did you give Merk any money yesterday?"

"We gave him twenty thousand each," Chuck said, "to seal the deal. He went to the bank at lunchtime to deposit the funds."

"How many cars does Merk have?" Daryl asked.

"Just one, the Chevy station wagon," Victor said. "That and a scooter."

"A scooter?" Daryl asked. "Where does he keep it?"

"In the garage with his car."

"What kind of scooter?"

"You know, one of those Japanese things that get rented all over town. Merk's was black, though, so he could tell it apart from all the rentals."

"I don't suppose you know the license number," Daryl said.

"That's easy," Victor replied, "it's Merk2. His car is Merk1."

"What's going on, Tommy?" Chuck asked.

"Never mind," Tommy said. "See you later."

The two detectives left.

In the car, Daryl asked, "What do you think?"

"There are two possibilities, as I see it," Tommy replied. "One, Clare and Merk have decamped together; or two, Merk is the schmuck who thought he could have Clare, and he was wrong."

"Have Clare again," Daryl said.

"Yeah, again." Tommy picked up the microphone. "Base, mobile four."

"Mobile four, base."

"I want a local APB on a motor scooter, probably Japanese, color black, license plate number mike, echo, romeo, kilo, one."

The dispatcher repeated the plate number.

"That's right; call me if somebody finds it."

"Roger."

"Over and out."

"What now?" Daryl asked.

"Let's go back to Clare's."

"Was she there all night?" Daryl asked.

"I saw her come home from the grocery store, I saw her lights go off about eleven, I saw her come out for the paper this morning. She was still there at eight-thirty."

"Bet you ten bucks she ain't there no more," Daryl said.

"I'm not taking that bet," Tommy replied.

They turned into Dey Street in time to see the big Mercedes back out of the driveway, Clare at the wheel.

"Drop back and tail her," Tommy said.

"At least she's still here," Daryl replied.

"Her bags may be in the trunk. Follow her."

They followed the Mercedes out Roosevelt Boulevard, where it turned into the parking lot of Scotty's, a huge building supply home improvement store. They sat a hundred yards away for half an hour, watched Clare get back into the Mercedes carrying a brown paper bag, then followed her back to Dey Street.

"Well, I'll be damned," Daryl said.

"Probably."

"Mobile four, base," the radio barked.

"Base, mobile four," Tommy replied.

"A black-and-white found your scooter at the Gulfstream marina on Stock Island."

"You know it?" Tommy asked Daryl.

"I know it."

"Thanks, base, over and out."

The black-and-white was waiting when they got there. There was a small pile of clothing on the footboard of the scooter.

"Thanks, guys," Tommy said to the two patrolmen. "You touch anything?"

"Not a thing," one of the cops said. "Can we go now?"

"Sure, we got it."

The two cops drove away.

Tommy picked up a polo shirt from the pile of clothing. He looked inside the collar. "Laundry mark says, 'Merk.'"

Daryl picked up the trousers and found a wallet. "It's Merk's. We got underwear, socks, and shoes here, too. Think he went for a swim?"

"I'm afraid he might have," Tommy replied. "Come on." He led the way to the dockmaster's shack at the head of the pontoon. A young man wearing nothing but cutoffs was inside, writing in a ledger.

"Morning," Tommy said, flashing his badge.

"What can I do you for?" the kid replied, gulping.

"Relax, we're not looking for weed."

The boy looked relieved. "I don't use the stuff myself."

"Yeah," Tommy said. "What's it like around here at night?"

"Pretty quiet." The boy pointed at a sign. "We

don't have no liveaboards. Mostly we got private fishing boats and that kind of thing."

"Any boats missing from the marina this morning?"

"Three or four have gone out since I been here; I came on at nine."

"I mean, any boats missing, like stolen?"

"Funny you should mention that," the kid replied. "A guy complained that a little Whaler and outboard was gone; looks like it was stolen."

"Any idea what time?"

"It was here when I closed up at seven last night, and it was gone this morning when I got here."

"You get many transients in here?" Daryl asked.

"Nah, they go to the other marinas where they got fuel, water, power, like that. All we got is slips."

"So everybody here is a local?"

"Pretty much; I don't know any boats that ain't."

Tommy pointed at the black scooter. "You see that come in here?"

"Nope, it wasn't here last night, but it was here this morning."

"You know the guy who drives it?"

"Never seen it before today; most of 'em's red around here."

From the car there came the squawk of the radio.

"I'll get it," Daryl said, and trotted toward the car.

Tommy gave the boy his card. "Call us if you talk to anybody who saw that scooter arrive, will you?"

"Sure," the boy said, and stuffed the card into a pocket of his cutoffs.

Tommy arrived back at the car in time to hear Daryl sign off. "What's up?" he asked.

"The Coast Guard picked up a body out near the reef. White male, six feet, one-seventy, brown hair, nude."

Tommy sighed. "Let's go take a look at him," he said.

CHAPTER

51

Tommy and Daryl arrived at the morgue just as the medical examiner was about to begin his postmortem examination. The man was standing next to the body, gowned, with a large scalpel in his hand.

"Doctor," Tommy said, "I don't mean to trespass on your turf, but do you mind if I look him over for a minute before you cut?"

The ME stepped back. "Help yourself," he said. "You fellows want some coffee?"

Daryl was staring at the white, swollen corpse that had been Merk Connor. He shook his head.

"No thanks," Tommy said. "You have some, though."

The doctor stepped a few paces away, poured himself a cup, picked up a pair of surgical gloves, came back to the table, and handed them to Tommy.

"Thanks," Tommy said, pulling on the thin gloves. He began with the hands.

"I'd like to know what you're looking for," Daryl said. "Might come in handy sometime."

"Just logical stuff." Tommy lifted the right hand. "There's no bruising to the knuckles or fingers; no broken fingernails." He looked up at the doctor. "Got some gloves for my friend here?"

"Sure." The doctor tossed Daryl the gloves.

"You take the other side," Tommy said. "Check the hand."

Daryl picked up the left hand gingerly and peered at it. "Same over here," he said.

"So he didn't put up a fight. Now let's check for puncture marks at vulnerable places, like around the heart." Tommy stretched the water-swollen skin. "We're looking for something not too obvious, like an icepick wound." He checked the throat as well, then he went down the body, looking for other evidence. "Help me turn him over," he said to Daryl.

The two men gently turned the body until it was facedown, and Tommy repeated his close

324

examination. He stopped at the back of the neck. "Look what we got here," he said.

Daryl and the doctor stepped forward to see.

"We got—what would you call that, Doc, massive bruising?"

"That's close enough," the doctor said.

"At the base of the skull," Tommy continued. "Okay, somebody tapped him one with something heavy, but not hard—not hard enough to break the skin, anyway." He was parting the hair on the back of the head. "Yeah, the bruising is confined to an area about, what, two and a half inches?"

"What sort of object are you talking about?" the doctor asked.

"Classically, a blackjack, but this is a little large for that. It was just something heavy, like a large wrench or a piece of pipe, probably wrapped in cloth. I'll bet you'll find some fibers there on closer examination."

"Very good, Detective."

"Okay, that does it for me, Doc; let's turn him over again, Daryl, so the pro can get at him with the knife." The two detectives rearranged the body for the doctor. "All yours, Doc."

"Before I get started, why don't you give me your best guess, Detective?" the doctor asked.

"Okay," Tommy said. "We know he was alive around, what, midnight, Daryl?"

"That was the last time I saw him."

"So the time of death would range from the early hours of the morning until, well, before dawn. My guess, from the condition of the body, is he wasn't alive much more than an hour after he was hit on the back of the head. He was lured to the marina, slugged, undressed, taken out near the reef, and dumped. Cause of death, drowning, following trauma to the head. Oh, and he was probably highly intoxicated."

The doctor's eyebrows went up. "Why do you say that?"

"Because whoever killed him wanted us to think that he got drunk, went for a boat ride, and got himself drowned."

"Well," the doctor said, "I don't get much in the way of murder around here, and when I do, it's a straightforward gunshot or knife wound. I might have missed the bruising at the back of the head. It probably would have worked if you hadn't been here to educate me."

Tommy shrugged.

An assistant came into the room. "Here's the blood alcohol," he said, handing the doctor a slip of paper. "It's off the scale."

The doctor looked at the document. "Point four three; point one zero is legally intoxicated. If somebody hadn't hit him, he'd have passed out anyway." The doctor retrieved his large scalpel, inserted it at the point of the chin, and sliced down the body to the pubic hair, then opened the stomach, and the smell of sweet alcohol filled the air.

"Rum," Tommy said.

Daryl stepped away from the table, his hand over his mouth.

"Well, I think we've got all we need, Doc. I'll look forward to your full report." He placed a hand on Daryl's shoulder. "Come on, kid; let's get out of here."

"I wasn't expecting that," Daryl said when they were back in the car. "That move with the knife, all the way down his . . ." He put his hand over his mouth again.

"Yeah, that's always the first cut," Tommy said. "Take some deep breaths." He put the car in gear and drove away.

"Where we going?" Daryl asked when he had recovered himself.

"Let's go talk to Chuck and Victor," Tommy said.

"Why them?"

"Because they're all we've got. I'm Clare's alibi, so she didn't do it."

"Oh."

"Don't worry, your brain will start working again in a minute."

Tommy found Chuck, Victor, and Meg in the clubhouse, counting socks, shorts, shirts and tennis racquets.

"Chuck, we need to talk to you and Victor separately. Daryl, you talk to Chuck; Victor, you come with me." Tommy led Victor outside and pointed at a courtside chair. "Sit," he said.

"What's going on, Tommy?"

"It's time you and I had a real serious talk, Victor."

"Shoot."

"You were here all day yesterday, is that right?"

"Except when I went to the bank, late in the morning."

"How long were you gone?"

"Oh, half an hour, forty-five minutes, I guess. I had to cash a CD to pay Merk. You hear anything from him?"

"What time did you finish last night?"

"At six."

"What did you do then?"

"I went home, showered and changed clothes, then I met Chuck and Meg at Louie's for dinner. We were celebrating our buying the club."

"How late were you there?"

"Well, now, that's where things get a little fuzzy," Victor said ruefully. "We sort of tied one on."

"You don't know what time you left Louie's?"

Victor shook his head. "Meg was sober enough to drive; ask her."

"You went home, then?"

"No, we went to Chuck's boat."

"How long were you there?"

"All night."

"Drinking? All night?"

"No, I slept there, in the saloon. Second night in a row."

Tommy stared at the man. If his story held up,

then the list of suspects was at an end. "How long have you known Clare Carras, Victor?"

"Since they came to town, late last year, I guess. I think they started playing here almost as soon as they arrived."

"Did you know Clare before that?"

"No. You asked me all this before, Tommy."

"Ever been to Las Vegas, Victor?"

"Yeah, a couple of times."

"How long ago?"

"Let's see, it was a convention of a tennis association, two years ago. I was there a couple of years before that, too, at a tournament."

"Is that where you met Merk?"

"Right. On the second trip."

"You became buddies then?"

"Not exactly; we had a few drinks, had dinner once in a group of people."

"Did you meet his wife at that time?"

Victor shook his head. "He told me he was going through a divorce, though."

"Do you know who his wife was?"

"Yep. But not until just recently."

"How recently?"

"Night before last. I had dinner aboard *Choke* and Chuck told me."

"And it came as a surprise that Merk and Clare had been married once?"

"*Did it ever!* Knocked me right off my stool, I can tell you. I mean, Merk never let on, never said a *word* to me about her."

"Give me your background since college, Victor."

"I didn't go to college."

"All right, since high school."

"I taught at a tennis camp the summers of my junior and senior years, and again the summer after high school, then I went into the marines."

"How long did you serve?"

"Two three-year hitches."

"Where?"

"Parris Island, Camp Pendleton, a tour of Vietnam, then to Quantico, where I joined a service tennis team. After that, all I did was play tennis."

"After the marines?"

"I taught at half a dozen clubs up and down the eastern seaboard, mostly in Florida."

"How did you happen to come to Key West?"

"Merk called me. He remembered me from our meeting in Vegas and he offered me the job, winters in Key West, summers in Santa Fe."

Tommy leaned forward. "Tell me about Vietnam."

"I was in a rifle company; we got shot at from time to time."

"Were you ever in Saigon?"

"Yeah, a dozen times, I guess."

"Did you ever meet Merk in Saigon?"

Victor shook his head. "Nah, Merk was an officer, running a program at an officers' club. I never rose above corporal, so we didn't move in the same circles. I knew he was there, though; he told me the first time we met."

"Victor, did the Marine Corps teach you how to use a knife?"

"Sure, they taught everybody."

"Did you ever kill anybody with a knife?"

Victor shook his head. "I never got that close to anybody I wanted to kill. Mostly I fired an M-16 at jungle. The only Vietcong I ever saw were at a distance or dead. Tommy, what's this all about?"

"Merk's dead."

Victor looked absolutely flabbergasted. "When? How?"

"Late last night, drowning."

"*Drowning?* He was swimming late last night?"

"Boating," Tommy said. "He didn't do any swimming."

Back in the car, Tommy and Daryl compared notes.

"The three of them seem to have spent most of the last forty-eight hours together," Daryl said. "But Victor was sleeping in the saloon on the boat. He could have sneaked out in the night."

Tommy nodded. "But if he did, he's got Meg, who was pretty sober, to testify as to how drunk he was. It would take a lot of doing to leave *Choke* and, without a car, get to a marina on Stock Island, slug Merk, dump him out on the reef, get back to the ma-rina, then back to *Choke*."

"Maybe he didn't go back to the marina,"

Daryl said. "Maybe he brought his boat into Key West Bight, then boarded *Choke* again."

"Or," Tommy said, "maybe he *left* Key West Bight in a boat and drove around to Stock Island. How long would that take?"

"Well, I'd say no more than an hour, even at night, if he knew what he was doing."

"So he could have done it," Tommy said.

"It's not impossible, but what's his motive? He and Chuck just bought the tennis club from Merk yesterday, and the money was already in the bank."

"You've got a point. By the way, he knew about Merk and Clare."

"Yeah, Chuck told me he told him."

"I wish he hadn't told him," Tommy said.

"Why?"

"Because Merk *might* still be alive."

"That's pretty far-fetched, Tommy."

Tommy nodded. "I know."

"Tommy, not to criticize your surveillance work, but Clare might have gotten past you last night, just like Merk got past me."

"How would she get to the marina and back?"

"Merk had a scooter; maybe she has some transportation we don't know about. It's possible."

"*Anything's* possible," Tommy replied. "That's the trouble with this case."

"Tommy, you predicted this; you said she had a man who was helping her; you said she'd waste him as soon as we nailed Chuck. Well, we nailed

Chuck, she thinks, and she wasted him. It's obvious to me."

Tommy sighed. "I wish it were as obvious to me, kid."

CHAPTER

52

Tommy was awakened by the telephone before dawn, but Rosie got to it first.

"Hello?" she said sleepily. Rosie was used to answering the phone for Tommy in the middle of the night. She listened for a moment, then nudged Tommy with an elbow. "It's for you," she said.

"Who is it?"

"It's a *woman*," she said venomously.

Tommy sat up in bed and took the phone. "Tommy Sculley," he said.

"Tommy, it's Rita," a small female voice said.

"Who?" Tommy replied, although he knew very well who it was."

"Rita Cortez, in L.A."

"Oh, yeah, how are you? What is it, the middle of the night out there?"

"It's a little after two," she said.

"What's up, Rita?"

"You're going to be very angry with me."

"Why should I be angry with you?"

"I told them."

"Told who, and what?"

"About Key West. I told them."

"Start at the beginning, Rita, and tell me everything."

"These two guys showed up at my house, and they said they wanted to know everything about Barry's time in Florida."

"Whatshisname, the lawyer sent them?"

"They didn't mention his name, but who else?"

"What, exactly, did they ask you?"

"They knew Barry had been to Florida, because he was killed there, and they knew you were from Key West. What they didn't know was the tip that Barry got about Key West. But they know it now."

"Oh," Tommy managed to say. His mind was racing.

"They hurt me, Tommy; I wouldn't have told them, but they hurt me."

"I'm sorry, Rita; I wish I could have been there to help. Are you all right?"

"I think they broke my arm."

"Oh, shit; do you want me to get you some help there? I'll call somebody on the LAPD and get you some help."

"No, don't do that; they might still be around, and they swore they'd come back if I called the cops."

"But you need help."

"I can get myself to the emergency room; Mount Sinai isn't far from my place."

"Can you drive?"

"I can make it, don't worry about me; worry about you."

"*Me*, why?"

"Because the lawyer knows you're from Key West, remember? They knew it, too. They're going to want to know what you know about Barry and Marinello and the Carras woman."

"Where did you hear that last name?"

"Carras? They mentioned it."

"What did the two guys look like? Give me a description."

"One of them was sharp-looking, a slick dresser; I think it was an Armani suit; dark hair, not too long, slicked back, straight nose, good teeth, a ladies' man. The other one was just a gorilla—big, hairy, smelled of garlic—right out of . . ."

"A description, Rita."

"Six-three, two-forty, black hair going gray, thick hair on the backs of his hands, hair everywhere, bad nose job."

"Okay, got it."

"You watch out, Tommy; they might show up there."

"I'll watch out, Rita; now you get to the ER right away, you hear me? And call me if you need anything, and I mean *anything*." He hung up.

"*So?*" Rosie said, and she was seething.

"Shut up, Rosie, it's business."

Her mouth dropped open, and she turned over and put her face in the pillow. He had never talked to her that way before.

He patted her on the bottom. "I'm sorry, sugar, but it was bad news."

Tommy and Daryl stood in the arrivals lounge, such as it was—at Key West International Airport, a long shedlike building, no air-conditioning. The good thing about it was that every flight pulled up and emptied at the same gate.

The two detectives watched the last passenger through the door.

"Nothing fitting the description," Daryl said. "Come on, Tommy, we can't meet every flight."

"Just the late afternoon, early evening ones," Tommy said. "That's when passengers from L.A. would arrive."

"Tommy, there are more than a hundred flights a day into this airport, from Miami, Orlando, Tampa, Naples. We can't meet even the late afternoon, early evening ones and get anything else done. The chief isn't going to stand for it."

"I haven't said anything to the chief."

"Thank God for that. If he thought you'd pulled two mob palookas down on us, he'd blow a bearing."

"A fuse, Daryl; you don't blow a bearing."

"You know what I mean."

"There's another flight due in seven minutes, from Orlando. That's where I'd change planes, if I was coming from L.A. I'd avoid the mess at Miami International. Let's sit down."

They sat down.

"I don't get it, Tommy, why are you so het up about this? Are you protecting Clare Carras?"

Tommy turned and looked at him. "They hurt Rita, Daryl; she's no more than a hundred pounds, and these two pieces of shit broke her arm!"

"So, what can we do about it? Beat them up? That's big trouble for us. Arrest them? On what charge?"

Tommy looked at his watch. "Listen to that; it's early." The sound was the whine of turboprop engines as the airplane approached the ramp. Tommy got up and stood near where the passengers would pass. "Come on, Daryl; let's check it out."

Daryl went and stood next to him.

"You remember the description?"

"I remember."

"If you spot them, don't look right at them; pretend you're looking for somebody behind them."

"Right, Tommy," Daryl said wearily.

Tommy looked at Daryl in his jeans and Hawaiian shirt. "They'd never make you, anyway; they've never seen a cop like you." He laughed.

"Well, I'm glad you've still got your sense of humor," Daryl grumbled.

"Heads up!" Tommy said. "Lookahere."

There they were, the younger one still in his Armani suit, the gorilla in a sport shirt with the tails out, looking weary and grumpy. They were carrying overnight bags.

"Don't look at them," Tommy commanded out of the side of his mouth.

"All right, Tommy," Daryl said, "I'm not looking at them."

The two men passed within inches of the detectives. Tommy watched as they headed for the rental car counter. "The big one's renting the car—he's using cash; the younger guy is on the hotel reservation phone. Let's go get in the car."

They went out to the car, parked close to where the rental cars were. A few minutes later the two hoods left the airport building, walked across the street, and got into a Lincoln Town Car.

"If they booked a hotel room, they must not know where she lives," Tommy said. "Otherwise, they'd just go do what they gotta do, then get out."

"They're tired," Daryl said. "It was a long flight. Maybe they're going to wait until morning."

Tommy stayed well back. He could see the younger man in the passenger seat, consulting a map and giving directions.

Tommy followed the car down Roosevelt Boulevard, which turned into Truman. The car slowed, the map was consulted, and they turned right on Elizabeth.

"I think I know where they're going," Tommy said.

"You could be right."

The Lincoln drove down Elizabeth, crossed Caroline, turned left on Dey Street, and stopped.

"Uh-oh," Daryl said.

But the Lincoln was moving again.

"They were just having a look," Tommy said as the Lincoln began moving again. He followed the car as it turned right on Simonton, then, a couple of blocks later, into the beachfront hotel near the Treasure Island marina. "They'll be back in the morning, though."

"Tommy, we're not going to babysit them all night, are we?"

Tommy grinned. "We'll take turns, kid."

CHAPTER

53

Tommy relieved Daryl at ten, and Daryl headed toward home, tired. Then he pulled the car over to the curb and stopped. Something was nagging at him, something about Merk's actions on the night he was killed. He thought about it for a minute, then pulled back into traffic and drove toward Duval Street.

He could hear the music two blocks before he

got there. A dozen bars up and down the street were blaring competing music into the night. There was a noise ordinance, but it didn't seem to matter. He thanked heaven he lived on the other side of town.

He found a parking place and went back to the bar on the corner, entering through the back door. The place was packed, and the music was loud. It was full of gay couples and stags, and Daryl's entrance was noted by most of them. He found a spot at the bar and ordered a beer. When the bartender brought it back, Daryl leaned over the bar and shouted into the man's ear, "Who owns the place?"

"Why do you want to know?" the bartender shouted back, in what passed for a whisper in the crowded bar.

"I have a badge," Daryl said. "You want me to show it to you in front of all these people?"

The bartender held up a finger. "Wait a minute," he hollered. He walked to the opposite end of the bar, near the rear of the room, and spoke to a small man seated on a stool. After a few words the bartender looked back toward Daryl and waved him over.

When Daryl reached the end of the bar, the stool next to the little man had been vacated. The owner was slender and very blond; he reminded Daryl of a photograph he had seen on a book jacket of the young Truman Capote.

"So?" the man shouted.

340

Daryl leaned toward him. "Is there somewhere a little quieter where we can talk?"

The man wagged a finger at him. "Now why would I want to go somewhere quiet with a cop?" He waved an arm at the room. "Maybe there's somebody you'd like to be introduced to?"

Daryl leaned in again. "Do you know a man named Merk Connor?"

"Sweetie," the man said, "I know absolutely *everybody* who's worth knowing. Is this Merk worth knowing?"

"Not anymore," Daryl shouted. "This Merk is dead."

The little man's face went very white.

Tommy walked through the hotel slowly, looking for the two men. He found them in the restaurant, tearing into large steaks and starting a second bottle of an expensive-looking Italian wine. He ordered a club soda at the bar and watched them through the rest of their dinner. They said almost nothing to each other during the meal. Finally, the handsome one paid the check with cash, and they left the table and went up in the elevator. Tommy followed them to the lobby and watched the numbers stop at four.

He went to the front desk, which was manned by a short, middle-aged man with an extreme comb-over. "I need some information about two people who checked in earlier this evening," he said.

"We don't *normally* give out information about our guests," the man said.

Tommy sighed and placed his badge on the counter, saying nothing.

"But for *you* I'll make an exception," the man said. "What is it you want to know?"

"The two men in question just left the dining room and went up to the fourth floor. I want to see their registration cards."

The desk clerk riffled through a stack of cards and placed two on the counter.

"Mr. Oliver and Mr. Twist," Tommy said aloud. "Somehow I didn't expect literary allusions. Of Kansas City, Missouri. And I see they're paying cash, no credit cards."

"We get some funny names now and then," the desk clerk said. "Usually it's a couple of salesmen from Miami who aren't out of the closet yet and think they're being discreet. They always pay cash; they don't want their wives checking the credit card bills."

"What were your impressions of them?" Tommy asked.

"The nice-looking one did all the talking," the clerk said. "I got the impression that the big one could only grunt."

"Accent?"

"None that I could place."

"Education?"

The man grinned slightly. "None that I could place. Funny, I expected him to sound New Yorky, but he didn't. His grammar was less than perfect." He picked up a clipboard and ran a finger down a list. "They left a wakeup call for nine A.M."

"Late sleepers, huh?"

"He said something about jet lag."

"Right. I want a room for the night, preferably on the ground floor, and I'd like your very best rate."

"For you, it's comped," the man said. "Anything to help out our mighty men on the force."

"You're sweet," Tommy said, accepting a key.

"Right down the hall there, on your left. You can see the elevators, if you peek through the little hole in the door. That's what you fellows do, isn't it? Peek through doors?"

"All the time," Tommy replied. "Thanks." He turned toward the room, and as he did, Daryl came through the front door, trying to look inconspicuous. "What?" he said when the younger man approached.

"Let's talk," Daryl said.

"I just got a room; come on." Tommy led the way down the hall, conscious of the gaze of the night clerk, opened the door, and showed Daryl in. It was one of the hotel's better rooms, he suspected; it was large, had a seating area with a sofa and a pair of easy chairs, and sliding doors opened directly onto a small beach.

"Not bad," Daryl said. "How'd you do it?"

"I think the desk clerk liked me," Tommy said.

343

"Have a seat; I've gotta call my wife." He dialed the number.

"You didn't show for dinner," she said without preamble.

"I'm sorry about that, hon, but this case is heating up. I'm having to stay in a hotel over at the beach tonight; Daryl and I are following two out-of-towners."

"Oh, is one of them the person on the phone in the middle of last night?"

"Rosie, baby, she was calling from L.A. Her information led us to these two guys. Now, I don't have time to run it all down for you, but here's where I am." He gave her the phone and room numbers. "Daryl and I are both going to be here all night."

"So now I have to worry about Daryl?"

"Sweetie, sleep tight, don't let the bedbugs bite." He hung up. "I'm starving; you want something from room service?" He tossed a menu at Daryl.

"Who's paying?"

"The hotel."

"Caesar salad, prime rib, apple pie á la mode and a good red wine."

"Same here." Tommy called in their orders, then hung up. "I'm going to take a short walk on the beach," he said, going to the sliding doors and slipping off his shoes and socks.

"Tommy, we have to talk."

"We'll talk over dinner. Right now I have to think some, and by myself."

"Suit yourself," Daryl said, opening the minibar and choosing a tiny bottle of good scotch.

They were into the roast beef before Tommy would allow any discussion.

"Now, what do we have to talk about?"

"We're going to have to rethink the secret man theory," Daryl said. "At least where Merk is concerned."

"Yeah? Why?"

"I got to thinking when I left here. You remember, I told you that the first time I followed Merk, he went in the front door of a bar and out the back door, and I thought he had gone to Clare's house?"

"Yeah. So?"

"He went to the same place the night he was murdered, too, only he didn't go out the back door. As a matter of fact, he didn't go out the back door the first time, either."

"So where did he go?"

"Upstairs with the owner."

"To do what?"

"Tommy, it's a gay bar."

Tommy swallowed hard. "Oh."

"He's been seeing the owner, a guy named Wilson Pater, for several weeks on a regular basis."

"I never would have figured him," Tommy said.

"Seems Merk was not exactly out of the closet yet. Pater said he was a little hard to get the first time."

"Well, that does seem to cast a slightly different light on his relationship with Clare, doesn't it?"

"Pater said the reason she gave him such a hard time in the divorce was he admitted he liked guys. She apparently didn't take it well."

"She wouldn't, would she?"

"You think she was so mad she would knock him off?"

"Maybe. I'm still more inclined to think he was involved somehow, and she knocked him off to keep us from connecting them."

Daryl polished off his apple pie. "So where does that leave us?"

"Our two palookas left a nine o'clock call; I left one for eight. Let's get some sleep and see where they lead us tomorrow."

"Suits me," Daryl said. "I'm bushed."

They each took a double bed and were immediately asleep.

CHAPTER

54

Clare Carras had just finished dressing when the doorbell rang. She opened the door to her bedroom and walked down the hall to the front door. A young man, rather handsome, dressed in a good Italian suit, stood at the door. He smiled.

"Mrs. Carras?"

"Yes."

"My name is Parma. I was a business associate of your husband, kind of. I just heard about his . . . passing, and I happened to be in town, and I wanted to pay my respects."

"Thank you," she said. She had never heard of anybody named Parma, but he was very good-looking and quite charming.

"Can I come in a minute? I'd like to use your phone, if it's okay."

"Sure," she said, unlatching the screen door. He was rather attractive, and it had been a while. She led him down the hall, past a phone on a small table. "Come upstairs," she said. "It's more comfortable."

"Yeah," he said, "comfortable is good."

She reached the top of the stairs and turned, smiling, to show him to a sofa. She had not yet completed her turn and didn't see the backhand coming. There was a loud noise as he struck her below the right ear, and she spilled backward into the room, her thin cotton dress riding up over her thighs. She scrambled backward, trying to get to her feet, but he caught her with his open right hand, and she fell again.

He came and stood over her, smiling. "Nice legs," he said. He reached down, grabbed the front of her dress, hauled her to her feet, then sent her reeling toward a sofa.

She struck the sofa with some force, making it slide backward.

He walked toward her, then took hold of the coffee table between them and, with a quick motion, sent it flying across the room. A vase of flowers on the table smashed against a wall.

She held her hands out in front of her. "What do you want?" she asked, and her voice was nearly uncontrollable. Then she looked toward the door and, as frightened as she already was, she saw a man who frightened her even more. "Who is he?" she asked.

"Oh, this is my associate, Mr. Bones. He got that name because he likes breaking them. He tells me it's something about the sound they make."

"Please tell me what you want," she said.

Parma dragged the other sofa toward her, then sat down, facing her. He reached into an inside pocket and retrieved a small kitchen knife. He removed a paper sleeve, revealing a blade only about two inches long. "I bought it this morning," he said, "just for you." He ran his thumb along the blade. "Razor sharp."

"What do you want?" she pleaded.

"It's like this, lady. I'm going to ask you some questions about your husband and his money, and if I don't get answers that please me a lot, I'm going to start using this cute little knife on your very pretty face." He threw the knife at the floor between them, and it stuck in the wide planking. "Then I'm going to fuck you in several places, maybe some you're not used to, but you'll get to like it. Then Mr. Bones here is going to fuck you, and he's not nearly as nice about it as I am. After that, when I've finished using the little knife on you, no man is ever going to want to fuck you again, and I don't think you would like that, because I think you like being fucked a lot. Am I right about that?"

"What do you want?" she asked again.

"*Am I right about that?*" he screamed.

"Yes," she said, trying to control her voice and think.

"Yes, *what?*"

"I like being fucked."

"Good; I think we're starting to understand each other. Now, let's get started with the questions. Your husband's name used to be Marinello, or sometimes Marin. You knew that, didn't you?"

"No," she said weakly.

He stood up and unzipped his fly. "I'm going to let you take it out for me," he said.

"Yes," she said quickly. "He told me that used to be his name."

"That's better," Parma said. "Your husband, back when his name was Marin, took some money from some people, didn't he?"

"Yes, he told me he did." She had to draw this out as long as possible, until she could regain control of herself.

"Did he tell you how much?"

"Not exactly. He only hinted that there was a lot." She sat up, got her feet under her.

"Well, let me mention a figure. *Twenty-seven million dollars.* Does that have a familiar ring?"

"More," she said. "He had more than that when he died."

"Boy, *that's* good news," he said. "The people I work for are going to like that. Where is the money?"

"It's . . . invested," she said, shifting her weight to the front of the sofa cushion.

"Invested where? In what?"

"I'll get the papers," she said, rising and starting toward the small desk a few paces away. She managed to take three steps before he reacted and started for her.

She got the drawer open and whipped around, pointing the automatic at his head.

He stopped moving, realizing he had made a big mistake. He backed up a step. "Now, listen, lady; that's going to hurt more than it's going to help. Give it to me." He held out a hand. "Unlike me, it's not even cocked."

Quickly, she worked the action and got off a round at his head. It caught him in the throat, and he staggered backward, wide-eyed.

Then, out of the corner of her eye, she saw the big man coming at her. She whipped around, assumed a firing stance, and put two rounds into his chest, knocking him off his feet. When she was sure he couldn't get at her, she turned her attention once more to Parma, who was still standing, clutching at his throat with both hands, vainly trying to stem the spurting blood, which had soaked the front of his suit and was gathering in a large pool at his feet. She took a step toward him, the pistol held out at arm's length.

He tried to speak but couldn't. Instead, he shook his head, spraying blood around him.

She lowered the pistol and put a round into his crotch. He staggered backward, knocked over a table, and fell facedown, twitching.

Then, before she could relax, another man appeared in the living room door. Clare spun and fired two rounds in his direction. He dove to the floor, his hands held out in front of him.

"Clare! Don't! It's Tommy Sculley!"

The younger cop appeared behind Tommy, aiming a pistol at her. "Drop it, Mrs. Carras! Drop it right now, or I'll fire!"

Clare dropped the pistol and fainted.

Tommy laid her on a sofa and slapped her cheeks lightly. "Daryl, get me some water. Oh, and you can call for an ambulance and a crime scene team."

Daryl brought the water. "No need for an ambulance; they're both dead."

"Too bad," Tommy said. "I would have liked to talk to them. Better call the ME."

Daryl went to the phone and started making calls.

Tommy gave Clare Carras some water, then took the glass, set it down, grabbed her under her armpits, and sat her up straight on the sofa.

He wanted to ask his questions before she had had time to recover her composure.

"All right, Clare, listen to me. I want to know exactly what happened, and I want to know before anybody else arrives. It's going to be a madhouse around here in a couple of minutes, and if I'm going to help you, I'm going to need to know it all right now."

She picked up the water and drank some more of it, then put a hand to her swollen face. "Could I have some ice in a cloth, please?"

Tommy had underestimated her coolness. "Daryl, ice!" he said. "Tell me what happened, Clare."

"It was all so strange," she said, breathing deeply. "A man—the younger one—appeared at my door and said he was a friend of Harry's." She accepted the bundle of ice from Daryl and applied it to her face.

"Go on, and be quick about it," Tommy said.

"He asked to use the phone, and I let him in."

"There's a phone downstairs. How'd he get up here?"

"I was going to have him use the downstairs phone, but he forced me up here and started hitting me. Then the other one showed up. I hadn't seen him at the door."

"Why was he hitting you? What did he want?"

"He said he wanted money, and he pulled out a knife—there." She pointed.

Tommy turned and looked at the small knife, still stuck in the floor. "Go on."

"He said he was going to do awful things to me if I didn't give him what he wanted. He said the other one liked to break bones. He said they would kill me."

"Go on."

"I remember running toward the desk, where the gun was. He was moving after me, and I think I shot him."

"From the sound of it, you shot him, then shot the other one twice, then shot the first one again. Why did you choose to shoot him in the groin?"

"I don't know, it all happened so fast. I'm not sure where I shot or when."

"Where'd you get the gun? It wasn't in the house when we searched it."

"From a local pawnshop; the receipt's in the desk drawer."

"Did either one of them mention the name Marinello or Marin?"

She shook her head. "No, I've never heard either of those names."

"Then why do you think these men were here?"

"They said they wanted money. They must have read something in the papers about Harry, heard he was rich."

Tommy got up in disgust and went to the kitchen, ran himself a glass of water. She was too good for him, this one. She was going to stick to that story, and nobody but he was going to question it, and there was nothing he could do about it.

And, he remembered, he was going to have an awful lot of explaining to do, himself, about how he had allowed this to happen.

CHAPTER

55

Chaos now ensued. The medical examiner arrived, followed closely by a crime scene team, followed closely by the chief of police. At some point, Clare Carras made a phone call, and shortly an attorney arrived and closeted himself with his client in her bedroom.

"Gee," Daryl said, "I wonder what they're doing in there."

"Shut up, Daryl," the chief said. He pulled the two detectives into the kitchen. "All right," he said to Tommy, "let's have it, all of it, and in the greatest possible detail."

Tommy began with the phone call from Rita and led the chief, step by step, to that morning in the beachfront hotel.

"Wait a minute," the chief said. "Am I to understand that you took a free hotel room?"

"Chief, there's a lot more important stuff here than hotel rooms," Tommy said.

"When we're finished here, you call the hotel manager and have the room charged to your credit card, then you can put in for expenses, and I'll decide how much you're entitled to."

"All right, Chief, I'll do that," Tommy replied. "Now can I go on with what happened?"

"Please do."

"So this morning we got into the hotel restaurant half an hour before the two palookas. We waited for them to finish breakfast, then we followed them. They stopped around the corner at that big hardware store; the younger guy went in for maybe five minutes, then came out and they drove here to Dey Street. We parked halfway down the block and watched them. The young guy knocked on the door while the big one waited out by the sidewalk. As soon as she let the young guy in, the big one followed."

"And that's when you moved, right?" the chief asked.

"No, sir; we waited another, I don't know, half a minute, a minute; I wasn't timing it. Then we heard this crash from the house, which I now think was the coffee table hitting the wall, and we started running. I didn't wait to ring the bell. Then, just as we got inside the house, the shooting started. There was one shot, which I think was the young guy getting it in the throat, followed a second later by two quick ones, which I think took out the big guy, followed another second later by the fourth shot, which I think the younger guy took in the crotch."

"Why do you think it happened like that? You couldn't see anything, could you?"

"No, sir, but it makes sense that way. I got to the top of the stairs just after the crotch shot, and she spun around and fired two at me."

"At *you?*"

"I don't blame her for that, Chief; she must have thought there were more of them. Anyway, I yelled at her, and Daryl yelled at her to drop it, and she dropped it. Then she kind of just keeled over. She came to after not very long and asked for some ice for her face. I think you saw she was pretty banged up. Then I questioned her. She gave me her account of what happened, but I think there was more said before the shooting started than she let on. I want to question her again."

"If she didn't give it to you then, why do you think she'll give it to you now, after she's seen an attorney?"

Tommy shrugged. "I don't know, I just want to talk to her again. I think she knows exactly who these people were and what they wanted."

"Don't you already know that?"

"Yes, sir, but I want to make sure she realizes the spot she's in. If I can bring that home to her, then she might make a mistake and give us something to go on."

"Yeah, well, lots of luck on that; she hasn't given you a goddamned thing so far."

Tommy felt himself blushing. "Nevertheless, Chief."

"Okay, if the lawyer will let her talk to you—and *I* wouldn't, if I were in his shoes—then you

356

can talk to her. But if he says you can't, you can't. Is that perfectly clear?"

"Perfectly, Chief."

The chief suddenly looked very vulnerable. "We don't have shootings of mob thugs in this town, and since we can't absolutely prove who they were, we're going to play dumb on this one. The lady was attacked in her home by two strange men, and she managed to shoot both of them. That's what I'm saying to the papers, and you'd better not give any reporter anything else, even off the record, clear?"

"Yes, sir."

"By the way, just how the hell do you think she managed to bring both of them down? Frankly, I don't think I would have done as well in the circumstances."

"That's one of the things I'd like to ask her, just for my own information, Chief."

The lawyer appeared at the top of the stairs. "Do you have any more questions for Mrs. Carras?" he asked the chief.

"I certainly do," Tommy said.

"Then come out by the pool; I'm not bringing her up here to view any more of this carnage."

Tommy, Daryl, and the chief trooped down the stairs and out to the pool. Clare Carras was sitting, perfectly composed, at a table, and they all drew up chairs.

"Mrs. Carras," Tommy began, "there are just one or two more things."

"I'll help if I can," Clare replied coolly.

357

"What, exactly, did the younger man say when he came to the door? Quote him, if you can."

She frowned. "He said something like, 'Mrs. Carras, my name is . . . Palma,' or Parma, something like that, 'and I knew your husband. I want to express my condolences.' I thanked him, and he asked to use the phone."

"Then what happened—as much detail as you can remember, please."

"I started down the hall, and I was about to show him the phone in the hall when he began pushing me up the stairs."

"Ma'am, why do you think he would push you up the stairs? Had he ever been in the house before?"

"Not to my knowledge. Harry never mentioned anybody by that name."

"Then why would he want to go upstairs?"

The lawyer broke in. "Really, Detective, how could she possibly know that?"

"All right, all right. What happened next?"

"When we were upstairs he hit me—twice, I think—and knocked me down. Then he threw me on a sofa and pulled out this little knife. It looked new, you know? It still had the little paper wrapper on the blade. He threw the knife at the floor and said that if I didn't . . . give him some money—I think that's what he said—he and the other man would rape me, and the other man would break my bones. He said the other man was called Mr. Bones, because he liked the sound bones make when they break. That frightened me greatly, of course."

"Then what happened?"

"I said I would get some money, and I started toward the desk."

"He let you get up?"

"I pretended that I was trying to be helpful. I reached the desk and got the pistol and pointed it at him. He held out his hand and said give it to him, and he started toward me, and I think I shot him twice."

"Where did you learn to use a gun?" Tommy asked.

"Harry taught me," she said.

"The gun is a nine-millimeter automatic. Was there a shell already in the chamber? Was the hammer back?"

She rubbed her forehead with a hand. Her face was starting to discolor now. "I . . . I'm not sure; I don't remember."

"Did the man mention the name Marinello or Marin?"

"I told you before, I've never heard either of those names before."

"You shot the big man twice, right in the middle of the chest, tight grouping," Tommy said. "That means you know how to shoot and where to shoot. Why did you shoot the younger man in the crotch?"

"I'm afraid it's all a blur," she said. "I just pointed and pulled the trigger. I don't feel I really had much effect on where the bullets went."

The lawyer spoke up. "Do you have anything else of *substance* to ask, Detective?"

"I think that'll be all," Tommy said. He, the chief, and Daryl all stood as Clare got up and was escorted back to her bedroom by the lawyer.

A criminalist from the crime scene team came out the back door. He walked over to the table and placed a zippered plastic bag containing a number of items on the table. "This is all they had," he said. "Neither of them had any of the usual things you'd expect a person to be carrying. Neither had a wallet. Each of them had one credit card; the big one's said Mark N. Jefferson, and the younger one's said John H. Williamson."

"They're stolen, you can bet on that," Tommy said.

"The big one had a handkerchief, dirty; they both had sunglasses."

"Oh, there's a Lincoln Town Car out on the street that'll have their luggage in it," Tommy said. "But I don't think you're going to find any ID. Let's just run the credit cards and run their prints and see what we come up with."

The chief nodded to the man. "Let's get it done. Is the ME ready to move the bodies?"

"Yes, sir; it's being done now."

"Get on with it, then."

The three men sat back down at the table.

"I didn't think she'd give you anything else," the chief said.

"Neither did I," Tommy replied.

Tommy waited until late that night before

making two phone calls. He found the home telephone number of Barton Winfield, the Los Angeles lawyer, and dialed it. He figured it would be about dinnertime in L.A.

"Hello?"

"Mr. Winfield?"

"Yes?"

"This is Detective Sculley of the Key West Police Department, do you remember me? You and I and Rita Cortez had a meeting a while back."

"Yes, I remember you. Why are you calling me at this hour?"

"I told you I'd let you know if I learned anything else about the Marin/Marinello incident."

"Yes? What have you learned?"

"I've learned all sorts of things about you and your business connections," Tommy said, "and I've turned over what I know to the Organized Crime Division of the Los Angeles Police Department."

"*What?*"

This was a lie, but he wanted to make the man sweat. "I expect you'll be hearing from them in due course," Tommy said. "You'll be hearing from me again in due course, too."

"What do you mean by that?"

"When you put your two thugs on to Rita Cortez, you made a very big mistake, Mr. Winfield, if that is your name. You made an even bigger mistake when you let them hurt her. I'm going to see that you pay for that."

"Now, listen here," Winfield began.

"Your two hoods are dead, pal, and I'm going to see that they're traced back to you."

"Dead? I mean, I don't have the slightest . . ."

"She took them both out, like a pro. You're going to have to send better talent next time."

"Detective, this conversation is over," Winfield sputtered.

"It ain't over 'til it's over," Tommy said, then hung up.

He had one more call to make; he dialed Clare Carras's number.

"Hello?"

"It's Tommy Sculley, Clare."

"My lawyer says I'm not to talk to you anymore," she said.

"You don't have to say a word; just listen."

She was silent for a moment. "All right, I'm listening."

"I know what happened at your house this morning, and I know why it happened. I know that you murdered Harry, and that you had help. I know you're responsible, somehow, for your ex-husband's death, too."

"Can you prove any of this?" she asked.

"I don't have to, not anymore. When you killed Harry, Clare, you grabbed a tiger by the tail, and you can't let go now. The people Harry stole the money from know he's dead, and they know you've got the money. And, as I think was demonstrated this morning, they know exactly where to find you. Now you can only do two things: you can run, and if you do I'll be on you like a pack of bloodhounds; or you can come in from the cold and try to cut a deal. I'll work with you on that, Clare. It's your last, best chance, believe me. If you don't play ball, you'll have me nipping at your ass, and the colleagues of the two men you killed this morning will be waiting for you at every turn.

"You're not Harry, remember; you don't know how to disappear and make money disappear. Without Merk's help, you're alone now, and you're in way over your head. I've already seen to it that the dead men's friends in L.A. know what happened. All I have to do now is wait. You got that?"

There was a brief silence, then Clare hung up.

Tommy called Daryl on his portable. "Hey," he said.

"What's up?"

"She knows the worst now; she'll probably bolt. You stick to her, you hear?"

"Like a limpet."

"Good kid. See you in the morning."

Tommy turned in, snuggled up to Rosie, and slept like a baby.

CHAPTER

56

Clare Carras moved at a little after 6:00 A.M. Daryl sat straight up in his car and watched her open the trunk to the Mercedes and toss in a small piece of luggage, then get into the car and back out of the driveway. Daryl waited until she was around the corner, then started his car and drove after her. He picked up his portable phone and started to call Tommy, then thought better of it. This might be a false alarm, and he didn't want to make a fool of himself.

She turned onto Roosevelt Boulevard and headed toward the end of the island and U.S. 1, but to his surprise, she turned into a large shopping center and went into an all-night supermarket. He parked at the other end of the lot and watched the Mercedes.

Twenty minutes passed, then Clare came out of the market pushing a shopping cart laden with grocery bags. An awful lot of groceries for one woman living alone, Daryl thought. She loaded the groceries into the trunk and returned the cart to the store, then got in and drove back toward Roosevelt. Rush hour traffic, such as it was in Key West, was beginning, and she had to wait for nearly a minute before she could turn left across traffic and onto the Boulevard. Daryl had to wait, too.

Finally, he was able to accelerate through a left turn, ending up in the right-hand lane. He figured she would take a right on Palm Avenue and cross Garrison Bight Bridge on her way home. There were at least fifteen cars between Daryl and the Mercedes now, and he kept an eye on the bridge to his right, waiting to pick her up after her turn. But she never appeared.

Suddenly, Daryl was aware of the Mercedes headed in the opposite direction on Roosevelt. She had made a U-turn and was headed north again, and he was in the right-hand lane. Traffic was solid, and he had to wait until the light ahead of him changed before he was able to get into the left-hand lane for a turn. It took another few seconds for him to bully his way into the north-bound traffic. He began weaving in and out of traffic, changing lanes at every opportunity to make some headway, but still the Mercedes was not in sight ahead of him.

When he reached the bridge to Stock Island and U.S. 1 North, he crossed the bridge and looked out at the straight stretch ahead of him. No Mercedes. She had doubled back on him. Shit!

Daryl put the red light on top of the car and tore into another U-turn, startling other drivers and creating a racket of screeching tires. Once headed south again, he brought the light inside;

he didn't want her to see that in her rearview mirror. He looked as far ahead as he could, searching the distance for the Mercedes, but he saw nothing but the usual early-morning stream of traffic. He was abreast of the Key West Yacht Club, moving fast, when he caught sight of the Mercedes out of the corner of his eye, parked behind the yacht club. He slammed on his brakes, switched lanes, and made yet another U-turn. If he kept driving like this, he thought, he'd get himself arrested.

He managed a left turn into the yacht club parking lot and screeched to a halt behind the car. It was parked as far as possible from the clubhouse, alongside a little canal that ran inland from Garrison Bight. The canal wasn't yacht club territory; the boats there mostly belonged to the houses that backed up onto the canal. He got out of the car and looked around. The trunk lid was ajar on the Mercedes, and he looked inside. Empty.

Then he looked up and saw a small cabin cruiser two hundred yards away, making a right turn out of Garrison Bight, toward the open sea. Clare Carras was at the wheel.

"Oh, my God," he moaned. He ran back to his car, got it started, stuck the red light on top again, and entered Roosevelt Boulevard at a high rate of speed, scattering traffic in his path. Once out of Garrison Bight, she could go anywhere, and by now she was invisible behind the arms of land that formed the entrance to the Bight.

Daryl swung right into Palm Avenue, his siren going, the red light flashing, overtook half a dozen cars, started up the bridge, and, at its highest point, slammed on the brakes. He opened the door and, oblivious of traffic backing up behind him, climbed on top of the car and stood up. He was ten feet higher than the bridge, and he could just see over the land to the dredged channel beyond. He caught sight of the little cruiser heading west just as she motored under a bridge, steaming along slowly, mindful of the posted order not to create a wake in the channel. He grabbed for his phone and dialed Tommy.

"Yeah?" A sleepy voice.

"Hit the deck, Tommy, she's on the move!"

"Where?"

"She had a boat we didn't know about, and right now she's headed toward the western end of the island. She'll go right past Key West Bight, and then she could go anywhere."

"Where is the police boat docked?"

"Stock Island. Not even remotely useful."

Tommy was quiet, seemed to be thinking. "Where are you? Can you see her boat now?"

"I'm at the top of the Garrison Bight Bridge, standing on top of my car. I can see the boat moving past the Coast Guard Station and on toward Key West Bight. Shall I call the Coast Guard?"

"No, no, we want to follow her if we can, not bust her. Not yet, anyway. Here's what you do."

Daryl listened to the instructions. "Right," he

367

said. He broke the connection and jumped down from the car.

Chuck was sleeping soundly when suddenly there was a loud thump aft, and *Choke* rocked in the water.

"What was that?" Meg said sleepily.

"Somebody on the afterdeck," Chuck replied, sitting up on an elbow. Now whoever it was was banging on the hatchway and shouting something. Chuck struggled out of bed, grabbed a nearby pair of tennis shorts, slipped into them, and went aft. "All right!" he yelled, "I'm coming." He got the hatch open, and Daryl Haynes spilled into the boat.

"Chuck, sorry to wake you," Daryl panted, "but Clare Carras is on the run, and Tommy said for you to get your engines started and get ready to let go your lines. He's on his way."

"What do you mean she's on the run?" Chuck asked, still sleepy.

"Just do it; Tommy will explain when he gets here."

"Oh, all right."

Meg stepped out of the forward cabin, dressed only in a T-shirt. "What's happening?"

"It appears we're going out for a boat ride," Chuck replied. "Better get some clothes on."

Chuck stepped up into the cockpit, switched on the ignition, and started both engines. After a moment they were idling smoothly. "Meg," he

368

called below, "will you make some coffee, please? I need it bad."

"The water's already on," she called back.

"Daryl, you go forward and let go the springs; just toss the lines aft to me. I'll get the gangplank in." Daryl followed his instructions, and just as Chuck got the gangplank stowed, Tommy appeared on the run and leaped aboard. Chuck brought in the stern lines and went to the pilot's seat. "Here we go," he said. "Fend off on both sides, Tommy, Daryl." In a moment they were free of their mooring and heading toward the little harbor's entrance.

"I guess you'd like to know what's going on," Tommy said.

"I guess I would," Chuck replied.

"Clare is running."

"From what?"

"From me."

"In what?"

Tommy turned to his partner. "In what, Daryl?"

"In a little cabin cruiser, maybe twenty-two feet, outboard engine, looked about forty horse-power from the size of it."

"Color?"

"White."

"Swell, everything's white around here."

"It has a light blue cabin top." Daryl was standing high on the cockpit rim, looking dead ahead. "Nothing out that way; better turn left once you're through the entrance."

Choke cleared the harbor entrance, and Chuck swung the helm left. "See anything?" he called to Daryl.

"Not much on the move this early," Daryl replied. "We ought to be able to pick her up; she can't be all that far ahead."

Clear of the Bight, Chuck applied more power, and shortly they were doing fifteen knots.

"We've got to find her," Tommy said quietly, almost to himself. "If she gives us the slip now, she's gone forever, you can believe that."

CHAPTER

57

Chuck handed his binoculars to Daryl. "Use these," he said. "She can go one of three ways: straight ahead to Sand Key, where the channel runs through the reef; left and up the east side of the Keys or to the Bahamas; or to the right."

"What's to the right?" Tommy asked. "I'm new here."

"A bunch of small, uninhabited islands with various names, then the Marquesas, which are another bunch of uninhabited islands with shallow water all around, and finally, about seventy, eighty miles out, the Dry Tortugas and Fort Jefferson."

"What's Fort Jefferson?"

"It's an island with a fortress on it, built during the Civil War. Remember Dr. Samuel Mudd, the guy who set John Wilkes Booth's broken leg after he assassinated Lincoln?"

"Yeah, vaguely."

"He was convicted as a conspirator in the assassination, although he was innocent, and he was imprisoned in Fort Jefferson, where he became a hero during a yellow fever epidemic."

"What's your best guess on which way Clare will go?" Tommy asked.

"Well, straight ahead is Cuba; I don't think she'll want to go there. My guess is she'll turn east and go up the Keys or to the Bahamas, maybe even the Turks and Caicos. I don't know how much fuel she's carrying."

"East, huh?"

"That's my best guess."

"There she is!" Daryl yelled, pointing west. "I can just barely see her in the distance."

"So much for my predictions," Chuck said.

Meg brought up coffee on a tray, and everybody had some. Chuck kept an eye on the speck in the distance that was their prey.

"This bothers me," Chuck said.

"What bothers you?" Tommy asked.

"That she's going west. Like I said, it's nothing but small, uninhabited islands, with no water. They're not called the Dry Tortugas for nothing. Even if she goes all the way to Fort Jefferson, where boats sometimes tie up and the sightseeing

371

seaplanes land, it's a dead end. It must be four hundred miles to Cancun, in Mexico, and nearly as much to the Gulf Coast. If she were going up the Keys, she sure wouldn't go to the Marquesas or the Dry Tortugas first; there's no reason to."

"She's got a reason," Tommy said. "The lady knows what she's doing."

"Do you want me to try and close in on her? She seems to be doing about twenty knots, and Choke can do thirty on a good day."

"No, just keep her in sight," Tommy replied.

"Hey," Daryl said, "I forgot to tell you; she went to the grocery store this morning and loaded up with food. The trunk of her car was empty when I found it."

"Maybe she is headed for Mexico," Chuck said. "She's got the reef to the south, so she can't turn left."

"Could a boat that little make it to Mexico?"

"If she's got enough fuel, and if the weather holds. This time of year, she'd have a good chance."

"Is she alone, Daryl?"

"I didn't see anybody else, Tommy."

"Can you see anybody else now, through the binoculars?"

"Nope, she's too far away."

"Are you sure we're following the right boat?"

"Pretty sure."

"Pretty *sure?*"

"Pretty sure."

"Swell. How much fuel we got, Chuck?"

372

"Nearly full tanks; we could run until midnight, at least."

Two hours passed, with *Choke* keeping pace with the little cruiser. Tommy looked at his watch. "I didn't think we'd be going this far," he said. "I think we'd better ask the Coast Guard for some surveillance, just in case."

Chuck pointed to an empty hole in the instrument panel. "Sorry, my VHF radio is in the shop."

"Swell."

Daryl produced his portable phone and switched it on. "No signal," he groaned. "We're too far from Key West."

Tommy pulled out his pistol and checked it. "One clip," he said to Daryl. "How about you?"

"The same."

"Chuck, you still got that shotgun aboard?"

"Yeah."

"Meg, would you bring it into the cockpit?"

Meg disappeared below and came back with the weapon.

"How much ammo you got?" Tommy asked.

"Just what's in the gun—four rounds, and it's birdshot."

"Swell," Tommy said.

"Well, I never wanted to kill anybody, just scare them if I had to. Do you think we're going to get into a shooting war?"

"She's going *somewhere*," Tommy said, "and if she's alone, she's meeting *somebody*, and you can bet she's got that nine-millimeter automatic with her, the one she used yesterday."

"What happened yesterday?" Chuck asked.

Tommy explained it to him. "And she did a real good job, too."

"I'm sorry to hear it," Chuck said. "Would anybody like to join me in some breakfast?"

"Sold," Daryl said.

"Meg, may we impose on you?" Chuck asked.

"I'm not scrambling any eggs or frying any bacon while we're under way," she replied. "But we've got some pastries."

"Sold," Chuck replied.

It was nearly midafternoon now, and they were still keeping pace with the little cruiser. They had slowed down to fifteen knots.

"She's changing course," Chuck said. "This doesn't make any sense at all. On her present heading she'll fetch up in South America in about a week, if she doesn't fetch up on the reef any minute."

"Wait a minute, she's changing course again," Tommy said. "Chuck, hold your original course; I think the lady is making a U-turn."

Daryl laughed. "She's good at that."

"She's making an end run around the reef; it must lie deeper out here."

They all watched as, slowly, the little boat came around to something like a reciprocal of her original course.

"Now she'll pass off our left beam at about the distance we've been following her," Chuck said.

"Hold your course," Tommy said again. "She may be doing this to see if we follow."

"Whatever you say," Chuck replied. "Hey, she's slowing down, too."

"Hold your speed." Tommy took the binoculars and focused on the little boat. "Still can't see anybody, just the boat," he said.

An hour later, the boat was no more than a speck on their quarter.

"Now," Tommy said, "come around and run toward her, but keep this distance; let your speed match hers."

"Aye aye, sir," Chuck said.

Tommy squinted into the distance. "Chuck, if she keeps her present heading, where would she end up?"

"Daryl, will you take the wheel?" Chuck asked. When the young detective was comfortable, Chuck got out a chart. "Look," he said to Tommy, pointing, "we've been running in a west by southwest direction all day. Now she's come onto a course that's east by southeast. On this heading the first land she'd see would be Key West way to her left, but if she kept on heading this way, she'd fetch up in the Turks and Caicos, and that's not even on the chart."

"Then what the hell is she doing?" Tommy asked.

"I don't know, but we've got kind of an advantage now. The sun is at our backs, and if she looks aft, it's unlikely she could pick us out." He looked at his watch. "It's going to start to get dark in an hour or so. Wherever we're going, it looks as though we're not going to get there in daylight."

"Reef ahead!" Daryl shouted.

"Daryl," Chuck yelled back, "slow down to two knots and watch my hand signals!" Chuck ran forward onto the foredeck and looked ahead. The reef wasn't as far submerged as he thought, and the sun was getting low in the sky, so the visibility from above was not great. The little cruiser, no doubt, drew less water than *Choke*, too. "Right!" he yelled at Daryl, signaling frantically, and a big coral head nearly scraped the port side. "Come left to here," he yelled, pointing. "Now this way." He held his breath; if they ripped the bottom out of the boat way out here, with no radio, they stood little chance of a rescue anytime soon. Then, suddenly, they were through and the water was deepening. Chuck ran back to the cockpit, took the helm from Daryl, and pushed the throttles forward until they were making ten knots. "Good job," he said to the young detective.

"How's our fuel?" Tommy asked.

Chuck looked at the gauges. "We've still got more than half tanks, and at this speed we're running very efficiently." He turned back to the chart, and his eyes widened slightly. "Tommy . . ."

Tommy turned and looked at him. "What's the matter, Chuck?"

"I think I know where Clare is going," he said.

CHAPTER

58

Tommy looked at the chart. "Okay, I give up, where's she going?"

"The wreck," Chuck said. "The one where Harry died." He circled a part of the chart with his finger. "It's around there somewhere, outside the reef. Clare didn't want to be seen turning west through the Sand Key cut, so she went way out to the west, then across the reef, and now she's heading back."

"If you don't know exactly where the wreck is, how could Clare?" Tommy asked.

"GPS. Global Positioning System." He pointed at the instrument above the steering wheel. "It's giving us a constant readout of latitude and longitude, to the nearest tenth of a minute."

"Satellite navigation?"

"Right. These days, you can buy a little box for a thousand dollars that would put you right on top of the wreck, give or take ten yards. If

Clare has the coordinates it won't take any talent to fetch up there."

"But why would she go back to the wreck?"

Chuck shrugged. "Who knows? I guess it has the advantage of being an isolated point where she could meet somebody. I can't think of any other reason."

Tommy looked out over the water. "She's gone," he said.

Chuck grabbed the binoculars and swept the horizon. "Shit! And it's going to be dark in half an hour."

"Her running lights will make it easier to see her," Daryl said.

"She won't turn on any lights," Tommy replied, "not if she's smart, and she's pretty goddamned smart."

"We'll just have to hold this heading and hope she doesn't change hers," Chuck said. "Chances are she won't. The reef is unpassable now, with no light to speak of, so she can't turn north, and if she turns south there's only Cuba."

"I'd give a lot right now to know what she's doing," Tommy said.

The sun dropped into the sea, and darkness came quickly.

"No lights," Tommy said. "If we come up on her, I don't want her to see us first."

Meg made sandwiches and passed out soft drinks, and they ate quietly while the boat chugged on, now making only eight knots.

"Tommy," Chuck said softly, "what are we going to do if we catch up to her? Arrest her?"

"I don't have a charge," Tommy said, "but I could take her in for questioning, I guess."

"We're well outside the twelve-mile limit; you don't have jurisdiction, do you?"

"We'll call it a hot pursuit," Tommy replied.

Chuck pulled the engines back to idle and switched off the ignition.

"What?" Tommy asked.

Chuck pointed ahead at the light. "It just came on," he said.

"How far?"

"Hard to judge distance at night, but the horizon's only two, three miles away, so she's closer than that; maybe only a mile, mile and a half."

"Why did you cut your engines?"

"There's no wind, and sound carries great distances over water." Chuck put the binoculars to his eyes. "Can't make out a shape, what with no moon. There's just the light."

"Listen," Tommy said. "Do you hear it?"

Chuck stuck his head outside the windshield. "Music."

"Latin," Daryl said.

"Maybe they're dancing," Tommy replied. "Would a boat the size of Clare's have music?"

"Sure," Chuck said. "She could have a car radio and some speakers, that's all you need."

"What do we do now?" Daryl asked. "We're

dead in the water, and we can't sneak up on them; they'll hear the engines."

Chuck looked up at the GPS, glowing in the dark. "We're doing eight-tenths of a knot over the bottom," he said. "We've got a little current under us, and we're headed in the general direction of the light. If she's anchored, and she appears to be, we'll drift down on her."

"How do we know it's Clare?" Daryl asked.

"We don't," Tommy replied, "but right now, the light is all we've got. Let's find out who it is."

Slowly, inexorably, *Choke* drifted downstream toward the light. Chuck raised the binoculars every ten or fifteen seconds, trying to make out the shape of the vessel.

"Listen," Tommy whispered. "They're talking."

Chuck listened, and he heard laughter. "Sounds like a woman and a man."

"Keep your voices down," Tommy whispered to everybody. "No unnecessary talking; if we can hear them, they can hear us."

Chuck stood on the pilot's seat, his head above the windshield, and pressed the binoculars to his eyes, then climbed down. "It's bigger than Clare's boat," he said. "Certainly forty feet, maybe bigger."

"Any sign of the little cruiser?" Tommy asked.

"No."

"I think we've wasted a hell of a lot of time with all this drifting."

"Maybe not," Chuck said. "She's lying across the current, beam on to us; the little boat could be tied up to her other side."

Tommy climbed up on the seat and took the binoculars, then got down again. "I think there are at least two people in there—it's hard to tell, because the windows are fogged up—and I think it's bigger than forty feet."

Chuck nodded. "Could be. What's the plan, Tommy? We're going to be on top of them in a few minutes."

Tommy motioned everybody to gather around him, then he whispered, "All right, first of all, nobody makes any noise of any kind. It looks like we're going to drift down on this other boat, and when we do, Daryl and I are going to board her, as quietly as we can. Chuck, I want you to stay here with Meg and be ready to start the engines at a moment's notice. Who knows, we may have to get out of here in a hurry."

Then they heard the sound of an engine.

"Have they started up?" Tommy asked.

"Sounds like a generator to me," Chuck replied. "Not low enough for the main engines."

"Good, that'll help cover any noise we make."

They were a hundred yards out from the big boat now, and Chuck tried to see through her windows, but they were misty. He could only see shapes moving inside and hear the music.

"Look," Tommy said, "there's a boarding ladder on her quarter, see it?"

"Yes," Chuck replied. "We're drifting sideways, so let's all four man the port side and fend off, make sure we don't make a big bump when we're alongside. Then we can hand the boat in position for you and Daryl to use the ladder. Move very slowly, because a man's weight can noticeably rock a boat even as big as this one." He slapped his forehead. "I've got an idea."

"What?"

Chuck went to an aft locker and retrieved a bucket with a thirty-foot line tied to the handle. "I'll try and cushion the blow," he said. He went to the starboard side of *Choke* and slowly lowered the bucket into the water, allowing it to fill, then played out the line. "Okay, we've got brakes of a sort now," he whispered. "You three get ready to fend off."

They were forty feet from the big motor yacht, then thirty. Chuck began to slowly haul in the bucket, which was now acting as a sea anchor. Just as he had his hand on the handle, three pairs of outstretched hands made contact with the white hull of the motor yacht, and *Choke* came to rest alongside her starboard bow without a sound. Chuck joined them, and gently they handed their boat along the bigger yacht's topsides, making sure the two hulls did not touch. When *Choke*'s stern was next to the ladder they stopped.

The music was quite loud now, but there were

no longer any voices to be heard. Tommy stepped lightly back into *Choke*'s cockpit, retrieved Chuck's shotgun, and went back to the ladder. Silently he laid the shotgun on the deck of the larger yacht, put a foot on the bottom rung of the boarding ladder, and started up, followed by Daryl.

Tommy got a leg over the side and hauled himself into the cockpit. He could see two figures in the saloon through the misted glass doors. Daryl came on board and brought the shotgun into the cockpit with him. Tommy leaned close to him and whispered, "I don't think you'll need the shotgun; there are only two of them."

Daryl quietly laid the shotgun on a cockpit cushion and drew his pistol.

Tommy drew his own pistol and motioned to Daryl to follow. He tiptoed to the sliding saloon doors, pushed them back, and stepped into the main saloon, his pistol out in front of him. A man and a woman stood in the middle of the cabin, locked in an embrace.

"Good evening," Tommy said, and as the two turned to face him, his mouth dropped open. "Well, look at this, Daryl," he said, "look who we got here."

CHAPTER

59

Tommy was grinning from ear to ear. "Hello, Clare," he said. "Hello, Victor." The two let each other go.

"Well, I'll be goddamned," Daryl said. "Victor is the schmuck?"

"Victor's the biggest schmuck you ever saw," Tommy said. "Tell Chuck and Meg they can come aboard."

Daryl stepped into the cockpit. "Chuck, Meg, come aboard! You're not going to believe it!"

A moment later Chuck and Meg came into the saloon. "Jesus, Victor," Chuck said, "what the hell are you doing here?"

Victor looked unhappy. "Just making my way in the world, pal."

"So now all is revealed," Tommy said. "In a blinding flash of light."

"Wait a minute, Tommy," Chuck said. "Will you please tell me what's going on here?"

"What's going on is that all along, Victor has been helping Clare do her dirty work. In fact, he's probably been doing it for her."

"Victor killed Harry?"

"That's right, with more than a little assistance

from Clare. He also knifed a man named Barry Carman—I don't believe you knew him—up near Miami. And he killed poor old Merk."

Chuck stared at Tommy. "Merk's dead?"

"That's right. Victor snuck off your boat a few nights ago, met Merk, slugged him, then drove him out to the reef and dumped him to drown. Nice guy, huh?"

Victor said nothing.

Chuck turned to face his new partner. "Victor, why?"

"For Clare," Tommy explained. "He did it all for Clare—and Harry's ill-gotten money, of course."

Victor shrugged. "I'm getting old," he said. "So are you, Chuck, for that matter, but unlike you, I didn't want to end my days teaching tennis in the hot sun."

"No," Tommy said, "Victor had other ideas about how to spend his days in the sun. Daryl, you pat Victor down real good and sit him down on that sofa over there, and if he gets desperate, you put a couple of rounds in him, and don't shoot to wound. Victor's a big, strong guy, and the Marines taught him a lot." There was no need to frisk Clare; she was wearing only one of her tiny bikinis.

Daryl turned Victor around, stuck the gun next to his spine, searched him thoroughly, and sat him down.

Tommy's eyes had never left Clare. "Clare," he said, "you turn off the music, and be very careful how you do it. If you have any ideas about going into that handbag next to the stereo, please remember that I'm not some jerk from L.A., and that I'll kill you where you stand."

Clare walked to an elaborate entertainment center and turned off the music, then went and sat by Victor.

"Chuck, you and Meg have a seat at the bar."

Chuck took Meg's hand, and they settled themselves on barstools. There was a fifth of rum resting on the bar, and Chuck looked as if he wanted some of it.

Tommy frowned and turned to Daryl. "Daryl, with the music off, do you hear water dripping? Is it raining outside?"

Another man's voice came from behind them. "It's not raining, Tommy." Then there was the sound of a shotgun being pumped. "Let your guns drop at your sides and put your hands on top of your heads."

Tommy did as he was told, then turned around. "Harry?" he said weakly.

Harry Carras was standing in the cockpit, dripping wet, wearing a wetsuit. His hair was blond, and he had a full beard; there was a large plastic cooler at his feet, sealed with tape, and Chuck's shotgun was in his hands.

Victor got up, retrieved the detectives' pistols, stuck them into his belt, and stood at the end of the bar next to Chuck.

"Now, Tommy," Harry said, "you and your

partner sit down on the deck, right where you are."

The two detectives sat down.

Tommy turned to Daryl. "I was wrong; Victor isn't the schmuck, I am."

Harry smiled. "Don't be too hard on yourself, Tommy. You weren't meant to figure it out."

"No," Tommy said, "I was meant to nail Chuck for murdering you, so you could be dead and Clare could disappear. By the way, Chuck, it was Victor who put the incriminating plastic hose in your car. And I thought it was Merk. What happens now, Harry?"

"I'll get to that in a minute, Tommy. Chuck, that beautiful little boat of yours runs on gasoline, doesn't it?"

Chuck nodded slowly.

"Victor, let's put your skills to work. Go aboard Chuck's boat and see if you can cause a lot of gasoline to leak into the bilges."

Victor left the saloon without a word.

"Harry," Tommy said, "while Victor's doing his dirty work, you mind answering a few questions?"

"Why not? My answers aren't going anywhere."

"Let's start with L.A. You *are* Marinello, aren't you?"

"I used to be, Tommy, but not anymore. I'm not even Harry Carras anymore. Clare and I have brand-new, quite genuine passports and a whole identity package to go with them."

"Let me give you a tip, Harry; this time make yourself a credit record. If you'd had a credit record when I checked, I might never have gotten near you."

"That's very good advice, Tommy. I'll put somebody to work on that. Did I make any other mistakes?"

"Yeah, but you first," Tommy said. "What's in the cooler?" He pointed to the cockpit.

"Twenty-two million dollars in bearer bonds, gold certificates, and other negotiable instruments," Harry said.

"It was all on the wreck?"

"That's right. You see, although I had a sizable sum in other, more visible investments, that was just to allow us to live well on the income while we were planning our final escape. I didn't want all the rest of it lying around the house."

Chuck spoke up. "Harry, I have a question, too. Why aren't you dead? You looked dead to me, lying down there on the deck of the wreck with a tank full of carbon monoxide and blood in your mask."

Harry smiled. "I was pretty convincing, huh?"

"You certainly were. How did you do it?"

"I had a little cylinder of clean air, just enough to get me to the wreck without breathing the noxious fumes."

"But how did you get off the wreck and . . . here?"

"I had a rebreather kit, which leaves no bubbles, stashed in a locker on the wreck," Harry explained. "When you popped up, I swam to the locker, started breathing oxygen, and got out of there."

"But you were an awfully long time with no air, weren't you? I mean, from the time I found you down there until I popped up."

"Less than two minutes; I can hold my breath for a little over three. It's a gift, like being able to run fast or jump high."

"Where did you go after that? There were no boats around that I could see."

"No, but there's a little island to the northwest, about two and a half miles."

"You swam two and a half miles underwater?" Chuck asked, incredulously.

"Partly. The last hour was on the surface; the Coast Guard had gone by then. I began swimming competitively at six; I would have made the Olympics, but my . . . personal sponsors didn't want me to become famous before I started practicing law. The trip took me nearly three hours, against the current, but then it had to be far enough that nobody would believe I could make it."

"And from the island, where?"

"I cruised around on the little boat that Clare used today—until we got this boat, which used to be *Fugitive,* out of Key West and to a little boatyard up the Keys, where we changed her name and made a few superficial alterations that would differentiate her from her old self. The three young men you encountered in the marina

389

were not a delivery crew; they were shipwrights. They're down in the wreck now, for some diver to find someday."

Victor came back on board. "There's about half a gallon a minute leaking into their bilges now," he said. "I didn't want to make it too big, in case anybody ever inspects the wreck. There'll be enough for a big explosion in a few minutes." He didn't look happy about it.

"I get the picture," Tommy said. "You take us out, put us aboard *Choke,* and then there's a terrible accident?"

"You're very quick, Tommy. We're pretty far out from Key West, and I doubt if anyone will even see the explosion. If they do, then by the time they reach the site, the boat will have burned to the waterline and sunk. Those old wooden boats burn quickly. By that time, we'll be thirty, forty miles south of here, headed for the Caymans, the other side of Cuba."

"I see," Tommy said. "Let's get back to your mistakes, Harry. You asked me if you made any more."

"By all means," Harry said. "I want to hear this."

"It's kind of a daisy chain of mistakes," Tommy said. "You trusted Clare, Clare trusted Victor, Victor trusted Clare."

"What do you mean?"

"Haven't you wondered how your mob friends found Clare?"

Harry frowned. "It was that detective, Carman."

"Yeah, but Carman was tipped. Clare tipped him."

Harry glanced at Clare. "Substantiate that."

"Carman told me he got a telephone call from what sounded like a young woman. Who but Clare? Who else knew?"

"That doesn't make any sense, Tommy; if they'd found me they would have found her."

Tommy was shaking his head. "The tip was before you faked your death. Clare was depending on your mob buddies to take you out so she'd be free to disappear with the money, but you solved her problem with your plan to die. She did know where the money was, didn't she, Harry?"

Harry looked appraisingly at Clare. "You have a rebuttal, sweetheart?"

"He's crazy, Harry. I want to be with you; you know that."

Tommy turned to Clare. "I'll bet that's not what you told Victor." He turned to the tennis pro. "By the way, Victor, Harry and Clare have brand-new passports and ID. Do you have a brand-new passport?"

Victor looked at Clare. "No," he said quietly.

"Victor, I have another question for you; when did you find out that Harry was alive?"

"The day before yesterday," Victor said.

"Must have come as quite a shock," Tommy

said. "And Harry, you've known about Victor all along, right?"

"Oh, yes." He looked thoughtful. "Well, nearly all along."

"Ahh," Tommy said, looking thoughtful, "so Clare has lied to both of you. You know, it strikes me that as soon as Chuck, Meg, Daryl, and I are out of the picture, somebody else is going to go." He turned to Clare. "Tell me, have you figured out which one is next? I mean, you need one of them to get out of here in this boat, but not both. Three's kind of a crowd, isn't it? And I doubt if two would be company for very long."

Harry turned toward Clare. "My dear, would you like to respond to that?"

"No," she said, getting to her feet, "I don't think I would." She started across the saloon toward her purse, next to the stereo. "What I'd like is some aspirin." She reached into the handbag.

Suddenly, there were guns everywhere. Clare's hand came out of the purse with an automatic in it, Victor clawed at his belt, where Tommy's and Daryl's guns were, and Harry had to make a choice.

Harry and Clare fired simultaneously; Harry staggered backward into the cockpit as Clare received a load of birdshot in the face and went down. Victor didn't seem to know what to do, and while he was thinking about it, Chuck used the moment to swing a bottle of rum at the back of his head.

Then it was very quiet. No one moved. Except Clare.

Bleeding, blinded, she raised herself on one elbow and began firing wildly. She got off half a clip before Chuck's dive ended on top of her. By the time he twisted the pistol from her grip, she had died.

"Daryl," Tommy said, getting up, "check on Harry, and be careful." He produced a pair of handcuffs and snapped them onto Victor's wrists. "Chuck, you go and stop the gas leak on your boat and pump out the bilges."

"Good idea."

"Meg, please find a bar towel and apply it to Victor's head. We don't want him to bleed to death before we get him back to Key West; he'll be useful in explaining what happened here."

Daryl came in from the cockpit. "Harry's bought it. Clare was a good shot with a handgun, wasn't she?"

"She was some piece of work," Tommy said. He walked behind the bar and started looking at bottles. "I believe I need a drink," he said. "Will anybody join me?"

While Daryl applied first aid to Victor's scalp in the saloon, Tommy, Chuck, and Meg sat in the cockpit of the big yacht, sipping rum and tonic and watching the Coast Guard cutter coming toward them.

"Tommy," Chuck said, "you know what

surprises me most in all this? Victor. I wouldn't have believed him capable of any of this."

"Victor's a sociopath," Tommy said. "He's a charmer, but he's one of those people who is completely without a conscience. I think Clare must have seen that in him. Remember, she dangled the bait in front of you, briefly, but you didn't take it. That's when she picked Victor. She knew the difference between the two of you."

Chuck shrugged. "If it hadn't been for you, Tommy, her plan would have worked. I'd have been a goner."

"Chuck," Tommy said, "if it hadn't been for *you* tonight, we'd *all* have been goners; Victor wouldn't have left anybody alive. You should always remember: When the pressure was on, when you had to come through, you didn't choke."

The three of them finished their drinks and got up to meet the Coast Guard.

February 20, 1995
Key West, Florida

Acknowledgments

I am grateful to Victor Mulcahy for being a good sport about all this and for teaching me everything he knows about tennis. If I got any of the tennis stuff wrong, it's his fault.

I am also grateful to my editor, HarperCollins vice president and associate publisher Gladys Justin Carr, and her staff for all their hard work, and to my literary agent, Morton Janklow, his principle associate, Anne Sibbald, and all the people at Janklow and Nesbit for their careful attention to my career over the years.

IF YOU HAVE ENJOYED READING THIS
LARGE PRINT BOOK AND YOU
WOULD LIKE MORE INFORMATION
ON HOW TO ORDER A WHEELER
LARGE PRINT BOOK, PLEASE WRITE
TO:

WHEELER PUBLISHING, INC.
P.O. BOX 531
ACCORD, MA 02018-0531